UNVEILED

Also by Ruth Vincent

Elixir

UNVEILED

A Changeling P.I. Novel

RUTH VINCENT

HARPER
VOYAGER
IMPULSE
An Imprint of HarperCollinsPublishers

This is a work of fiction. Names, characters, places, and incidents are products of the author's imagination or are used fictitiously and are not to be construed as real. Any resemblance to actual events, locales, organizations, or persons, living or dead, is entirely coincidental.

Digital Edition DECEMBER 2016 ISBN: 978-0-06-246620-4

Print Edition ISBN: 978-0-06-246621-1

Harper Voyager, the Harper Voyager logo, and Harper Voyager Impulse are trademarks of HarperCollins Publishers.

HarperCollins is a registered trademark of HarperCollins Publishers in the United States of America and other countries.

FIRST EDITION

10 9 8 7 6 5 4 3 2

To Matt, for making real life so magical

UNVEILED

UNVEILED

CHAPTER 1

Not everyone's mother leaves a knife on their pillow, but not everyone's mother is the Fairy Queen.

It was only 7:00 a.m. I had just emerged in a burst of steam from the bathroom I shared with my room-mate and best friend, Eva, my hair wrapped in a towel turban, racing to get ready for work, when I saw it out of the corner of my eye. There was something dark and glinting on the immaculate whiteness of my pillowcase: a stone blade with a copper handle, shaped like the crescent moon. And all I could think was, *Please no. Not now.*

I knew exactly what the knife was—and what it meant. For a brief moment, I tried to ignore the fairy knife and continue getting ready for work. I shimmied into my tights, buttoned the tiny, translucent buttons on my crisp white shirt until I realized my hands were shaking. Cursing, I turned back to the knife on my pillow.

I couldn't just *not* deal with it. I'd spent the past eight months not dealing with things: hundreds of human children held hostage in a death-like sleep in the Vale, the drought of Elixir that was killing the fairies, and a looming vacancy for the worst job in the universe—the Fey throne, which my mother, the Queen, expected me to fill. But I didn't know how to deal with any of those things. Eight months since I'd journeyed to the Vale, and I still had no idea how to fix the mess we were in. No amount of brainstorming with my boyfriend, Obadiah, had gotten us any closer to a solution. I didn't want to go back without a plan.

The knife hadn't been there on the pillow when the alarm clock jangled me awake this morning. Which meant somehow, in the span of my shower, a fairy had entered my bedroom, left this "gift" and exited. The thought unnerved me. Even in my own home I couldn't ever truly get away from my mother or the role I'd been born to play.

Half-dressed, my hands on my hips, I stared at the knife. The morning sun from the curtainless window made a brilliant white square on the pillowcase, but nothing was able to illuminate the black obsidian blade. It was creepy in its ancientness, from a time before there were Fairy Queens, before the Vale itself. The stone blade was sharper than steel. It would cut from one world into the next. It was a knife that could take me back to the Vale, back home.

Except New York City was my home now. And the Queen had almost tricked my boyfriend into stabbing himself to death with this knife's lookalike, I thought bitterly.

I picked up the blade. It was warm in my fingers, unnaturally so. Stone should be cold, so should copper, but the blade was hot as human skin, as if something living pulsed beneath the cold minerals and metals. It very well might be alive.

Staring down at it, I noticed there was writing scratched faintly into the side of the blade. I lifted it up to examine it more closely, trying to ignore the awful feeling in my fingertips.

It was indeed writing, the first line in English, the second line in High Faerie. The message was the same, like a Rosetta stone. It read simply:

Please come home.

A lump rose in my throat and I swallowed it down, hard. I knew my mother missed me. That didn't mean I was ready or that it was a good idea to go.

I was about to place the knife back on the pillow when I thought to check the opposite side of the blade. There was more writing:

It's gotten worse.

I resisted the urge to fling the knife across the room. What did my mother mean? What had gotten worse? The drought? The deaths? Whatever it was, it was definitely bad news.

It wasn't that I didn't care; I still had nightmares about all those tiny, too-still faces trapped in their enchanted cocoons. But I didn't have a plan to help them yet. And I wasn't ready to leave my human life behind. I'd been a fairy once, but I'd been a changeling for the past twenty-three years; I was closer to human now than anything else.

I looked at the clock. If I didn't leave soon, I'd be late for work with Reggie. There was no way I could go back to the Vale without at least checking in with my boss first, I reasoned. I'd deal with the knife tonight. When Obadiah came over after work, we could talk about it.

Wincing, I slipped the knife underneath my pillow, so that if Eva entered my room while I was out she wouldn't see it. It would definitely freak her out. I continued getting dressed. Still, I could feel the presence of the blade, even when I turned my back to the bed to slip into black pumps. It was like the knife could sense my moments and was watching me.

I shivered, but grabbed my purse and tiptoed out into the hallway of our apartment, hoping the sound of my heels wouldn't wake up Eva, who had likely worked a night shift. She hadn't been around when I'd gone to bed last night. She'd gotten a new job, and it seemed like I barely saw her anymore.

I'd just turned towards the kitchen when I noticed there was an unfamiliar pair of shoes next to the welcome mat. Men's shoes. And not Obadiah's. He didn't favor obnoxiously loud sneakers, orange and teal with neon swooshes; he was an old-world, leather-loafer kind of guy. Eva must have had a boy over last night,

I thought. Which didn't perturb me. She deserved a fling. Except she normally told me first as a courtesy. Then again, Eva and I had barely seen each other the whole past month; she was always working.

And then suddenly Eva's bead curtain door burst open, jangling the strands. An unfamiliar young man was standing in the kitchen, staring at me with a kind of dazed, terrified, deer-in-headlights expression. Cute, I thought appraisingly, looking up at the tall, blond, muscular, blue-eyed boy. Though his cheeks were a bit too cherubic for my taste. I liked my men a little rough around the edges, like Obadiah. Still, he was attractive, in a "recently retired teen idol" sort of a way. His shirt was rumpled, hastily put on, and those cherubic cheeks were blushing. Clearly he knew I knew that they'd been up to something highly un-cherubic behind Eva's swinging bead door. Like I cared.

"Oh, I'm heading out," he stammered, his voice changing midway from high-pitched squeak to low rumble. How old was this guy? But he was probably Eva's and my age, just really nervous.

I gave him a friendly smile.

"It's fine. You don't have to leave because of me."

He still looked terrified, however. Maybe he didn't believe me.

"Seriously," I said. "I made a pot of coffee. You can have some if you want. I always leave some for Eva. There's milk in the fridge."

My effort to ease his terror didn't seem to be working, though, by the look on his face.

"Uh, no, thanks, I'd better be going."

And in a terrible hurry, he put on his sneakers, not even bothering to tie the neon laces. He got halfway to the door, stopped and awkwardly rush-tied them, and then literally ran out, with no more than a quick, wincing nod goodbye.

The door slammed shut behind him.

I stood there for a moment, staring at the closed door, listening to the clomp of his feet as he bounded down the three flights of stairs ending in the bang of the front door. The whole interaction had been so weird and awkward. My intuition prickled with worry. Why was this guy so quick to run off? Had he said goodbye to Eva first? Was she okay?

I walked over to the curtain of beads that separated her room, and paused in front of the shimmering strands, wondering if I should go in. I was about to part the curtain when I heard Eva's voice, singing.

My shoulders relaxed, and I turned away. A singing Eva was a happy Eva, I'd learned after two years of living together. Her voice drifted through the shared wall between her closet and the kitchen as I poured coffee into my to-go mug, snatches of old Spanish folksongs belted out in her deep, imperfect but soulful way. When Eva sang in her first language, it meant she was especially content. That boy must have had to leave early for a job, I thought, fastening the lid on my coffee cup. Likely he'd said goodbye to her before she'd gotten up to dress for work. I was probably worried over nothing, as usual. I hoped this one would work out for Eva. Maybe she'd finally have a relationship that lasted longer than six weeks.

One glance at the wall clock made me rush for the door. As I bounced down the stairs, I couldn't shake that naggy-twisty feeling in my gut that there was something not quite right about that boy. But I couldn't figure out what had triggered it. Telling myself I'd call Eva on my lunch break, I stepped outside into the warm Indian summer morning, the cheerful blue September sky at odds with my uneasy heart.

I arrived at the dingy office building on West 37th Street exactly, to the minute, on time. When I strode in, my boss, Reggie, had his feet propped up on his filing cabinet. A banquet of breakfast items was scattered across the desk. I'd learned already that Reggie did not begin the work of the day until he'd consumed at least one egg sandwich, a large coffee stretched to two cups with about a carton of heavy cream and a fresh-squeezed orange juice. Only when proteined, carbed and caffeinated could the mind properly begin its work, Reggie always said. His fuzzy, caterpillar-like eyebrows twitched up as I walked through the door. For a moment, seeing his eagerly expectant face, I almost forgot about the knife under my pillow.

"Mab, glad you're here. We got a new case," he said excitedly, his mouth still full. "Breakfast sandwich?"

"Sure." I acquiesced to the overstuffed everything

bagel in his proffered hand, and took a seat in the chair across the desk from him.

As Reggie thoughtfully chewed, I let my breakfast sandwich sit there in its foil wrapper for a moment, twisting my hands beneath my desk. I wished I could tell him about the knife. Eventually I would have to say something, when I asked for the time off from work to go visit the Vale, but I wished I could tell him where I was really going. That could never be, though. Reggie was the last person on earth I could ever imagine believing in magic. Actually, that was the reason I liked him: his charm was in his earthiness, his humanity. But it did make some things difficult.

"Eat up, Mab, gotta clear this away in fifteen minutes. She'll be here soon."

He threw away the remains of his breakfast, wiping the grease stains from his fingers on a paper napkin.

"Who will be here?" I asked, digging into my sandwich.

"Our new client. From the little bit she told me on the phone, I think this will be the perfect first independent case for you. The girl is around your age. Not the one who's coming, that's her mother. But the daughter is twenty-something."

"Not another missing-persons case, is it?" I asked, grimacing, thinking of our last case. That poor girl had been found dead.

"No, this one is alive. So you can talk to her. That's

why I think it's a perfect match for you. Maybe you can get her to open up to you."

I leaned in closer to the mahogany desk, excited to hear more. This was the work I was really cut out for—detective work, not becoming the next Fairy Queen.

"What's the case about?" I asked.

Reggie frowned. "I'll let the mother explain it when she comes in. She wasn't entirely forthcoming over the phone."

He was just finishing the words when the buzzer rang.

"Boy, is she ever punctual," Reggie exclaimed, looking at the clock and giving his fingers a final wipe with a paper napkin. I quickly discarded the remains of my sandwich as he picked up the phone to let her in.

Moments later, a woman in her early fifties appeared at the glass door of Reggie's office. She was impeccably dressed, in the sort of casual elegance that spoke of old money, affluence without the gaucheness of trying too hard. Her rumpled white linen blouse was deceptively informal, but the designer sunglasses and red-soled shoes, with a matching handbag, made her money perfectly plain. She was in excellent shape for her age, her hair an artfully highlighted blond. She looked like she'd had a bit of work done on her face too—just a tad, not enough to seem unnatural. It gave a slight stiffness to her smile, though that could have been there to begin with. She greeted us cheerfully, but I detected the disparaging glance she gave to the tired, out-of-fashion sofa in Reggie's waiting room.

"Good morning, I'm Brenda Sheffield." She extended a pearly pink manicured hand, first to Reggie, then to me.

"Reggie Ruggiero." Reggie shook her hand heartily.

"Mabily Jones." I smiled.

Her fingers were weak in my grasp, and she fidgeted when I met her eye. This woman was nervous, really nervous. I could see it through her flutters of "Lovely to meet you."

"Can I get you a coffee?" Reggie asked. "A bagel? We got bagels."

"I'm fine." The woman gave Reggie a tight-lipped smile, plastered over disgust, that said, *I don't eat that sort of thing. I subsist entirely upon organic mesclun greens.*

The three of us stood around awkwardly for a moment, till Reggie took a seat behind his desk. I assumed my usual seat beside him, and Brenda daintily lowered herself into Reggie's client chair. She seemed distinctly uncomfortable and kept glancing through the glass doors into the lobby, as if she was worried someone would walk in and see that she was here. There was a slight redness around her perfectly contoured cheekbones, and I didn't think it was sunburn: it was shame.

"So, Brenda," Reggie began, breaking the awkward silence. "What can we help you with? You said on the phone about your daughter . . ." His voice trailed off, waiting for her to speak.

But the woman didn't answer. She flinched ever so slightly. Then she turned her head to the window, facing away from us. It struck me as a shockingly rude gesture from someone who seemed so intent on being polite.

And then I saw her shoulders were shaking.

There was a little hushed peep, like the cry of a smothered baby bird.

And that's when I realized she was sobbing.

"I'm sorry, I'm so sorry," she managed to say, the words hiccupped and choked through her tears.

Reggie and I both reached for his silver plated tissue box at the same time, banging knuckles.

I plucked one out and offered it to her.

She snatched it quickly from my hand. When she finally looked up at us, her face was flushed red in clear embarrassment.

"I'm so sorry," she muttered again.

"Please don't apologize. There's no need," I said gently. It had always bothered me how much human women apologized. And it bothered me more how the habit had rubbed off on me during my time as a human.

She blew her nose as daintily as one could blow one's nose, which was not very.

"I'm sorry," she said again, "it's just . . . I don't do this. Ever. Well, not in public."

I offered her another tissue, and held my breath for what she would say next. I knew it had to be bad if she was letting us see her this vulnerable. I may have known Brenda Sheffield for all of three minutes but I knew she was telling us the truth: this was not a woman who let her emotions show easily, and definitely not with strangers. Something must be deeply wrong in this woman's life, and I felt guilty for having judged her about her shoes.

At last Brenda collected herself.

"Something is wrong with my daughter," she said quietly.

"What's going on?" I asked.

Brenda shook her head. "I don't know. That's why I came here. My friend Jessie Goldstein recommended you. I know you had great success when her husband, well, you know what he did . . ." Her voice trailed off. "I just . . . I don't know where else to turn."

"Tell us a little more about your daughter." Reggie cast me a quick glance and I could tell he knew I was studying him, absorbing the way he handled clients, the way he questioned them, so that I could eventually do it on my own.

Brenda's face brightened at the mention of her daughter, though there was still pain behind her eyes.

"Our daughter, Quinn, is twenty-one. She's a senior in college at Vassar. Or she was. Until recently. She dropped out halfway through her last semester."

Oh man, I thought. That must have been tough on her parents. The Sheffields, at least going by her mother, did not seem like the type of people who had a child drop out of school.

"But that's not even what has me worried. I mean, it's Quinn's life; she can live it however she wants." There was something a bit forced in Brenda's voice when she made this statement. "But what has us concerned is that Quinn's whole personality . . . it just *changed* overnight. It's terrifying. For the past few months, Quinn has just laid in bed all day. She won't come out of her room. She won't go to class. She won't speak to her friends. She won't even speak to me. She's catatonic."

"Mrs. Sheffield, if I may?" Reggie interrupted her gently. "I'm not sure if we, as a private detective agency, are really the best party to help you, or your daughter. You should probably talk to a different kind of professional about this, a doctor, maybe, or . . ."

I knew he was about to say "a psychiatrist" and clearly Brenda knew that too, because she interrupted him, shaking her head almost violently.

"Don't you think I've tried that already?" she said harshly. When I flinched, the tone was instantly gone, replaced by her previously demure expression. "I'm sorry, it's just . . . we've been to see everyone: doctors, therapists, psychiatrists, neurologists. None of them have been able to help."

Reggie's caterpillar eyebrows furrowed, and he nodded thoughtfully. I did too.

"Mrs. Sheffield, how do you envision us being able to help?" I asked gently. "What would you want us to do that these other professionals haven't been able to?"

Brenda looked slightly askance at me for speaking up, maybe because of my youth, but Reggie was nodding approvingly. He always encouraged me to take a lead in these conversations.

She was silent.

"If you think your daughter is depressed . . ." I started, but she cut me off.

"I don't think it's like that."

I glanced at Reggie, and we exchanged a look. Depression sounded exactly what it was like.

"She's never been like this before," Brenda went on.

"Depression can strike at any time," I said, but Brenda cut me off again.

"No, what I meant is"—she pursed her lips—"I think she's on some sort of drugs. She started seeing a new boyfriend, right before the change occurred. I think he gave her something. How else would someone who was an honors student, class president, outgoing, social, just suddenly change overnight?"

Reggie steepled his fingers.

"I understand your concern, Brenda," he said diplomatically. "Have you taken your daughter to a medical professional, gotten her tested for drugs?"

Brenda gazed out the window at the steam billowing up from the pipes on the roof below. She was silent for a moment. "I performed a home test."

"Your daughter consented to that?" Reggie asked, one caterpillar eyebrow raising.

Brenda bit her lip. "Well, no. But it was for her own good."

Reggie must have seen the frown on my face, because he shot me a look that said, *Stay silent, don't judge her.* I could tell by the furrowing of his brows that he didn't approve of Quinn's mother drug testing her daughter without the girl's permission either. Reggie seemed like the kind of dad who would have just *talked* to his daughter, like my human dad would have. It was one of the things I liked about him. But he stayed silent.

Much as I wanted to speak, I bit my tongue too. I'd seen too many people hurt by things done "for their own good," without asking them. But I let Reggie continue.

"All the tests came back negative," Brenda said.

"Well, then," Reggie began, but she interrupted him.

"It might have been something the test didn't cover. I mean, the home kits only test for a few things."

Reggie crossed his arms over his chest. I did too.

Brenda looked at both of us desperately. "Call it a mother's intuition," she said, breaking the silence, "but I know something is wrong. My daughter is under the influence of something. This isn't normal behavior for her. She's always been this bright, bubbly, vivacious girl. Now"—her voice began to crack, and I could tell there were more tears behind it—"it's like she's dead, going through the motions of being alive."

The raw pain and love behind this woman's airy, feminine voice took me aback. I genuinely felt for her, and wanted to help her and Quinn.

"So, what exactly would you like us to do?" I said at last.

Brenda hung her head. She was silent for a long moment, and that pink flush of shame crept back over her cheeks.

"I want you to do what you do best."

I was about to ask what that was, but I was afraid I already knew the answer. I frowned.

Finally, Brenda summoned up the nerve to say it out loud.

"I want you to spy on her."

Seeing the look on my face, she backpedaled. "I want you to see if she's taking anything, see if there's any substance involved. For her own health and safety."

The reasons behind this spying were noble, but still, I bit my lip.

Reggie's eyebrows furrowed. We were private detectives; this kind of work was our bread and butter. Hanging out in parked cars outside of buildings, watching for visitors, going through trash cans, planting spy cams. But it was one thing to do it on a cheating spouse, or someone suspected of insurance fraud. I'd never done it for a parent on a child before. It made me queasy, and I could tell by Reggie's eyes it bothered him too.

At last he spoke.

"Brenda, I say what I'm about to say because I think it's in your daughter's best interest. I think you should take her to another doctor, someone who really specializes in substance abuse, or a drug treatment center, something like that, before you hire us. Look, I'm turning down potential work by saying this, but it would be unconscionable not to. Can't you just talk to your daughter? Ask her what's wrong?"

"Don't you think I've tried?" Brenda said again. "I've tried to take her to doctors, counselors, programs. She won't leave her room; she won't leave her bed. Her father and I have picked her up and literally carried her to the car and driven her there, but she won't talk. We can't force her. The last resort is calling someone to commit her, and I won't do that to my daughter, I won't!"

She was on the verge of crying again, and I bit my lip.

Clearly Reggie had been won over too.

"Alright, we'll see what we can do. Can we come over to your home and speak with your daughter directly?"

He paused, and all the breath rushed out of me at his next words. "I would like my colleague, Mabily Jones, to interview her, one-on-one. I wouldn't be there; it would be just Mabily."

He still wanted me to lead the investigation? He was trusting me to handle a case like this all by myself? I wanted to jump out of my chair and hug him, but in deference to Mrs. Sheffield's pain, I stayed silent.

Brenda, however, did not sound pleased. "I assumed *you* would be conducting the investigation," she fluttered, looking at Reggie. I could tell my youth and inexperience bothered her.

"Ms. Jones is only a few years older than your daughter. Quinn might relate to her more as a peer. She might be more likely to open up and talk to her than she would be to somebody like me." Reggie gestured to his fifty-something-year-old frame. "You and me aren't exactly of her generation." He smiled at Brenda, and she gave a tense nod, but her expression towards me softened.

"Ms. Jones may be a junior P.I., but she has already proven herself on cases of a highly sensitive nature," said Reggie, and I flushed with pride.

"I'd be happy to have you come speak to my daughter," Brenda acquiesced at last.

"When would be convenient?" I asked.

Brenda sighed. "She never leaves her room, so I guess one time is as good as another. Tomorrow? Could you come tomorrow morning?"

I nodded.

"We live in West Tulip, New Jersey," said Brenda. "I can pick you up at the train station."

We said our goodbyes to Brenda, who looked visibly softer than when she came in. She put on her designer sunglasses, like a mask to hide her emotion from the world, and bid us a stiff farewell.

Reggie and I waited in silence, watching on the security camera as she got into the elevator and exited onto the street.

Then he turned to me.

"So what do you think is really going on here?"

I pinched my lip. I had some ideas, but they were just that, ideas, without proof. "I'll need to go see her to know anything for sure."

Reggie nodded sagely. "I think her mom could be on to something about the drug thing. She's right that, without knowing what type of drug to test for, she's not going to have luck with a home test. What if it's something uncommon, like that drug you found at that club last year? That stuff was crazy. To think that there are things like that out there, that we don't even know about."

I gulped. The NYPD's lab had found the vials of Elixir—i.e., fairy magic—at Obadiah's club, and were still studying it, thinking it was a new narcotic. No one knew what to think of the mysterious substance that had made lab mice levitate. Who knew what they were going to find if they kept examining it? But I stayed silent.

"What we have to do," Reggie continued, "is get some kind of photographic evidence. Get video of the boyfriend slipping her something, or whatever. Plant a spy-cam."

"Is that legal?" I asked. "To spy on someone in their own home without their permission?"

Reggie shrugged, his expression saying without words that everything we did as private eyes fell into that great legal gray area.

"It's not *illegal*," he said. "Jersey is a 'one party consent state.'"

I scowled.

"But is it right? How is it any different than drug testing her without her consent?"

It was bold of me to be arguing with my boss like this, but Reggie respected that I had my own opinions and voiced them, and I respected him for respecting that.

"You're right, it's not different, but we weren't the ones who did that. Personally, I can sympathize with her mother's motivations. If something doesn't change, this kid could die. We'd be helping her."

Helping, yeah, I'd heard that line before.

The whole case made me slightly queasy. Maybe it just reminded me too much of the way the Fairy Queen spied on me.

I stared out at the window at the steam rising from the pipes of the building roof across the street, silently thinking.

Reggie's voice startled me out of my thoughts. "I hope it was okay I volunteered you to go out there. But I wanted you to know, I trust you on your own. I think this case is perfect for you. Maybe this kid will open up to you. If it is the boyfriend, she's not going to open up about her love life to some old geezer like me, or to her mom. Maybe she'll confess to you about whatever this new boyfriend has been doing, and you won't even have to do any spying. Wouldn't that be nice?"

Nice, yes. Likely to happen? Probably not. But I gave Reggie a thin-lipped smile.

"Her mother seems like a real piece of work." Reggie sighed. "But the poor woman is beside herself. I get it. I'd be going nuts if it was my daughter."

I glanced over at the photo on Reggie's desk of Nicole Ruggiero, who had to be about the same age as Quinn. I'd never met the girl, but I'd seen a lot of pictures. She looked just like her father: the same dark, Italian eyes, the same prominent nose, though if she had the same eyebrows, they'd been plucked, waxed or threaded into near oblivion. She had a beaming grin on her face in this photo, just like in all others.

I glanced back at Reggie. I think he saw his daughter in every one of these cases that involved a young woman. He always told me we couldn't get personally invested in our cases—"That's death," he'd say. But I think he violated that rule about as often as the crew of *Star Trek* violates the Prime Directive.

And so I found myself caring about this girl, Quinn, too, who, I supposed, wasn't that different from me.

"Well, I'll go out there, talk to her and see what I can do," I said. The lack of a concrete plan made me nervous. Reggie had more faith in my abilities than I did in myself. But I had to try.

"Great. I'll get the paperwork started." I rose from my chair.

"Hey, your first case on your own," Reggie said brightly. There was something almost paternal about the pride in his smile.

My first real case on my own. I hoped I didn't screw this up. I was afraid I would. But more than that, I was afraid I would have to leave before seeing it through. Dammit, now was a really terrible time to go back to the Vale. But the Fairy Queen's note on the knife said things were getting worse. How much time did I have?

I sighed, rubbing my brow as I walked back to the makeshift desk Reggie had set up for me since I'd officially started here. Staring at the familiar piles of paper, a thought occurred to me. I tried to dismiss it, but it wouldn't go away, buzzing around like a fly in my mind.

I could hear Brenda Sheffield's words in my head: *It's like she's dead, going through the motions of being alive.*

That sounded a whole lot like a Fetch. The Fairy Queen always replaced the human children she kidnapped with Fetches—copies made of enchanted wood that looked alive but *weren't.* I'd been the only exception, the only live changeling replacement. But Quinn was twenty-one, far too old to be a stolen child. And it wasn't like when the Queen had briefly replaced Eva with a Fetch to get my attention. Quinn had no connection to me. The Fairy Queen would have no motive for messing up her life. Would she?

I turned back to the pile of paperwork in front of me. The events of the past year were making me see every case in a supernatural light, even the ones that were just plain old grunt detective work. I'd gotten burned personally and now I was trigger-shy. I'd never forget the sight of that living corpse in the hospital bed that looked like Eva but *wasn't*, alive and yet lifeless. And that was the way Brenda described Quinn: listless, silent, catatonic.

But those could all also be symptoms of severe depression. That was a much likelier cause. Or substance abuse, like her mother and Reggie suspected. If the symptoms started after seeing the new boyfriend, it very well could have something to do with him. Either the guy wasn't good for her and was having this negative effect on her emotions, or he was giving her something that was making her this way.

Still, I couldn't let go of the thought that maybe this "overnight" change in Quinn's personality could have a magical origin. Probably my own paranoia, but it was worth ruling out. If she was a Fetch, we didn't have much time.

There was only one way to find out. And that was to go out to West Tulip, meet the girl and see for myself. If I could look in her eyes, touch her skin, talk to her, I could tell whether she was real or a copy. That was the only way to know. And Reggie was right, though he didn't know it: this was one area of our work that I was uniquely suited for, and no one else. I felt like I could never escape my supernatural life, even when I tried to bury my head in my human one. I tried to dismiss the thought, and instead focus on looking up train schedules from Penn Station to West Tulip, but I couldn't quell the growing feeling of unease this case was giving me. It was just reminding me of the fact that I was living in the human world on borrowed time. Sometime, and soon, I had to go home.

When I got back from work that evening, Obadiah was already there waiting for me. I'd given him his own key; we were at that point now, and Eva didn't mind. She was thrilled for us, even though she made a great show of pretending to gag whenever we acted ultra-lovey-dovey around each other. When I opened the door and saw him, lounging awkwardly in the tiny IKEA dining room chairs that were much too small for his tall frame, my heart leapt. It didn't matter how many times I saw him, there was still that rush when his eyes met mine. He got up from the chair, walked over to me and folded me into his arms. I leaned into him, pressing my cheek against his leather jacket, closing my eyes and inhaling the spice of his cologne. He leaned down; I lifted my face, hungrily reaching for his mouth. His stubble was a delightful prickle against my lips. He gave me a playful bit of tongue, and when we pulled back for air, we were both smiling.

"How was your day, love?" he asked, and the

warm, melty feeling that came over me whenever he called me "love" crept over me, like maple sugar in my soul.

"Good. Reggie's putting me on a new case. He wants me to do this one on my own."

I set down my purse and sat at the table while Obadiah went to fetch two hard ciders from the fridge, the perfect thing on a warm September evening.

He poured them into glasses for both of us, and I relayed to him our whole conversation with Brenda about Quinn.

"It makes me nervous," I said at last.

"Why?" he asked.

I frowned, watching the tiny gold bubbles rise to burst on the surface of my glass.

"Because it's spying. It's wrong."

"You're a P.I.," he countered gently. "Isn't spying what you do?"

"Yeah, but it's one thing when it's cheating spouses, or stalking exes or insurance fraud or whatever. Those people are adults at least."

"Twenty-one is technically an adult," Obadiah said. But I shot him a look.

"Come on. Almost no one acts like an adult at twenty-one. Plus, a parent spying on their grown child?" I frowned.

"Does it remind you too much of what your mother did to you? What she's probably still doing right now?"

My stomach went cold at his words, and I pushed

my cider away. I was still unnerved by how that knife had appeared on my pillow. I hadn't seen a floater in my eye, the telltale sign that the Fairy Queen was watching me via one of her pixie spies. But she or one of her minions had obviously visited without my knowledge or permission. I was never completely out of her control, and it made it feel like there was a leash on my free will. Quinn's case rubbed at that old sore, because we were acting like her own personal Fairy Queen.

"Maybe you're right," I admitted. "But it's different. This case is temporary. We'll observe, learn and leave. It's not for life, not like with me."

"True." Obadiah nodded. "So, are you going to go out there?"

"Tomorrow. She's out in West Tulip." I grimaced. I didn't like the suburbs of New York, all those perfectly manicured lawns, the too-large houses, the big empty space of it all. It felt cold, in a way the warm, pulsing life of the city never did. Still, it was one day. I didn't have to live out there. I wondered if being stuck in a suburban house in the middle of New Jersey with one's parents would be enough to make anyone depressed. I adored my human parents, but I would have gone mad if I was still stuck living with them out in Grover Heights.

"You got any tips for my interview?" I asked Obadiah. He was good with this sort of thing. I sort of wished he could come with me. But Reggie would never allow that.

"Be yourself."

I rolled my eyes at the cliché.

"No, seriously. And make sure the parents are out of the room, and not listening at the door either, when you interview her. This girl has had her privacy violated a lot. I'm sure her level of trust isn't high. You'll have to earn it."

"Thanks. Now I feel even more intimidated than I did going in." I grimaced.

He took my hand under the table and squeezed it. "You have nothing to fear here. You're good at earning people's trust."

I shook my head as I set my cider down on the table. "How do you know?"

"You did a pretty good job earning mine. And I'm sure I'm a far tougher nut to crack than this girl."

That warm melty feeling came over me again at his words, and I smiled, nudging his knee under the table.

We held hands beside our half-drunk ciders for a moment, not saying anything, just looking into each other's eyes.

His took a mischievous gleam.

"You're not going out to see her tonight, are you?"

"No, tomorrow."

"So tonight you're free?"

"Mm-hmm, what did you have in mind?"

He winked at me, that wink saying everything. Then he got up from the table, and I followed suit. He hooked his thumbs through the belt loops of my jeans, and tugged suggestively towards the bedroom. I let him lead me, laughing, my heartbeat quickening as we made our way down the dark hall. He stopped at the entrance to my bedroom.

"Is Eva going to be home tonight?" he asked, glancing at her closed door.

"Pretty sure she's working late."

"So we've got the apartment to ourselves, then," Obadiah whispered into my ear, nibbling on it, sending a pleasurable shiver through me.

I leaned back, arching my spine against the firmness of his body, feeling arousal already pooling in me. "To the bedroom, then."

He nudged the door open with one foot, his hands warm around my waist, and there we were, standing over my unmade bed. I fell down on my familiar ribbon quilt, and he joined me, the narrow twin-size mattress that was far too small for the two of us sinking under his weight. His mouth found mine, and all of a sudden I stopped laughing, closing my eyes as our mouths met, his kiss urgent and hungry.

His weight pushed me into the bed. My head fell back against the pillow and I winced as I felt something hard.

"Ow," I gasped, rubbing the back of my head.

I'd forgotten the knife.

Obadiah looked up.

"What's a'matter?" he asked, concerned.

"Oh, it's nothing," I said. "Let's continue where we left off, shall we?"

I tried to make my voice sound light. I was trying to fool myself more than him, to squelch the dread the knife had brought back to me.

But Obadiah raised one eyebrow.

"What is it? You're as transparent as glass, Mab, something is up."

I sighed. Sheepishly I reached under my pillow and pulled out the knife. "This showed up in my room this morning."

Obadiah jerked back. Instantly I regretted showing it to him. I knew he was reliving the memory of when my mother had forced him to stab himself with that thing, and he had, not knowing if it was the Vale Cleaver and he'd pop back into the human world, or it wasn't and he would die. I put my hand on his shoulder.

"That's why I didn't want to show it to you," I said quietly. "I won't ever try to hide things from you. I just didn't want to make you upset."

"It's okay." He managed a smile. "I'd rather you be honest."

He looked down at the knife lying beside my pillow.

"So I guess it is what I think it is?" he said, eying it warily. I noticed he didn't touch it. The human-like warmth of it probably freaked him out. It freaked *me* out.

"I'm pretty sure. I guess I couldn't be a hundred percent sure till you saw it, since you've seen it a lot more recently than I have." I grimaced, regretting the words. "It's the knife my mother offered you, isn't it? The Vale Cleaver?"

"Has to be. I've never seen another one like it. Well, except for its double."

We both stared at the ancient blade, so out of place against my soft percale sheets.

"There's a message written on it." I held up the blade to Obadiah, so that he could read the text in English.

He scanned the writing. "Your mother misses you."

"I know."

Dammit, the old lump was back in my throat. Sometimes I felt bad about the way I treated her. Then again, she'd also killed people. She'd killed *children*. But I was her daughter, as much as I tried to forget that fact. Thinking about it, I realized how many days it had been since I'd called my human mom too, who'd done nothing wrong. Now I felt doubly guilty.

I turned the knife over, so that he could read the message on the reverse side, then thrust it back under my pillow, figuring Obadiah had seen enough, and because I couldn't bear that pulsing warmth in my hands.

"Do you think there's any truth to the message on the other side, about things getting worse in the Vale?"

"I don't know." Obadiah sighed. "Things were pretty bad already."

"Or is that just a ploy to get me to come home faster?" I asked.

"Could be either, knowing her. But she very well could be telling the truth. You saw how bad things got with the Elixir drought. I doubt it's gotten better."

"What can we do?" I said.

"Nothing," Obadiah said. "We've had this conversation before. We still don't have a plan."

The heat of desire was leaving me, worry beginning to pick away at it.

Then a change came over his eyes, the familiar spark I loved so much.

"Look," he said tenderly. "If you want to go back, or feel you need to go back, you can go back. I'm sure Reggie will give you the time off. And I'll come with you."

I warmed at his words. I wanted him to come with me, and yet I heard my voice saying, "You really don't have to. I know you don't like to leave your club alone for that long."

But he pressed his finger lightly to my lips.

"In any case, you can't leave tonight, or tomorrow, because you promised Mrs. Whatshername that you'd meet her out in West T."

He paused, and I saw the roguish spark in his eyes growing. I knew exactly where he was going with this, and I blushed, liking it very much. "You know, there is something we can do that could take your mind off your worries in the meantime."

He bent down, nibbling at my ear, and then his hot lips traveled down to kiss my neck.

It worked. All the thoughts that had been going

round and round in ineffective circles in my mind vanished in the trail of kisses down my shoulder.

We leaned back onto the soft cotton sheets.

I reached up, entwining my fingers in the tendrils of his hair, bringing his lips even closer against mine. This was what I'd been looking forward to all day.

He leaned over me, the weight of his body pressing me down into the mattress. He pinned my wrists playfully behind my head.

He loomed above me now, and I gazed up at him, drinking in the way the last rays of sun made his crisp white shirt almost glow. Leaning over me, his hands pressed over my wrists, *that* look in his eyes, he was a god in man's clothing—or lack of clothing—as, never breaking eye contact, he began to slowly unbutton his shirt.

I smiled, gazing up at him.

And then I stopped.

Something had caught my attention, and now that I had seen it, I couldn't *un*-see it. All the desire that had been building inside me froze in an instant.

"Obadiah, what's wrong?" I asked.

"Nothing," he said, smiling down at me, but I knew what I'd just seen.

His hand, undoing the buttons, was shaking.

Not shaking in a nervous way. Shaking in a full-on, tremor sort of way, like a "something was medically wrong" sort of a way. The muscles beneath his skin were flinching and twitching in a jerky offbeat rhythm from the tips of his fingers down the length of his arm.

"Obadiah, what's going on? Are you okay?"

He looked at me, then down at his hand, and sat up, shifting away from me. He must have seen the tremor I was seeing, because he removed his hand from his button flap and thrust it into the pocket of his blue jeans, hiding it from me. There was a small flinch in his eyes, a tightening in his brow.

"I'm fine," he said. He bent down and began to kiss my neck again.

The alternating swirls of his tongue with a nibble of teeth always felt delicious, but I was not going to let him distract me like this, not till he told me what was wrong.

I sat up abruptly in bed, pulling the sheets around myself, and looked at him squarely.

"What were we just saying? About not hiding things from each other? Hmm?" I raised one eyebrow, as best I could, in imitation of his classic one-eyebrow-raising maneuver, although I couldn't do it nearly as well as he could.

He smiled, but didn't meet my eyes.

"No," he said quietly, sitting back upright, "we don't." He gazed out the window at the little sliver of sunset we could glimpse between the neighboring buildings.

"Seriously," I said, "what's wrong?"

He sighed. "It really is nothing, love. Nothing to worry about."

But I noticed he was sitting on his hands.

"Come on, just tell me."

There was a small sheen of sweat on his brow that I could see gleaming in the fading light. It wasn't from anything we'd been doing yet, and it wasn't from heat. It was chilly in the apartment now.

"I promise I'll tell you, but can we wait to talk about it? Can we first . . . ?" He smiled charmingly at me. "I don't want to think for a while."

But as good as his lips had felt, I couldn't just turn my brain off. It was one of the downsides of being human.

"I'm not going to be able to relax unless you tell me."

Obadiah sighed.

"You're not going to let me get away without telling you right now, are you?"

"Of course not. I don't let you get away with b.s., any more than you let me, and that's why we love each other." I smiled up at him, and his face broke out into a smile in return.

"So why were your hands shaking like that?" I pressed him gently.

Slowly Obadiah brought his hands back into his lap. They were still trembling like leaves in November.

"It's just a little tremor I get sometimes," he said, his tone light, but he wasn't meeting my eye.

"Just a little tremor you get sometimes? That's not normal; that's concerning. Do you need to go to a doctor?"

"It's not a, um, health problem," Obadiah muttered.

"Then what is it?"

At last he looked at me, his expression almost guilty.

"You know, ever since we got back from the Vale eight months ago, I haven't touched Elixir. I mean, not a drop. It's not just that the cops raided my stash. Now that I know where it comes from, what the Queen does to her captives, I just can't, you know? And I want to cultivate my own magic, instead of having to steal it from others. So that's why I quit taking the stuff."

"I know." I smiled at him. "I'm proud of you."

"Don't be so proud," he said, his eyes downcast again.

I touched his cheek, turning his head to face me. "Obadiah, if you had a little Elixir, it's not the end of the world. One drink isn't what's keeping those kids in prison. It's the Fairy Queen who . . ."

"I will NEVER drink Elixir again."

The sudden volume of his voice startled me and I drew my hand back.

Instantly he lowered it. "I can't. How could I? Knowing what I know now? Mab, I have nightmares about them. All those children—their sleeping, dead faces. I can't, I can't, I just can't."

"I know," I said. "I can't either."

We'd both woken each other up in the night from bad dreams about the fairies' human captives we'd seen in the Vale—whom we'd been unable to save. He held me and rocked me when I came to, screaming and clawing at invisible cocoons, and I held him when it was his turn.

"I understand why you don't drink Elixir. But if you've fallen off the wagon once, you shouldn't beat yourself up," I started, but he interrupted me.

"It's not that. I *haven't* 'fallen off the wagon,' as you say. I haven't had any Elixir."

"So what is it?"

"I think that's the problem. The problem is I *haven't* had any."

I looked up at him, not understanding.

"These symptoms started when I stopped drinking Elixir," he said quietly.

A lump of cold dread filled my stomach.

What if Obadiah needed the Elixir? I'd seen the symptoms of Elixir sickness in the victims of the Elixir drought. I'd just never thought of it with Obadiah, because he seemed so human. The "Thirst," as the fairies called Elixir sickness, had four stages. The first one was tremors. The second was weakness. The third was madness. The last was death.

"Oh my god," I whispered. "You're half fairy. You must need the Elixir to survive. Obadiah, you've got to drink some. I understand your ethical objections; I have them too. But you won't help the cause if you don't have your health. If this is the first symptom of Elixir Thirst, you can't let it get a foothold. You need to take some Elixir immediately."

Obadiah was starting to get dressed, and I noticed he shoved his hands back in his pockets whenever he could, so I wouldn't see him shaking. "That's the thing, though. I don't know if I actually need it. I'm not like other fairies. I'm half human too. Maybe that makes me hardier? Maybe it means I can live without it?"

He wrapped his arms around me, and I leaned back against him, thinking. His heart was a warm, steady presence at my back, but my mind was whirling. *Did* he need Elixir as a half Fey? I wasn't sure, given that he was the only half fairy I'd ever met, the only one I'd ever known existed. But I didn't want to find out the hard way. I couldn't let him take that risk.

I twisted my hips so that we were face-to-face.

"Obadiah, until we figure out what it is that's causing these symptoms and what to do about it, drink a little Elixir, okay?"

He shook his head in disgust.

"No, I'm serious. It's for your health."

"I'm *fine*." The edge was back in his voice.

"No, you're not fine."

"I'll *be* fine. The shakes aren't that bad; they're not interfering with my life. Occasionally I'll drop a glass in the club. Reuben calls me a klutz, but it's not like I can't do my job. I don't need to drink any Elixir."

I frowned at him. "The shakes are just stage one of the Elixir Thirst and you know it. You can't take that risk."

He frowned at me. "I'm not drinking any Elixir. I couldn't live with myself if I did. I can handle the shakes and the . . . other stuff. I'm fine."

"What other stuff?" I asked.

But he refused to answer me.

"I said, I'm *fine*."

I shot him a look that said I didn't believe it one bit. "I love you. That means I worry about you. Those two go hand in hand. Come on, if it was me who was shaking and sweating and worse, you'd be worried about me."

"I'd be going out of my mind, love," Obadiah said quietly, cradling me against him, my cheek pressed against his chest, feeling the rhythm of his heart.

I ran my fingers through his curly hair.

"So if you won't do it for your own health and well-being, do it for me?"

"Don't say that. That's not fair."

"I'm just saying, don't take the risk. A little Elixir wouldn't kill you." I nuzzled against him. "And I don't think it will kill any kids in the Vale either. It's the Fairy Queen who's responsible for their deaths, not you."

"I used to drink Elixir ignorantly, but now I know it comes from human suffering."

It didn't used to come from human suffering. Not in the golden age, when the Elixir streams replenished themselves, when fairies deserved their magic, I thought glumly. But since the drought, he was right.

"There has to be another way," I said. "There has to be another way to get fairies, and half fairies, their Elixir, without killing people."

Obadiah was silent.

I gazed up at him, studying the face of the man I was growing to love.

And in that moment I made my decision.

I couldn't let him get sick from the Thirst. I didn't want him to risk his life for his principles.. My hands clenched in the folds of the sheets.

"I have to go back," I whispered. I wasn't sure exactly when I would leave, but I couldn't put it off. Obadiah's condition had pushed me over the edge. I had to deal with everything that was wrong in my world.

"You don't have to go back," Obadiah said, knowing exactly where I meant.

"I had to go back eventually. This just gave me extra motivation. I mean, I wasn't going to let all those kids sit and rot there. And my Shadow too."

I still had nightmares about the girl, whose place I had taken in the human world when I became a changeling. In my dreams she was always chasing after me through dark tunnels of stone.

"I have to save them all," I said.

"Mab, you can't save everyone."

I opened my mouth to reply, but shut it. He was right, but that didn't change the need I felt in my heart.

"When we go back, what's your plan?" Clearly he realized I'd made up my mind.

"Wait, what's the 'we' you're talking about? Obadiah, it's my problem; it's my fight."

"No, we're in this together."

"You are not coming with me. My mother tried to kill you the last time you were there. It's not safe for you. I need to go alone."

"No, you don't." Obadiah looked almost offended by the suggestion. "If I'm a boyfriend worth my salt, I'm not going to let you face your biggest demons alone."

I wasn't going to let him risk his life for me, but it touched me to the quick that he wanted to, that he was instantly willing, for *me*. I hadn't realized how lonely I had been all these years on my own, without a connection to the Fey world. And now for the first time, I wasn't alone. I had someone to share these burdens with. But still, I cared about him far too much to let him do something stupid, just because he loved me.

"We'll see," was all I could manage to say in reply, and we smiled at each other, clearly both feeling like we'd won.

Obadiah lay back against the bed, and I rested my head on his chest. He pulled the comforter up over us as we lay together, clothed and staring at the ceiling.

"Well, I'm not going anywhere yet," I said. "I can't. First I have to go out to West Tulip. I have to at least check out the Quinn case, see if there's anything I can do before I leave." I glanced at him. "Are you going into the club tomorrow? I don't want to leave you by yourself."

Obadiah stroked my hair. "Relax, Mab. I'm totally fine on my own. This isn't the first time I've had these symptoms. I've been having them for months." He must have seen the expression on my face, because he looked abashed. "I didn't want to worry you."

"Please promise me you'll never keep anything like that from me again," I said, and I could tell he was serious when he nodded.

"I promise."

As we undressed for bed that night, though, dread crept back into my heart. I'd seen firsthand what the Thirst could do. Memories of my old life as a fairy kept flooding back to me in the darkness: watching my fellow Fey waste away, collapsing by the sides of the gilded roads, or terror-eyed and screaming with madness. Now that I knew about Obadiah's symptoms, I couldn't stop my brain from returning there, like a tongue to a sore tooth. The glowing red lines on the bedside alarm clocked changed, minutes passing into hours. In the filter of the moonlight through the curtains, I watched Obadiah lying next to me, the shape of him slowly rising up and down with his breaths.

Obadiah murmured something in his sleep, and twitched. His nightmares had been growing more frequent lately, I'd noticed, and I wondered if it was the Elixir sickness. He cried out, and I pressed my hand to the small of his back, gentling him. Still half-asleep, he rolled over to spoon me. Dammit, I had to do something to help him. The thought of the Thirst getting him stopped my breath, made me want to curl into a ball and scream. It had been a little less than a year since we'd first met, and yet, I could no longer imagine life without Obadiah in it. It was noble of him to try to abstain from Elixir, but I wouldn't let him do something stupid, just to be noble. And if he wouldn't drink Elixir, I had to find a cure for the Elixir Thirst, before it was too late.

CHAPTER 2

I must have drifted off into a worried sleep myself because the blaring alarm clock woke me, and I groaned, reaching over to punch it off. I sat up and stretched.

"Morning, beautiful," Obadiah whispered, handsomely grizzled in the blue light of early morning.

I kissed the top of his head. "You feeling better?"

"Yeah," he said brightly.

But I looked askance at him. I couldn't forget what I'd seen last night.

"I wish I didn't have to go out there."

"What time do you have to leave?" Obadiah asked.

"Soon." I frowned. "I'm doing the interview first thing, then heading to Reggie's office."

Obadiah eyed me from where he lay sprawled out like a lion in the rumpled sheets. "Are you going to ask him about taking time off, to go back to the Vale?"

I shook my head. "Next week is Labor Day weekend. I'll have Monday off and Reggie always closes the office early on that Friday. It's enough time to make a quick trip back, enough to see what this bad thing is that the Queen's talking about, and try to find out some answers." *And maybe steal some Elixir for you, directly from the streams, so you know it doesn't come from the Queen's captives*, I thought, getting out of bed and shivering as my bare feet touched the floorboards.

"I hadn't realized the holiday was coming up so soon. It would be the perfect time for a trip," Obadiah said, rising from the bed after me.

"I wish I could tell Reggie where I was really going," I said wistfully, putting on my robe.

"That you're taking a long weekend to Fairyland?" Obadiah replied, raising his eyebrow.

"You're right. There's no way to really tell him, is there?" I sighed as I headed for the shower.

When I kissed Obadiah goodbye that morning, he was headed back to his club. He said he'd received a text from Reuben in the night that there was some trouble with the werewolves.

"Do you think everything's okay?" I asked as he buttoned the cuffs to his crisp business shirt like a knight preparing for battle.

Obadiah shrugged. "I'm sure it'll be fine. The Wolfmen are always having spats with each other. Too much testosterone." He rolled his eyes, finishing the cuff. "But I'd better go out there and check it out. I don't want Reuben to have to deal with it all on his own. He can't be bad cop to his own pack, but I can."

"I don't want you to have to play bad cop," I said, continuing to get ready for work myself.

"Why? I like playing bad cop." He winked at me.

"Text me when you're there just to let me know everything's alright?" I said.

"Of course," he said, "and good luck with the interview. I know you'll do great."

He kissed me again, filling me with warmth all over. The way Obadiah looked at me when he pulled back from the kiss made me feel strong, brave, capable.

"I'll call you on my lunch break." I smiled at him, still singing inside from his kiss as I bounced down the stairs.

Penn Station was a throng of pushing, shoving New Yorkers, but as I made my way to the Jersey Transit side, the crowd thinned out. The train glided towards me on the platform, and I walked on board, taking a seat on the top level of the double-decker. I settled my bag in my lap. The car was cleaner and more spacious than a subway car, but only slightly.

I was dressed in a freshly ironed, navy blue suit. Reggie had told me a suit wouldn't be necessary. He told me I didn't even need to dress up as much as I did to go to work, considering he himself lived in rumpled khakis. But I had met Brenda Sheffield; I saw how *she* dressed, and I knew my relative youth and inexperience were going to count against me here. At least I could *look* like an adult, even if I seldom *felt* like one.

The train lurched into motion. We rocked and swayed through the tunnel for a long time, at last popping out on the other side of the Hudson River. Newark seemed very much the same as New York City from the train: a maze of office buildings, dirty and gritty, until it all thinned out into a vast, industrial wasteland. But then twenty minutes later we had entered a different world.

I stared out the window in wonder as the green suburbs whirred by. It had been too long, I realized, since I'd seen trees. I'd forgotten what a difference looking out on nothing but green made to my heart. The last time I'd seen a forest, not a park but a real forest, was the last time I was in the Vale. I tried not to think about it, peering out at the houses: Tudors, Victorians and colonials, which grew larger and statelier as we sped along. Little commuter towns with picturesque names like "Bellefleur," and "Griffin Park," sped by, but after a while, they all blended in to each other, and I missed homely, homey Brooklyn.

The conductor's voice boomed out, "West Tulip, next stop!" and my heart fluttered nervously. If this girl hadn't opened up to the dozen other professionals her mother had dragged her to, who had many more degrees, and years of experience, what chance did I think I had?

But you have magic, a little voice inside me whispered. Not really. What I had was the *memory* of magic, the knowledge that there was another world outside our mundane realm. I didn't know if that would help me in this case or not. But it was the only leg up I had.

The train rolled to a stop at the pretty brick station house of West Tulip, and I scrambled to my feet, smoothing the sitting wrinkles from my trousers, my pulse quickening. Brenda Sheffield met me at the station, as promised. Her Mercedes Benz was beige. In fact, it sort of matched her outfit, which was also beige: Coach purse, khaki pants, a blouse and stilettos. Here I was wearing a suit, and yet I still felt underdressed around the woman.

"Thank you for coming out," she said stiffly, opening the door for me.

"Thanks for the ride," I replied. Taking a seat, I tried to not stare too obviously. I'd never been in a car this expensive before, and I resisted the impulse to run my hands down the curves of the buttery soft leather seats.

We drove through the picturesque village of West Tulip. The sidewalks were punctuated by streetlights fashioned to look like old-fashioned gas lamps, each one of them supporting a basket of blooming begonias. The tidy little shops flanking the street sold designer baby clothes, artisanal ice creams, interior decor and various other lovely but impractical things.

It didn't take long to leave the town center and drive through the green, sun-dappled lanes of residential West T to arrive at the Sheffields' house.

My eyes widened as we pulled up at the gate. Yes, there was a gate, which should have been the first tell. It was a stately colonial, like the other houses in the block, set off from the road by large, sculpted hedges, and tastefully colored blooms lining the slate walk.

Brenda let me into the house through a side entrance, and the first thing I noticed was how immaculately clean it was. I mean, she knew I was coming, but still. It was intimidating. Eva's and my domestic standards were basically if it didn't violate any health codes it was probably okay. This house looked ready to be shown by a Realtor. The effect was cold and unlived-in.

"May I get you something to drink? Iced tea? Perrier?" Brenda asked amiably, but she was still looking askance at me, like she was disappointed Reggie hadn't come out himself. It made me more nervous than I already was.

"Oh, um, just some water, thanks," I said, trying to act natural.

As Brenda filled a crystal glass with bottled water, I glanced around her kitchen, trying to not let my jaw drop open in amazement. It was almost the size of our entire apartment, full of gleaming granite countertops and a six burner Viking range. Eva would have flipped, yet I got the distinct impression that the only kitchen implement that got used in here was the small microwave recessed into the cream-colored wainscoted cabinetry.

She led me to take a seat in the living room, which was wall-to-wall beige couches, with a huge abstract painting over the fireplace that looked like it had been purchased more because it matched the colors in the window treatments than out of any love for the art itself.

"Is your daughter home?" I asked, fiddling with my glass.

Brenda frowned, the worry and strain showing through the perfect mask of her makeup. "Yes, of course, she's upstairs, in her room."

I looked Brenda right in the eye. "She's expecting me, right? You *did* tell her I was coming?"

"Oh yes, I told her," Brenda said quietly, her eyes drifting off to the window, where the remains of a child's playhouse stood in the backyard. The wood was a pale weathered gray, and the shingled roof was beginning to sag. It contrasted so sharply with the otherwise immaculately manicured back lawn that at first it surprised me they hadn't torn it down. But there are some things none of us can quite let go of.

"I told her you were coming," Brenda continued. "But I'm not sure if she heard. I'm never sure anymore what gets through."

I nodded. This interview wasn't going to be easy.

"May I go see her?" I asked. I was nervous about

my conversation with Quinn, but at the same time, I didn't want to prolong the awkwardness of sitting here on this too-clean sofa drinking bottled water with her tightly wound mother.

Brenda nodded, biting her lip hard. It was hard for her to let a stranger into her house, hard for her to let me see how bad things really were with her daughter. I could tell by the haunted expression in her mascaraed eyes, the fact she was letting me was a sign of how desperate she was.

"Come upstairs with me. I'll show you where her room is."

I followed Brenda's clacking heels up the stairs. The landing was decorated with framed family photographs. The center of all of them was a beaming, towheaded little girl, in ballet outfits and Christmas sweaters and elementary school graduation gowns. Quinn was adorable and had the glow of a well-loved child. I noticed the photos stopped around the age of twelve, though, and I wondered what kind of teenager this little Shirley Temple blonde had grown into.

There were three closed doors at the top of the stairs. Brenda pointed to the middle. "It's, um, that one."

She paused outside the door awkwardly.

"Would you like me to be present for the interview?" she asked hopefully.

"Actually, I think it would be better if we speak one-on-one," I said, and her face fell. "I'll stay and talk with you after, if I have additional questions," I added.

I had an instinct Quinn might be more forthcoming with a stranger than her own family.

Brenda headed back downstairs. Once she was out of earshot, I knocked softly on the door.

There was no answer.

I knocked again, louder this time.

"Quinn?" I called through the door. "It's Mabily Jones from Reginald Ruggiero Investigative Services."

I paused. Still no answer.

Brenda called up from downstairs. "You can just open it. She'd not going to answer."

I realized she was probably right, but still, I felt bad. This whole assignment made me feel queasy inside.

"Quinn, I'm assuming you can hear me. I'm going to come in, okay?" I said, and slowly and hesitantly I opened the door.

When the door swung open, I caught my breath.

A young woman was lying on the bed, fully dressed, her eyes staring up vacantly at the ceiling.

For a brief, terrifying moment, I was afraid I was looking at a corpse, and then I saw the slow rise and fall of her chest.

"Hi, Quinn," I said with all the friendliness I could muster.

She made no response. Just continued to lie there and stare.

The first thought that came to me as I saw her was how utterly different she was from her mother.

It wasn't just that her blond hair had been dyed an unnaturally maroon red, or the fact that she dressed mostly in black. It was the complete lack of politeness and social pretense. She didn't even glance in my direction; she just ignored me, staring at the ceiling plaster.

Of course, Fetches just lay there catatonically too, I told myself. But I dismissed the thought.

Since Quinn wasn't talking or looking at me, I cast a quick glimpse at the room in which I found myself.

Quinn's room was another world entirely from downstairs.

The place was a complete mess. It seemed almost an act of defiance against the immaculately tidy downstairs. Black clothes were strewn across the floor like decaying leaves. Stacks of books and magazines collided haphazardly in the corners like collapsing skyscrapers. The whole room was a battleground between Brenda's aesthetic taste and Quinn's, symbolized by Nightwish posters tacked up over the pretty pink floral wallpaper. They met in the middle on some posters of Pre-Raphaelite paintings, one with Persephone thoughtfully holding a pomegranate, the other of Ophelia drowning in the stream, her hair spread out around her like a halo. It occurred to me as I glanced over at Quinn that she looked a lot like Millais' painting: her pale face staring so vacantly up into space, her red hair sprawling out over the black flowered pattern of her comforter.

There was a chair by the bed, an elaborate Victorian-styled stuffed thing made of red velvet and black lace, perhaps a gift from her parents with a nod to their daughter's tastes. If I sat down, I'd be more at eye level with the girl on the bed.

"May I take a seat?" I asked.

Again no response.

Awkwardly, I sat down. Sitting, I could see now that there was a shelf over her bed containing an altar much like Eva's, although Quinn's little statues of goddesses seemed a lot less friendly.

Quinn still wouldn't look at me. I wondered if she knew I was there. Could it really be that she was a Fetch? The only way to find out would be to get her to talk, or to touch her, but I didn't want to do the latter without her permission. "May I talk to you?"

She didn't respond. Of course she didn't. But after a second, she slowly twisted her head to the side, so that one eye was looking at me.

That didn't tell me whether or not she was a Fetch. Even a Fetch could still track with their eyes, mindlessly, like how plants move to follow the sun.

"Did your mom tell you who I am?"

"Yeah."

I almost jumped at the sound of her voice. I hadn't known she could speak. It almost wasn't a word, just a low whisper, the shadow of a word. But she'd spoken. I'd heard that Fetches could speak sometimes, well, sort of. Yeses and nos at least. I need to get more of a complete conversation out of her to know for sure.

"What did your mom tell you about me?" I asked, trying not to ask yes or no questions.

Quinn turned her head another few inches to look at me directly. Her blue eyes were blank, soulless. She didn't respond.

After a beat of silence, I tried again.

"Your parents hired my boss and me because they're worried about you," I began.

"They hired you to spy on me."

It was the first full sentence she'd spoken, and it let me know definitively she wasn't a Fetch. That was a level of complex thought that a wooden replacement could never handle. No, there was no magic here. This girl was just garden variety not okay.

I couldn't help it; my heart sank a little. It would have almost been easier if she had been a Fetch. At least then I might have felt qualified to help her. I could have put some of my supernatural knowledge to use. Now I was going to rely on just old-fashioned detective work, something I'd been doing less than a year, something Reggie thought I was far better at than I feared I really was. But I'd been assigned this case, and I was going to do something to help this girl, or at least try.

"I'm not going to spy on you," I said quietly.

Quinn starred at me, clearly not convinced.

I tried a different strategy. "If I wanted to spy on you, I could have already. We have cameras the size of a pinky fingernail. I could have already planted one."

Her eyes widened slightly, but she didn't say anything.

"But I didn't plant any spy cams."

She still didn't say anything. Slowly she moved to turn her head back towards the wall.

"I wanted to talk to you. You're an adult. So am I. Maybe our parents don't think we are, but we are, and I'm not going to treat you as less than that."

I couldn't tell if my words were getting through or not, with her head facing away from me, but I kept going.

"So, are you willing to talk to me?"

Quinn kept her face turned to the wall, silent, and I sighed, feeling like I'd lost what little ground I'd made.

And then, with her face still to the wall, I heard her voice, so quiet it was almost inaudible.

"I can't talk about it. You wouldn't understand. If you spy, you won't see anything anyway. So don't bother with me."

This was a lot more than she'd been saying previously, and I felt like it was progress.

"Quinn, I'm not going to spy. I just want to talk. Your parents are worried about you. That's the only reason they hired me. They're worried that you dropped out of school, that you haven't left your room. They're worried something happened, that you're hurt."

She didn't reply.

"They're worried your new boyfriend . . ."

"I'm not seeing him anymore," Quinn interrupted me, her voice emotionless.

Something about the utter flatness in her voice told me the end of that relationship had been bad.

I didn't say anything for a while, steepling my fingers on the arms of the red velvet chair. I supposed it was a good thing that they had broken up, if the boy was the source of the drugs. Then again, the boy was out of the picture now, but Quinn's symptoms continued.

I studied her. She turned back to me, her knees gradually drawing up into a kind of fetal position. Her eyes still had that same, dead, haunted look.

A terrible possibility was dawning in my mind, but I didn't know how to talk about it. And I didn't know how to get Quinn to trust me. I mean, who was I to this girl? A stranger, and one hired by her parents ostensibly to spy on her to boot. Why should she trust me?

But as I looked at her, I thought of Eva, I thought of my Shadow, so outwardly hostile and so inwardly hurt. I wanted to help this girl too. Would she see that my intentions were good? Would that matter? I had to say what I was thinking. I tried to put it gently.

"Quinn," I said softly. "Did he . . . ?" My words trailed off. How could I say it: hurt, abuse, rape?

"Did he hurt you?" was all I could manage.

Quinn didn't reply. Her whole body had gone stiff, wooden again.

But I noticed a glistening in her eyes, a tear pooling, unheeded.

"If he hurt you, there are things we can do," I tried desperately. "I can help."

But she shook her head, almost violently.

"It wasn't like that," she said quickly.

I was silent.

"No, I mean it. It wasn't like that." She struggled to find the words. "He didn't hurt me. I mean, he *hurt* me, I guess, but it wasn't . . ." She paused, grimacing, searching in our paucity of language for emotional pain to describe whatever had happened. "It wasn't like that," she finished.

I believed her. I had to take her at her word, because what other choice did I have? But then it left me wondering what to say next, what would help?

"Quinn, you don't have to talk to me. I mean, I know I'm just a stranger. But I hope you will talk to someone."

She didn't reply.

"I know your parents took you, forced you to go, to therapists. But what if it wasn't someone they picked, what if it was someone *you* picked?"

She was silent.

"Maybe it would help," I started, but she cut me off, her voice utterly cold.

"They wouldn't believe me."

"But . . ."

"They wouldn't believe me because *I* wouldn't believe me if I heard myself. It's too unbelievable."

I waited, breathless for her to go on.

But she didn't.

Clearly, she'd decided she'd said too much. She

rolled herself onto her other side and faced the wall again, away from me. I put my head in my hands.

At last I asked, "Would you be willing to try me?"

I heard a "no" in her silence. But then to my surprise she spoke. With her head still turned to the wall, her voice sounded disembodied.

"Listen, Mabily, you seem like a nice person. And I know my mom and dad are trying to help. That's why they keep bringing people in to see me: doctors, therapists and now, I guess, private detectives." I couldn't see her face, turned as it was to the wall, but I could imagine she was rolling her eyes at the last one. I tried not to be insulted.

"It's very well meaning and sweet. I'm sorry I worry them."

I sat there, just crossing my fingers that she would keep speaking. It was the most she'd spoken since I'd arrived.

"I'm sure I do seem *worrisome*," she added. "They can't understand it. But I don't even understand it, really, what happened. It's just like all the joy got sucked right out of me . . ."

I sat very still on the edge of the velvet chair, holding my breath. I could tell she was debating whether or not to open up, whether or not to trust me with more, and if I said the wrong thing now, she'd never say another genuine thing to me again. So I said nothing, sitting on my hands and praying that the little crack of light I'd seen in Quinn's thick wall would open wide enough for me to come inside.

"Maybe I should have told someone," she muttered, her head to the wall. "But there's no way to find him now. No telling where he is. I never even knew his real name." Her voice trailed off into silence.

"Um, Quinn, that's where I, as a private detective, might have an advantage over the other *professionals* your parents hired. If you want to track someone down, that's our strong suit."

"You wouldn't be able to find him. Not someone like this."

"We can try. Give me as much information as you can about him," I said. "Do you have any photos of him? Anything you remember him telling you about his life, occupation, where he was from, any biographical details? And whatever name he gave you, even if it was a fake name, it's a start."

But she shook her head again, her back still to me. "I'm not even sure if he's *alive*."

"We can find out," I said gently. "There are databases we can search that can help us find out if he's still living."

"He's not like other people. I'm telling you it won't help, okay?"

I couldn't tell what it was I'd done or said, but I could feel the wall around her slowly rolling down like a garage door, and there was nothing I could do to stop it.

"Look"—she turned her head to stare straight at me—"your intentions seem good, but I'm not going to tell you anything. I'm not because I *can't*.

So you can go, because you're just wasting your time with me."

The defensiveness in her tone was asking me to quit, but I wasn't giving up so easily.

Then again, I didn't know what to do next.

Quinn turned her face back to the wall.

Her words rang in my mind.

I'm not going to tell you anything . . . because I can't, she'd said. Was she worried about retribution for talking to me? Did she think this man would come after her to hurt her, if she revealed his identity? If that was the issue, this made it an entirely different conversation.

"If you're worried he's going to come back and hurt you because of something you tell me, we have ways to keep you safe," I started, trying to reassure her.

"That's not what I'm worried about. I don't think he's even in this world anymore."

I wondered what had happened that made Quinn think her ex-boyfriend might be dead.

That was what she meant when she said "not in this world," right?

It was an odd choice of phrase, a haunted emphasis on the word *world*, and a thought occurred to me as I gazed at the prostrate girl on the bed. Could Quinn possibly be talking about another world, *my* world? But it didn't make sense. She clearly wasn't a Fetch, if she was having a conversation with me. There was no way a human like her would have access to the Vale. And fairies didn't linger in the human world when they visited; they didn't like spending time here. Perhaps Quinn's mysterious man was a Sanguinari—a vampire—or a Wolfman? I looked at her pale white neck, exposed where her hair fell back upon the pillow. *No.* She didn't have any of the telltale scars.

I sighed, rubbing my forehead. There was nothing supernatural here. All there was was a depressed girl, who'd had a bad breakup, and now refused to talk about it.

I opened my mouth to speak, but Quinn turned to me with dead, desperate eyes.

"Please leave my room," she said quietly. "I feel like shit, and I want to be alone."

I hesitated for a moment, wanting so badly to talk to her more, hating that I was leaving with no more information than I'd started with.

"If there's any information you could provide . . ." I started, but she cut me off.

"No. Please leave now."

"Okay," I said softly, "thank you for talking to me."

She gave me the tiniest nod. "Thank you," she whispered, and I could see through her pain, and her anger, her despair and self-loathing, that the thanks had been genuine. There was that tiny crack in her wall again.

"Would it be okay if I come back again and talk to you later?" I asked.

She shrugged.

I realized I wasn't going to get any more out of her.

"Here's my card," I said, pulling one out of my purse and setting it on her bedside table. "Please call me if there's anything I can do." I highly doubted Quinn would ever call me. It would be me calling her. She acknowledged the card with the tiniest flicker of her eyes, but didn't say anything. So I said goodbye and let myself out of the bedroom, and the stale air of despair it reeked with. Shutting the door behind me, I closed my eyes and let out a long sigh. I felt like I'd failed. I'd come all the way out here, talked to her for a half an hour and gotten *nothing* useful. Why had I ever thought I could be a P.I.?

But maybe there wasn't even a case here? Clearly this ex of hers had hurt her, but the wound seemed primarily emotional. Maybe I just saw the supernaturally sinister everywhere I turned because of my past experience, even where it wasn't.

There was the telltale click-clacking of heels and Brenda stood at the base of the stairs.

"Well, how did it go?" she said with cheerful desperation.

What could I say? I walked down the stairs to her, past the rows of photos.

"It was an initial conversation. Quinn wasn't . . ." I paused, trying to put it diplomatically. "She wasn't very forthcoming. But I certainly haven't given up. I'd like to go back and talk to my boss, and then we'll let you know if and how we want to proceed."

It was as delicate an answer as I could give, but Brenda obviously heard failure in it, because her face fell.

"Well, thank you for trying," she said. Yet somehow her voice was kinder now, as if she didn't blame me for not being able to get through to her daughter. We were in the same boat.

"None of the doctors or therapists or anyone else were able to get her to talk either; it's not just you," she said quickly as she led me towards the door. Well, that was a small comfort.

"I'll call you about next steps," I said, but I could tell in her eyes she'd already checked us off her mental list as one more failed attempt, and she was running out of options.

We sat in silence in the Mercedes, soft rock playing faintly from the stereo as she drove me back to the train station.

"Thanks for the ride," I said as I got out. Her polite smile was a bright facade, but I looked her straight in the eye. "Your daughter knows you're worried about her, and she's sorry," I shared, thinking maybe it was the one helpful thing I could say. "She told me so."

"Oh, thank you." Brenda bit her lip and looked like she was about to cry. She gave a quick nod, buttoning up her emotions, but I could tell I'd touched a nerve, and her posture was different when she drove away.

The whole train ride back to Penn Station I thought over the conversation, wondering if maybe Quinn had revealed something without meaning to reveal it, like her evasive answers could be some kind of code. But I got nothing. The train jolted and rocked as it sped through the suburbs and industrial parks towards the beckoning skyscrapers of Manhattan. What had I even come out here for?

CHAPTER 3

I was in a dark mood the rest of the day at the office, and nothing Reggie could say about it only being an initial interview, and that I shouldn't be so hard on myself, or that there were brownies in the break room (food was Reggie's answer to all conundrums), seemed to be able to affect my gloom. I just felt so helpless. I didn't know what was worse, if magic was somehow involved in Quinn's case or it wasn't. If there was something otherworldly here, it didn't match up with anything in my experience. And if it was just an ordinary case, then I was just a fledgling P.I. in way over my head. Either way, I had nothing. I appreciated Reggie's faith in me, but I wasn't sure I deserved it.

Eva met up with me after work. She had texted me that she would be in the city, something to do with this new mysterious job that was taking up all her time, but that she still wouldn't talk about. I was eager to see her. It had been too long since we'd had a face-to-face conversation. When the elevator doors opened and I saw her in the lobby, it dispelled my gloom about Quinn's case. She threw her arms around me in a hearty hug, and we walked arm and arm out onto 37th Street.

Eva looked happy. There was a glow to her skin, and a light in her eyes, despite the bags of exhaustion under them. This new job, whatever it was, was clearly agreeing with her.

We walked towards Broadway. There was a street fair set up about half a block down from Reggie's building, and I could already smell the arepas sizzling. Street fairs were fairly ubiquitous in midtown in the summer. But it was September now, which meant this might be the last one until next season. That gave the meat-scented sausage smoke and pounding reggaeton a kind of melancholy feel.

"You want to walk through it?" Eva asked. We had both lived in New York City just long enough to no longer be surprised by street fairs, but not so long that we viewed them merely as a traffic blocking nuisance.

"Sure," I said, figuring it would take my mind off things.

We strolled along through the colorful booths, wandering meanderingly in the direction of the subway. We passed smoking kabab grills, and signs advertising Thai food for the terrifyingly low price of "$1," and a booth selling flimsy batik dresses that would shrink down to the size to fit an infant as soon as you put them in the dryer.

I turned to Eva. "I met the boy you had over. We didn't get to talk very much, though. He said he was on his way out."

Eva's face crumpled up at the mention of the boy, and she averted her eyes from me. "I don't think you'll be seeing him again," she said quietly.

"Oh, Eva." I put my arm around her. I felt so bad that she had gotten hurt again. She was just starting to get over Ramsey.

"Did he not even say goodbye to you when he ran out the door like that?" I asked, incensed.

"Nope," she said, still not meeting my eye, feigning an interest in the batik dresses.

"Bastard." I squeezed her hand. "I'm so sorry, honey. You deserve so much better than that."

Eva nodded, but that crushed look was still on her face when she finally raised her eyes to mine. For a moment she gazed off into the colorful booths, not saying anything.

"I guess I shouldn't have been surprised," she said at last. "But I thought he was different. The thing is, he *was* different."

I looked at her skeptically.

"I know you don't believe me, but trust me, he wasn't like other guys. I met him through my, um, group." She turned away from me, flushing.

I nodded, understanding. I knew about Eva's "group." She didn't seem to want to call it what it was: a coven. Eva had always been a seeker, and she'd found a group of other twenty-somethings who shared her spiritual interests. They got together once a month and meditated and chanted and took day trips upstate to dance around bonfires, etc. . . . It all seemed like pretty good, clean fun, honestly, but Eva's Catholic grandmother viewed it as Satan worship, and had given Eva a bit of a guilt complex about the things she most dearly loved.

"That's great," I said. "I'm glad you're meeting people there. People with whom you have something in common. No offense, but you and Ramsey?"

"I know." She rolled her eyes. "That was a mistake. But anyway, this guy, Cory"—her eyes looked far away, dreamlike, as she spoke of him—"we only spent that one night together but it was . . . magical. *He* was magical. I'm worried now he's ruined me for merely mortal men."

She laughed, but there was a darkness to it.

"Eva, don't say that," I cajoled.

"I thought if it was that good, it had to be love, I guess. I thought he was special. Maybe he is. I just wasn't special to him."

"Eva, stop it. If this guy didn't see how great you are, he's an idiot and you're better off without him."

First Ramsey, and now this Cory jerk. I wished she could be with someone who saw how special she was, someone who could see her like I saw her.

She shook her head, as if she could shake off the pain in her heart.

Then she walked over to one of the nearby booths. It was one of the ones that sold bed linens of impossibly high thread counts at impossibly low prices.

"Do you remember when we were setting up house, when we first moved into the apartment together, and we bought a set of those things?" Eva said to me, changing the subject.

"And we both woke up the next morning with a horrific rash, and vowed to never buy sheets off the street again?" I laughed, and she did too.

"We really have come a long way together, Mab," Eva said at last, and I nodded, a deep sadness in my chest. This was one of the things I would miss most if I ever moved to the Vale permanently, the comforting domesticity of my life with Eva. Dammit, I couldn't think about that right now.

"Ooh, look, they have funnel cakes," Eva cried, interrupting my thoughts. She pointed towards the sign. I could smell the hot sweet grease in the air. I was glad that she seemed to be distracted from the memory of Cory.

Eva turned to me. "I do not need a funnel cake."

"Eva, no one *needs* a funnel cake. But *wants* . . ."

"You're not helping," said Eva, forking over a couple bucks to the vendor, and being rewarded with bomb of powdered sugar in a red-checked paper container.

We walked in companionable silence for a while, pulling off bits of hot, sugary dough and munching on them.

At last I wiped my fingers on a paper napkin and spoke.

"Will you tell me about this new job that's taking up all your time? Where have you been?"

Eva's eyes brightened. "I'm sorry I haven't told you before now. It's just . . . I wanted to wait until I knew for sure it was really happening, until I was a hundred percent certain I'd get in."

"Get in? What are you talking about?"

"It's not just a new job. Although it's that too." She grinned. "I'm continuing with school. I'm not going to stop with my associate's degree in nursing. I'm going to go for my bachelor's."

"Eva, that's wonderful!" I threw my arms around her and we hugged in the middle of the street, annoyed crowds of pedestrians grumbling past.

Eva blushed, and shrugged. "I guess I'd never really thought of it before. I never thought I'd make it this far. I mean, I know more people from my high school class who are dead than who went to college."

She said the words lightly, turning her attention to one of the used book vendors, but I looked at her horrified. Eva and I had grown up a hop-skip across the Hudson from each other, in the South Bronx and Grover Heights, New Jersey, respectively, and yet we might as well have been raised in different universes. And I didn't mean the human world and Fairyland. Most of the time I forgot that, and then she'd say something like this, casually offhand, and I'd see the chasm that separated us.

"But my new boss, Tamira," Eva continued, running her hand along the book spines, "she's amazing. I told her how much I loved all my science classes and she encouraged me to switch majors to bioengineering. I didn't have all the prerequisites, but Tamira wrote some letters for me, and told the department she thought I could handle it. The last few weeks I've barely slept—it's why I haven't seen you—but even though it's hard, it's so fascinating. You know how I got the job with Tamira?" she asked me.

I shook my head.

"Remember when that guy from the NYPD wanted to interview us about that drug they found in Obadiah's club?"

My stomach tightened, the funnel cake I had eaten turning to lead. I remembered all too well. The NYPD had questioned us in connection to their investigation of the vials found in the club. Our participation had been voluntary, but Reggie had encouraged me to talk to them. It had been the most awkward conversation of my life. How could I tell the well-meaning investigators that the substance they thought was a new street drug was really Elixir? I told them I didn't know anything about it, and they'd seemed satisfied with my non-answers. I'd assumed Eva hadn't been any more forthcoming. She'd told me she had no memory of what had happened that night at Obadiah's, because of her subsequent injury.

"What did you tell them?" I asked.

"Nothing important. I told them I didn't have any

memory of what happened that night, after someone put something in my drink. I was just grateful
that nothing worse happened to me than my fall.
But anyway, I really hit it off with the detective who
interviewed me." She smiled, her dark, long-lashed
eyes beguiling. Eva could always charm the pants off
whatever man she happened to talk to—often quite
literally. "Anyway, he was so sweet and nerdy. I was
telling him about my nursing school classes, how mi-
crobiology was my favorite subject. And he told me
that the head of the lab they were going to be using in
their investigation was looking for a part-time assis-
tant. That's how I met my boss, Tamira. I didn't want
to tell you till I was sure they were going to hire me,
but now it's official."

"That's amazing," I said, excitement and fear trilling through me. Eva was going to be working at the
lab that was investigating Elixir. On the one hand it
was perfect; I'd have an inside source to keep tabs on
their research. But what were they going to find? This
stuff must be terrifying the researchers. They had no
idea what they were dealing with.

We continued walking among the booths, but I
could no longer see them. I was so caught up with the
idea that Eva was going to be right there in the lab
that was researching Elixir.

"Tamira thinks I could be a real researcher if I stay
in school and work at it," Eva went on. "She's willing
to mentor me. The work itself is pretty tedious for the
most part; that's what people don't understand about

science. But the work we're doing, it's truly ground-breaking."

I bet, I thought fearfully, not saying anything. *You're studying magic. You just don't know it.*

But judging by the wideness of Eva's eyes as she talked, I wondered if she hadn't begun to suspect something. Oh god, would she or her colleagues realize they were dealing with something that wasn't from the human world at all?

An idea was occurring to me.

"Eva?" I asked. "Is your lab open to the public? Could I come visit?"

"It's not really open to the public, but I bet Tamira would let you visit me there. I'm sure some stuff would be off-limits, of course, anything that's volatile or undergoing active research. But if you want to just take a look around the facilities, that would probably be okay." She shrugged. "I'm not sure it'll be very interesting for you; all there is to see is lots of racks of agar-jell and vials."

"Still," I said, "I really would like to visit." I wanted to meet the people who were working with Elixir. Glean as much knowledge about their experiments as I could. I could always ask Eva questions about it, but there was no substitute for being there, seeing their work for myself. It was a long shot, but it was worth asking.

"Let me check with my boss," Eva said.

"Thanks," I said. "But only ask if it feels comfortable. I don't want you to do anything to jeopardize your job. You seem really happy there."

"Yeah," Eva said. "I guess I feel like the work I'm doing actually matters. That's precious."

It *was* precious. And all I could think about as she said these words was what was that type of work for me? I mean, being a P.I. was fun, and challenging, but did it matter in that *ultimate* way? It mattered to our clients, like Brenda and Quinn, but did it matter to the world? Like being the next Fairy Queen mattered to the Vale? No matter where my thoughts turned, my mind kept circling back to that.

Eva got the go-ahead from her boss and set up my meeting at the lab two days later. I had never been inside a real research laboratory before, and had no idea what to expect. I met Eva in the vicinity of NYU, and she pointed me towards an unassuming brick building. There was nothing in its external appearance that screamed "lab." We proceeded through the double doors and down a long, winding hallway of squeaky linoleum, then down the elevator to the lower level.

There was no natural light down here, and the fluorescent strips were a harsh, buzzing flicker. At last we came to a door. Eva swiped her badge to it, and we went inside.

The room was large and surprisingly quiet, considering how many people were working there. They stood side by side, at their own stations along the counter-height, black, soapstone lab benches. A few goggled eyes peered curiously at us as we entered. Clearly they weren't used to having visitors. But a moment later their heads were down again, intent on their work. I felt guilty interrupting the atmosphere of hushed concentration. They all wore white lab coats, but under that, their clothes were surprisingly casual for my mental image of a scientist; one man even wore shorts. Behind the soapstone benches were racks of vials with brightly colored lids, and racks of clear circular dishes. The only sound was a mechanical whirring coming from one corner of the room. The whole place had the sharp, citrusy scent of benzene.

A tall, middle-aged African American woman looked up from her station and stepped out to greet us. She raised her goggles, which she'd placed over a pair of funky blue cat-eye glasses, and extended her hand.

"Tamira, this is the friend I was telling you about, Mabily Jones," Eva said.

"It's wonderful to meet you, Ms. Campbell." Tamira's fingers were icy cold but she gave my hand a hearty squeeze. "Thank you so much for letting me visit your lab."

"It's my pleasure," said Tamira. Her voice was soft and lilting, with the tiniest hint of an accent that said she was originally from somewhere in the Caribbean.

My cheeks flushed as I felt the scrutiny of her eyes. Her quick intelligent gaze seemed to take in everything about me in an instant. I could bet whether by career or just personal inclination Tamira was much more observant than most people.

"I'm happy to do a favor for any friend of Eva's," Tamira said. "She's one of the best lab assistants we've ever had here."

Eva glowed with pride. I hoped that maybe Eva could hear it when Tamira said that she was smart and capable, since she never seemed to be able to hear it from me.

"There are parts of the lab that are off-limits to visitors for safety reason, as I'm sure you understand," Tamira continued. "But Eva knows where she can take you around. I'm afraid there's not much to see. Real research isn't very exciting." She laughed self-deprecatingly, but there was a twinkle in her eye that belied how exciting she actually found it. I could see why Eva liked her so much.

"Let's take a quick break for coffee."

She led us into a small room off the main lab. It was sparsely furnished with a Formica table, a handful of bright plastic chairs and a little kitchenette where a coffeemaker burbled cheerfully. The strong scent of good coffee infused the room. Tamira poured for Eva and herself and offered me some but I declined. I was nervous enough as it was just being here.

"There are obviously some aspects of our research that I can't discuss," she began diplomatically, warming her long, delicate fingers against the mug, "but I am happy to help wherever I can. I know your boss actually, Reggie Ruggiero."

"Oh, really?" I sat up, surprised by this. "He mentioned he knew someone at the NYPD's forensics lab, but I didn't know he knew you."

"Oh, he probably wasn't talking about me. It's been years since I worked at the forensics lab, but Reggie isn't a person you easily forget." She laughed. "He referred a couple of cases to me when he was a detective with the NYPD. Obscure cases that their regular lab needed some outside assistance with. I was very sorry when I heard that he was no longer with the NYPD. I'm glad he's doing well in the private sector."

I smiled politely, but I couldn't help but wonder if Tamira knew the real reason Reggie had been let go from the force. It was the one thing Reggie would never talk about, that scandal. Knowing Reggie, I couldn't believe it was anything too bad, but I couldn't help but be curious. If Tamira knew anything, I was sure she had far too much discretion to talk about it.

"So what was it that you wanted to ask me?" Tamira set down her mug and peered at me through her turquoise rims.

"Reggie and I encountered the substance you're studying," I began, not the whole truth, but not a lie. "One of our clients' twenty-one-year-old daughter died in what was ruled a suicide, but we have reason to believe she might have ingested some of this substance beforehand." I left out the part about Charlotte flying. "I know the NYPD's forensics lab stopped their investigation when it didn't match any known narcotic. But if you're willing to share, I would love to learn more about what you've discovered about this substance." I was trying so hard not to say the word "Elixir." "We want to be prepared in case we have another case where this substance might be involved."

"I wish I could be of more help." Tamira sighed. "I told the NYPD that there's every reason to believe this substance might still be at large. But that aspect isn't the focus of our research here. We're really focused on the chemical composition."

"What is its chemical composition?" I asked. Truthfully, as a fairy I didn't even know what Elixir was made of. The old stories were that Elixir was made of Feydust moistened with the fairy goddesses' tears of joy when they created the Vale, but that wasn't exactly helpful to a scientist. I cast a glance over at Eva, sitting quietly in her chair, and waited breathlessly for Tamira to go on.

"Well, I suppose you could say it's a combination of different things. One part of it is human dopamine."

"Dopamine? Like the chemical in your brain that makes you happy?"

Tamira smiled, seeming amused by my cursory knowledge. "In a manner of speaking, yes. That's what led us to initially view this substance as a narcotic. Because many known narcotics stimulate a dopamine response, I suppose it was only a matter of time before someone invented a street drug made from dopamine directly. But this is different. I'm not sure it is a narcotic at all, even though some of its victims may have used it that way. The dopamine isn't synthetic; it's human derived. And that's just one component. There's another component as well. Usually dopamine has a very short half-life, but this other component has been able to preserve it, almost indefinitely. It's been a real boon to our research."

"What's the other component?" I asked

Tamira was quiet, frowning. The look on her face suggested that she was debating how much she should tell me. There was a long moment of silence as the clock on the wall slowly ticked seconds away. I had just about assumed that I wouldn't get any more information out of Tamira when she spoke.

"We don't know," she said at last. "We're only in the very preliminary stages of our research, you see. A full investigation will take a long time. Science is very slow, I'm afraid. It's not like it is in the movies."

She smiled, but I could tell she was distancing herself from me.

"I'm sorry I don't have more helpful information to share."

I thanked her for her time but inwardly I grimaced. She obviously had more information than she was willing to tell me about what this other, unknown component of Elixir was. Maybe I could get Eva to be more forthcoming when we were alone. Surely Eva had been privy to some of this information, working in Tamira's lab?

Tamira was getting up to go back to work, rinsing her used coffee mug in the sink.

I decided to ask a different question, one she might be more likely to answer honestly. An idea was occurring to me. I didn't want it to be true, but I feared it was.

"Um, Tamira, if I could ask one more question? Is dopamine by any chance more prevalent in children than in adults?"

"Why, yes, in a way. Children have many more dopamine receptors than adults do. Why do you ask?" She looked at me curiously.

"Oh, just wondering." I smiled at her but my heart was pounding. Was this why the Fairy Queen kidnapped kids and not grown-ups? They had more of the joyful chemicals she needed to make magic? I felt nauseous.

Tamira was walking towards the door of the break room to go back into the lab.

This was my last chance to ask her what I'd come here for.

"Tamira?" I asked. "Do you think at any point in the near future your researchers will want to do a human trial of this substance? I know that the NYPD forensics lab did an experiment with rats. If it's not a narcotic, maybe it has some positive use in medicine?"

My heart was in my mouth as I said it, but I had to ask. If I could get Obadiah to come to the lab and take some Elixir, it could quell his Thirst symptoms, at least for a little while.

He felt it was unethical to consume Elixir when it came from the Vale, but maybe he'd agree to take some again if it was in the name of science?

Tamira shook her head, almost violently.

"We're years away from any experiment involving human subjects," she said. "That would be completely unethical. I was surprised the NYPD's lab even did an animal experiment as early as they did. Though the results were certainly *extraordinary*." She didn't elaborate, but I could tell she was thinking about the levitating lab rats Reggie had told me about. "We're still trying to identify the chemical composition of this substance. We would never give it to a research subject, not knowing what it is."

I'd expected her to say as much. It had been a last vain hope.

"I understand," I said. "Thank you again for your time."

She smiled at me. "You're welcome."

She disappeared through the double doors and I stood for a long time in silence with Eva, till I could no longer here the click-clack of Tamira's heels in the hall.

Knowing she was out of earshot, I turned to Eva.

"I hope I didn't sound like a complete idiot talking to your boss, asking about a human trial," I said. "I should have known it would be far too soon. It's just . . . Promise you won't tell anyone about what I'm about to say," I started, and Eva nodded.

"I think Obadiah's addicted to this stuff. He's

stopped drinking it since the NYPD searched his club. I think he's scared of the repercussions," I told the half-truth, leaving out the part about the Fairy Queen's captives. "But without it, he's starting to have withdrawal symptoms. His hands start shaking and he can't stop it."

I pressed my fingers against my face, fighting back the panic that clutched at me every time I thought about Obadiah's condition. Eva was looking at me, her eyes wide and serious.

"You should take him to one of those drug treatment centers," she said.

"He refuses to go. And honestly, I don't think they could help him. This isn't a normal narcotic. It's not any known substance. Those places are designed to combat heroin, meth, coke, whatever. But this isn't like that."

Eva was silent, nodding.

I listened for signs of anyone out in the hall and then spoke.

"What's Tamira not telling me? The other component of this substance, the one she wouldn't talk about, do you know what it is?"

Eva frowned. "I think Tamira just didn't want to talk about it because she's telling the truth. We really *don't* know. It wouldn't be right for her to make a definitive statement about something that's still mostly conjecture."

I nodded, but I wasn't satisfied.

"You must have some ideas, though. I mean, I won't

hold you to anything you say—I'm just curious. What do you think this stuff is? I mean, you personally?"

Eva glanced behind her back to make sure no one was coming.

"I'm worried one of the other members of the team might come in the break room and overhear us," she said. "Come on. I know a part of the lab that Tamira would have no problem with me showing you, and we'd have total privacy there."

We left the break room and walked down the hall. Eva opened a door and turned on the lights.

The room was full of cages. Fluffy white lab rats scampered around inside. The whole room had a musky, animal smell. There were sounds of squeaking and scuffling, and curious rats stood up on their hind legs, pressing their pink noses between the bars and peering at us with their beady black eyes, whiskers twitching back and forth.

"I hope they don't freak you out," Eva said apologetically.

"No, I think they're cute." I smiled at the small furry face snuffling next to me.

"One of my jobs here, as the lowest person on the totem pole at the lab, is to feed and clean their cages, when they're not in use in an experiment. No one is going to be coming in here today. It's probably the most soundproof place we have in the lab for us to talk."

She paused, and I could hear the soft clang of a rat running on a wheel.

"I've been wanting to talk to you, Mab. In the last couple months, some of the memories have been coming back to me, since my accident at Obadiah's club."

I nodded, my heart beating faster. It shouldn't have been a surprise; I'd always heard that memory loss from head injuries was often temporary. What had Eva remembered? Had she remembered the Vale? Did she remember what I'd told her, about being a changeling?

"I keep thinking that surely I'm not really remembering, surely I'm just recalling a dream," she said, and I bit my tongue. Of course Eva would doubt herself, if memories of magic had resurfaced.

"Honestly, though, that's the real reason I'm so excited to be working at this lab. I mean, Tamira is amazing, and I'm really looking forward to doing my graduate work, but when I found out what Reggie told you, that the lab rats the NYPD gave Elixir to had *levitated*, I felt I had to research this stuff myself."

I cast a glance at the furry little bodies running around in the cages beside us. Whoever had done that experiment the first time must have doubted their own senses.

"They did a repeat of the first trial, just to make sure the people who reported those initial results weren't crazy," Eva went on. "It worked again. That's when I knew I had to take this job."

"Of course you'd want to be on the cutting edge of studying something that extraordinary," I said.

Her face looked grave. "Yes, but that's not the only reason."

She hesitated for a moment, then spoke.

"I remembered something about the night of the accident. I hadn't told anyone, because I figured no one would believe me. But I remember *flying*. I thought I'd gone nuts—but if this substance made the lab rats levitate after they drank it, I guess it's no crazier than the same thing happening to me."

She laughed, a hysterical little laugh. "You probably don't believe any of this. If you saw the tapes of the rats levitating, though . . ."

I cut her off. "Eva, I believe you."

She was silent, her arms crossed tightly over her chest, her eyes skeptical.

"I was there that night, remember?"

"You saw me fly?"

I nodded.

She stared at me wide-eyed, barely breathing.

"Well, thank you for not thinking I'm nuts," she said at last.

"Of course."

She was silent for a moment, staring down at the rows of cages.

"I meant what I said to you at the street fair. We could be doing research that will change the world. I mean, this substance, whatever it is, it's totally new. I bet that a hundred years from now, kids will be reading about Tamira Campbell in their science textbooks, the way we read about Marie Curie. She'll go down in history for discovering this stuff."

I nodded, feeling suddenly afraid. Humans were going to "discover" magic. What would the implications to that even be?

I began to pace back and forth between the racks of cages.

"The thing that Tamira didn't want to tell you," said Eva, "is that we do sort of know what the other component of this substance is. Or, at least, we know what it *isn't*."

"What do you mean?" I asked breathlessly.

"Well, she told you how this substance is made up of two parts, right? For the sake of example, let's call them X and Y. X is human dopamine, or similar enough to it. And the problem is we don't know what the hell Y is. At first we thought Y was strands of DNA," she explained, "because the structure looked similar. But then when we examined it more closely, it wasn't. At least Y wasn't *human* DNA, or the DNA of any other animal. Like I said, we've never seen anything like it before."

I held my breath, thinking.

"The only thing we've been able to figure out so far is that whatever Y is, it lives in some kind of symbiotic relationship with X, the dopamine. If we add more dopamine to it, Y multiplies. It's like the dopamine feeds it. But that still doesn't tell us what Y is."

What if it was *fairy* DNA? I'd be hard-pressed to

explain that to Tamira or even to Eva, but it was the most likely explanation I could think of. Was Elixir a mixture of fairy DNA and dopamine? What if Fey-dust was really fairy DNA, in human terms? And what if the goddesses' tears of joy was a metaphor for a dopamine-like chemical? Maybe our world had been rich with this chemical until the drought, and then the Queen had to start supplementing it with the dopamine she derived from the children? It was so wrong. But it sort of made sense.

I looked at Eva. She was standing next to one of the cages, reaching a finger through the bars to scratch the head of a large white rat that was nuzzling into her, its eyes closed in bliss at her touch.

How in the world could I tell Eva that the Y-factor they were studying wasn't even from this world? She might believe she had flown, but already that was stretching her credulity to capacity. How could I tell her what Tamira had in her agar-jell dishes down the hall right now was *fairy* DNA? And yet, if I didn't say something, Tamira and her team would forever be on the wrong track in their investigation as to what the mysterious Y-factor was.

"I should be getting back to work," Eva said, glancing at her watch. She gave a behind-the-ears scratch goodbye to the rat. I could tell that one was her favorite. "Thanks for letting me talk about all this stuff. There's no one else I can talk to about it, really."

"Thank *you*," I said.

I walked with Eva back to the room with all the researchers, and thanked Tamira again for her time.

Walking past the racks of colorful capped vials, I kept wondering if the clear substance contained in them was Elixir. I couldn't smell it, sealed like that.

A highly improper thought crossed my mind. Obadiah didn't have any Elixir in his store anymore, since the cops had raided his stash. If I could get him a vial or two, would it hold off the symptoms of Thirst for a while? At least till I figured out a better plan? Tamira and her team all had their eyes down at their stations focusing on their work. But I dismissed the thought quickly, feeling ashamed. I'd never stolen anything in my life, and despite how badly I wanted to help Obadiah, it wouldn't be right. Tamira and Eva had trusted me. I wasn't going to betray that trust.

I walked with empty pockets back out the long corridors of the lab and out into the street.

Back in our apartment that night, to distract myself from thinking about the Elixir experiments, I decided to give Quinn a call. I didn't think she'd pick up. Why would she be more responsive over the phone than she had been in person? But I had to try something. I didn't want to come back to Reggie with my tail between my legs. What I wanted was for Quinn to send me a picture of her boyfriend, the one she'd started seeing when all the trouble started. Facial recognition software was getting better and better, and if Quinn wouldn't give me any info about him, maybe I could find him that way?

I sat down on my bed and dialed the number her mother had given me.

As expected, the phone rang and rang but she didn't pick up. All I got was a voicemail with a one hundred and eighty degree more cheerful version of Quinn's voice on it. The chipper greeting, with the hint of a giggle on the end, showed me just how much Quinn had changed. She hadn't always been a half-alive girl who barely left her room. The contrast was so sharp it made my heart ache and strengthened my resolve to do something to help her.

Not giving up that she wasn't taking calls, I also sent her a text:

Please send a photo of your ex, if you have one. Much appreciated. Thanks, Mab Jones.

I waited for a while but nothing came through. Likely nothing would. If she didn't take calls, why would she take texts either?

I set my phone down on the nightstand and was halfway to the kitchen, wondering why I'd bothered to contact her at all, when I heard a ping. I turned around.

There was a message from Quinn:

Okay. But it won't help.

Well, there was the optimism characteristic of the malaise that had swallowed her, I thought sardonically, opening the message. But there were photos.

I almost leaped with joy. As my gaze fell on the first picture, my eyebrows rose. There was no denying he was strikingly handsome, like movie-star good-looking. I was a trifle surprised. Usually people dated someone in the same strata of attractiveness as themselves, and Quinn, even in the old photos of her happy and smiling with makeup on and in a stylish dress, was no more than average. Somehow, perhaps irrationally, it made me think better of this guy. A man that spectacularly attractive could have had any girl he wanted, could have had all the prettiest arm candy. If he'd chosen Quinn, it must have meant he actually liked her for who she really was, didn't it? That didn't mean he hadn't hurt her, though.

Then I realized there were more pictures. She'd sent me more than one. I scrolled down to view the other photos. But they weren't more photos of the same guy. They were photos of different guys. Why had she sent me these? They had to be other guys she'd dated recently. I hadn't asked for that, but it was nice of her to send them to me. She was actually trying to be helpful and *forthcoming*. It was such a contrast to the utterly walled-off girl in the bed. It felt like progress.

I scrolled through the photos. All of these guys were total hotties. *Damn, Quinn*, I thought, kind of in awe at her dating prowess. Then again, it could all be fake. Maybe she'd copied and pasted up-and-coming idols off IMDB and passed them off as her boyfriends? I kept scrolling through what looked like the casting auditions for male leads in the latest YA dystopian blockbuster. And then I saw the last photo. I shrieked, almost dropping my phone.

I recognized him at once. It was the guy Eva had had over the other night, the good-looking one I'd seen putting on his shoes in the hall, the one who walked out on Eva without even saying goodbye.

I raced into the kitchen.

Eva was standing by the stove. She was making her famous *pollo guisado*, Dominican stewed chicken. The air was warm from the preheating oven, and smelled pungently of the garlic she was chopping with deft, rhythmic strokes.

"Eva," I called out.

She looked over at me without even losing the rhythm of her dice. Anyone else, I'd worry they were about to cut their fingers off, but not Eva.

"That guy you had over the other night, the jerk, by any chance is this him?"

I held up the picture on my phone.

The knife slid from Eva's fingers, and she barely caught it before it fell to the floor. She stared at the picture, one hand clutched to her mouth.

"Holy shit, yeah, it is. Mab, how did you get this photo?"

I told her in a few words about Quinn.

Eva's eyes grew very big. She didn't say anything. The knife hovered motionless in her hands, her lips in a thin white line.

My heart was beating very fast, a fear looming in

my mind. This was the man who might have hurt Quinn. Oh god, had he done something to Eva, more than just walking out on her? I would hunt him down and kill him. But she had seemed so happy after their one-night stand.

"Eva, he never *hurt* you, did he?"

My heart was in my mouth as I looked at my best friend.

"No, it wasn't like that." She used the exact same words Quinn had, but when Eva said it the conviction seemed genuine.

I asked the question directly.

"He never did anything . . . not consensual, did he?"

"No, not at all." When Eva looked into my eyes I could tell she was telling the truth.

"I mean, I was hurt when he left," she said. "But during, it was nothing but good. It was magical."

She kept using that word, I noticed, to describe this man.

"So Quinn and I dated the same guy?" she said. "What are the odds of that?"

But something in her voice sounded afraid. Like it wasn't just coincidence.

She went back to chopping garlic. But her heart wasn't in it. She kept pausing, the knife dangling in her fingers.

I watched her. Even though Eva seemed devastated that this Cory had dumped her, she wasn't taking it like Quinn. She was still herself. She was hurt, yes, sad maybe, but not depressed. There was a world of difference between the two. Whatever had happened to Quinn hadn't happened to Eva. So if there was a boy behind Quinn's mysterious descent into despair, it must have been one of the other boys in the photos, not Cory. That was all I could think. Unless Quinn's experience had just been totally different than Eva's.

Eva washed the garlic from her hands and then turned to me.

"May I see that photo again, Mab?"

I handed her the phone.

She stared at his picture for a long moment, frowning.

"Does it bother you to see him?" I asked. "I shouldn't have shown it to you."

"No," she said quietly. "I'm glad you did. I never took a photo of Cory, during the brief time we were together. I wish I had."

She turned to me and there was an expression on her face I couldn't quite read.

"So since Cory dated Quinn," she asked at last, "are you considering him a suspect in your case?"

I nodded, hoping this wasn't too close to home for Eva.

"We have been investigating anyone Quinn might have dated, since her mom said her symptoms started after seeing a new boyfriend," I said. "But that doesn't mean it's Cory. There are four other photos of guys that she sent me. It could be any of them too."

Eva still had that strange look on her face.

"Did Quinn tell you where she met these guys?" she asked me.

"No. Trying to extract information from Quinn is like trying to get blood from a stone. But I'm planning to work on her more about it. Maybe I can get something useful. You said you met Cory at your group, right?"

Eva nodded. She had abandoned her cooking and taken a seat at our tiny kitchen table, steepling her fingers, clearly lost in thoughts she wasn't sharing with me.

I took a seat opposite her. An idea was occurring to me.

"How big is your group?" I asked. "How many people typically show up for your monthly events?"

"There's a core group of about a dozen of us, but at some of the big rituals, we could easily get fifty or a hundred people. Some people show up once and don't come back."

"So it's possible Quinn might have come to your group? Maybe she met Cory the same place that you did?" Of course, it was also possible Quinn had met Cory somewhere else. And who knows how she'd found the other four guys. But now I had another potential "in" into Quinn: Eva's group. What were the odds? And yet New York, for being a city of eight million, sometimes functioned uncannily like a small town in terms of the unlikely coincidences of running into people. It was a vast metropolis of thousands of tiny, tiny subcultures, and if you shared one of those, the world was actually quite small.

"I wonder if anyone else in your group might remember Quinn, might have some information about her." I felt bad asking Eva for another favor. Here I'd just asked to see her workplace, and now I was asking for an invitation to her group.

Eva took the hint. "I'm sure Tiffany, the girl who runs our group, would be fine with you coming, if I vouched for you."

But that strange look was back in her face, her eyes wide, lips set in a thin hard line.

"Eva, is it upsetting you to talk about this?" I asked. "I mean, I know everything with Cory is really fresh. We don't have to discuss it right now. And if it's not comfortable for me to come to your group, I have other ways I can work on to track Quinn's exes down. It was just a thought."

"No, that's not it at all."

She was silent, biting her lip, and suddenly she looked almost as if she would cry. She turned away from me, towards the window.

"What's wrong?" I asked, extending my hand across the table and placing it gently on her arm.

When she looked back up at me, I could see in her eyes that there was a lot she hadn't told me. Eva was always so transparent, so willing and ready to share. I'd never seen this secretive part of her before, and it frightened me. I'd glibly assumed, since we were such good friends, and roommates for goodness' sake, that she told me everything. And I could see plainly in her eyes that assumption had been wrong.

"What is it?" I asked.

She pressed her hands to her face. When she slowly lowered her fingers from her eyes, she opened her mouth, and then closed it, a few times in quick succession, as if she wasn't sure how to begin.

"Mab," she started uncertainly. "I didn't tell you everything about Cory. I mean, I may have left out the most essential thing."

I waited breathlessly for her to tell me more.

She had turned her face back towards the window. A pigeon was strutting up and down on the fire escape, head bobbing, making a trilling coo; for a moment I wondered if it was one of Obadiah's messenger pigeons, but I didn't see any tag on its leg.

"You're going to think I'm crazy," Eva muttered, turning back to me.

"Have I ever thought you were crazy?" I said, and she must have heard the sincerity in my voice, because her face relaxed.

"When we were talking in the lab," she began, "and I told you about the crazy results of our experiments, how the lab rats levitated, you believed me then. So maybe you'll believe this . . ."

"It's not about belief," I said. "It's just the facts. As unbelievable as it may seem to people, that's what happened. You know it, I know it. So I'm not believing; I'm just accepting what's true," I said.

"And you accept that I really was flying that night over Obadiah's club, that it wasn't just a hallucination."

I nodded. "I do, because I saw it."

Eva pressed her fingers together tightly, as if summoning up the courage for what she was about to say.

"So you understand that there's more going on in the world than meets the eye."

"Where are you going with this?" I asked.

"Something happened in my group," Eva said. "It started about eight months ago. I didn't say anything to you because I didn't know how to explain it. And I was afraid you'd think I was crazy."

I opened my mouth to protest, but she went on. "When I tell you, you'll understand why I didn't mention it before. It wasn't just that I was afraid you'd think I was nuts. *I* thought I was nuts. That's why I didn't say anything. If there hadn't been so many other witnesses there that night, I would have thought it was all a dream. It's that unbelievable. But as you say, when you see something with your own eyes, it's not about belief anymore, just accepting what's there."

"Go on," I said, my voice so quiet as to be almost inaudible. I was afraid of what she was going to tell me next.

"May I see your phone again?" she asked. "May I see the pictures of the other four guys Quinn sent you?"

I handed my phone to her and she scrolled through them. Her hand went to her mouth, her eyes growing wider and wider.

"Eva, what's wrong?" I asked.

"I knew it," she whispered. "I didn't want to be-lieve it, but I knew it. And there's the proof."

"Eva, what's going on?"

She turned to me, her face grave.

"Mab," she began, fear in her eyes, "what if I told you that all five of these guys were the same guy?"

CHAPTER 4

"Wait, what?"

I grabbed the phone back from Eva and scrolled through the five photos again. They couldn't all be the same guy. They were totally different people. The only thing they had in common was that they were all conventionally attractive. But it wasn't just that one was blond, one was dark haired, one's eyes were blue and the other's brown. The structures of their faces were different. There was no way, even with the best disguise and hefty theatrical makeup, that they could all be the same person. It just couldn't be.

"Eva, I don't think so. Look at the shapes of their brows, their jawlines, their ears. You couldn't do that good of a job even with silicone. They're not disguises."

"It's not a disguise like that," Eva whispered softly.

I stared at her, not understanding.

She put her head in her hands.

"I've been afraid to tell you."

I gently touched her arm across the kitchen table, trying to get her to stop covering her eyes and look at me.

"We've always said we could tell each other anything," I said.

She sighed. "There are some things you can't explain."

I understood about that better than she knew. My own guilt still twinged that I hadn't been honest with Eva about being a fairy. Or rather, I *had* been honest, but then she'd lost all those memories in her accident in the Vale. I wanted to tell her the truth again, but I didn't know how. I felt like I'd lost that opportunity, and I didn't know how to get it back.

Eva got up from the table. She began to walk restlessly around the room. She resumed her cooking, gathering a bunch of cilantro that was balanced in a glass of water and beginning to chop the mess of green leaves. I wanted to stop her; everything she was doing was just a distraction from what she really wanted to say.

"When I told you that the memories are starting to come back to me from the time of the accident," she said, looking over at me at last, "I didn't just mean that night of being able to fly at Obadiah's club."

I stared at her, fear and hope battling it out within me. What if Eva suddenly remembered her trip to the Vale, remembered me telling her I was really a fairy? What would happen; how would she react?

"Things have been coming back to me in bits and pieces," she continued, beginning to chop again. "But the things I'm remembering—if you could call it that— they can't be memories, because they don't make sense. They're more like dreams. They couldn't *be*."

Oh god, Eva was remembering the Vale. I had to tell her the truth or she'd believe she really was losing her mind.

"Eva, what if I told you that you really *are* remembering. Everything you saw, everything you experienced, is true."

Eva stared at me, her eyes moist and glistening. She set down the knife and wiped at her eyes.

"That would mean there really is a whole other world. Is that what you're saying?"

I took a deep breath. I could almost hear my mother the Fairy Queen screaming in my ears, begging me not to tell our secrets to a human. "Yes, there is."

Eva looked at me. I could tell she wanted so badly to believe what I was saying, but she was having such trouble letting herself. Her rational mind just couldn't let go, even though she'd seen it with her own eyes. But she spoke.

"Remember I told you about my group?"

"Your coven?" I said.

Blushing, she nodded.

"We do a ritual every full moon," she said, beginning to chop up a red bell pepper. She threw her other chopped ingredients in the blender. They made a pretty mélange of red and green. I realized she was making a sofrito, and when she turned the blender on, the piquant smell wafted up, making my mouth water. She stopped, turning to me. "We call upon the spirits of nature: the four directions, the sun and the moon. We invoke different nature deities." She scraped down the bowl. "I know it probably sounds really tree-huggery."

"Nothing wrong with hugging trees," I said. *I used to live in one*, I thought, suddenly homesick.

"Well, Tiffany led a ritual where we did a summoning. Don't worry, we didn't summon demons, or anything like that. It wasn't anything scary. The ritual was about connecting with nature and the natural world, which is important in New York City, I guess. So we summoned nature spirits. You know, *fairies*."

Oh no, they didn't. I felt like I was going to faint. This was bad; this was really, really bad.

"Please don't try to summon fairies," I said, my voice quiet with fear. "You'd honestly be better off with a demon."

But Eva went on. "I thought it was just a metaphor, though, right? I mean, it wasn't like we were *really* going to 'summon fairies.'" She made air quotes around the words, with her hands. "Because that's ridiculous. Summoning fairies was just a metaphor for connecting with nature. We were just *symbolically* summoning fairies. Or so I thought."

My stomach felt leaden. Oh god, what had they done? Who had they summoned?

Eva's voice was full of fear as she spoke. Her eyes had taken on a faraway quality as she leaned up against the kitchen counter, staring at nothing. I knew she was seeing it all clearly in her mind. "We were all arranged in a circle," she said. "Tiffany was leading us in the chants. She kept saying, 'Come into our midst, come into our midst . . . spirit of nature, we welcome you here,' and then . . . If I hadn't seen it with my own eyes I wouldn't have believed it, just like those lab rats levitating . . ."

"What happened?"

"This guy, I guess you could call him a guy. He looked like a man, but so beautiful. His skin, his body, everything was just perfect. He was like one of those Greek statues in the Met come to life. He appeared in the middle of our circle. One moment he wasn't there. And then the next moment he was *there*. I know you probably think I've lost my mind but . . ."

"No," I said, breathing hard. "No, I don't." But I was terrified. Who had they summoned?

"Well, we were all screaming, of course. People were falling to their knees. A couple of the girls and even some of the guys fainted. I almost did too. And this *man* told us he was from the fairy realm. That he couldn't tell us his real name, but we could call him 'Cory.' And that he was here to help us, if we would help him."

My throat went dry, my stomach a ball of weight. I had a dreadful feeling about this "Cory." I didn't know who he really was. He could have been anyone, given fairies' infinite capacity for disguise. But the whole "help" thing scared me. A fairy's bargain was always a dangerous thing, especially to a bunch of idealistic young twenty-somethings who had no idea what they were messing with.

"You didn't agree to help him, did you?"

Eva was silent, wiping her hands on the dishrag. For a moment she didn't meet my eye.

"Well, yeah, of course we agreed to help him. I mean, we were all so flabbergasted that he'd come into our circle. When a freakin' fairy shows up and asks for your help, I mean, you say yes."

I put my head in my hands. "This is bad," I whispered.

Eva leaned down so she could look at me over the gaps of my fingers, "So, wait, you believe me? You believe all this?"

I lowered my hands and sighed.

"I believe you."

Eva looked at me skeptically.

"I really do believe you."

"*I* wouldn't believe me if I was you."

I sighed. "I believe you because . . ." I took a deep breath. "Come on, sit down. The stew can wait. Do you want a cup of coffee?" I didn't even know how to begin what I had to say. Eva shook her head, but she sat down with me at the kitchen table.

"I told you this once, but your injury made you forget." I squinted my eyes for a moment, and then blurted it out. "I'm from that other world."

Eva clutched her hands to her face. She stared at me over the tops of her fingertips, her dark eyes huge with fear and something else I couldn't name. I waited breathlessly for how she would respond.

I wasn't prepared for what she would say next.

"So it's true, what I remembered?"

"You remember me telling you I was a fairy?"

Eva nodded around her fingers. "I thought I'd dreamed it."

"You didn't."

"Everything I remember: waking up in that cocoon, you rescuing me and then you telling me that you were a . . . . I didn't dream that?"

"No," I whispered.

Eva began to laugh and cry at the same time, until she was almost choking. "It's all true?"

"It's all true."

All she could do was shake her head over and over, squeezing my hand across the table. She couldn't form words.

"I know this is a lot for you to process all at once. But promise me one thing. Whatever you do, tell everyone in your group to stay away from this 'Cory.' I don't know who he is or what he wants. But fairies are dangerous. We're not innocent little nature spirits. Fairies are powerful. And you can't trust them."

"But you just said you were a . . . and I can trust you," she gasped.

"I'm different." I sighed. "I'm a changeling. So I'm human too, as well as fairy. And that mellows it out, I guess. Really, fairies are terrifying. Their minds, their motives, they're not comprehensible to us. Just stay away from him. I don't want you to get hurt. I don't want anyone else in your group to get hurt either."

Eva bit her lip. "I think it may be too late for that," she whispered.

"Eva?" I asked, afraid to know the answer.

She hung her head. "Cory came back after the initial summoning. He came back multiple times. He became a member of our group. I think we were all a little in love with him. I mean, here we were, saying we believed in magic, and then all of a sudden magic was real and standing in front of us in the form of this gorgeous man. Every time he came to our group he looked different—different faces, different features— but always flawlessly beautiful. That's what I meant when I said all of Quinn's pictures are all the same guy. I recognized four out of the five. He took on all those disguises in our group."

My stomach clenched. They really were all the same "man."

This was what Quinn had meant when she said, "You wouldn't understand. No one would understand. It's too unbelievable." This poor girl. It didn't matter what kind of professionals her parents took her to, no one *would* believe her if she told them what had really happened. Everyone would think she was nuts. And she knew it. I resolved to call her. I had to tell her the truth. I had to tell her that I *knew*.

"Well," Eva continued, "he came up to some of

the girls in the group. He told them he wanted to be their lover."

"No, no, no." I put my head in my hands, shaking my head. This was going to end badly.

"You don't say no to a gorgeous supernatural deity."

"And then he came to you," I said. "And you . . ."

She blushed.

"How could I not? I mean . . ."

"Listen, I get it. I get why you'd want to. But he's dangerous. If he's a fairy, he's inherently dangerous."

"I didn't think so at the time. We only spent that one night together. Like I said, it was magical. I've never experienced anything like it. I really am afraid he may have ruined me for human men." She laughed, but there was a tinge of fear in it. "But then like I told you, the next morning he ran off while I was getting ready. I haven't seen him since. I don't know if any of the other girls in the group have seen him. I'm far from the only one who he was with. I heard that for some of the girls he wasn't just a one-night stand, that he dated them for weeks, months even."

Quinn, I thought. Was it the duration of time she'd seen Cory that had made all the difference, that had made him so much more destructive to her than he had been to Eva?

"So wait, Quinn must be or have been a member of your group," I said. "Unless she met him elsewhere?"

"It's very possible. We have our long-standing members, like Tiffany and, well, me, kind of at this point," she said with a modicum of pride in her eyes. "But we get a ton of drop-ins, people who show up a few times and never come back. It's very possible she's been there. Do you have a picture of her?"

I went to the bedroom and got my laptop, opening the file with the picture Reggie had gotten from Brenda when we started the case. It was an old picture, from before whatever unshakable gloom had descended over Quinn. She was wearing her college sweatshirt and grinning.

Eva scrunched up her face. "She does look familiar. I know I've seen her before but I'm not sure where. I think she may have come to our Beltane ritual a few months back. I didn't get to know her; we probably just chatted for a few minutes." Eva looked up at me, a shadow of sympathy crossing her face. "So you think this girl is not okay? You think Cory hurt her?"

"I don't know." I frowned. "At first I thought it was abuse or rape or domestic violence. But now that we know he's a fairy, what if the crime was something magical?"

I could hear Tamira's voice in my mind, talking about the human dopamine that was one part of the Elixir she studied. Children might have more dopamine receptors. But adults produced dopamine too. And they produced more after sex. A terrifying idea was occurring to me.

"Oh my god," I said, my hands going to my mouth.

"What is it?" said Eva. "What's wrong?"

The Queen put humans in her cocoons, forcing

them into a death-like sleep to steal their "life energy" as she called it to make Elixir, until the process actually killed them. Quinn wasn't dead. Yet she was *like* dead: catatonic, listless, malaised. I could hear her voice, flat and monotone, in my mind: *It's like all the joy got sucked right out of me.* But what if it had? What if it literally had? What if this Cory, whoever he was, had found a way to steal Elixir's "X-factor" from human women, through sex? I looked up at Eva. She'd slept with Cory too, but didn't have any of Quinn's symptoms. Then again, Eva had only slept with him once, not many times over the course of months. Maybe it was the prolonged exposure that depleted Cory's victims of their dopamine? Or maybe, for whatever reason, he'd decided not to prey on Eva like he had on the others? Maybe Eva was truly just a lover to Cory, and not a means to an end? Maybe despite all her protestations to the contrary, Eva might have truly been special to Cory, and so he hadn't stolen her joy like he had with Quinn.

"Eva, how have you felt since that night with Cory?" I asked her. "Did you notice any changes in how you're feeling physically, mentally, emotionally?"

"I've felt fine. I mean, I felt disappointed. But it's not the kind of depression this girl Quinn seems to be suffering from."

"So it doesn't seem like this fairy did anything to you that way?"

"No. I don't think I'm any worse off, that I can tell."

It was strange. Did he only prey on certain girls he slept with and not others? And what was the rational for the difference? Was there something within Eva that made her able to withstand whatever it was he did?

I didn't know. But a disturbing possibility was occurring to me. If this rogue fairy "Cory" was trying to fix the Elixir drought by stealing human X-factor through sex, he needed a lot. How many human girls had he slept with? It could be dozens. Hundreds. There would be no way to know, because most of victims' families and friends wouldn't have called a private detective. They'd merely think that their loved one was suddenly, severely depressed, and blame it on the breakup or some quirk of brain chemistry, because who could ever guess that the source of their joy had been literally, maliciously, stolen from them?

"Eva, I have to find out who this is and stop him," I said, our eyes meeting across the table.

"How the hell are you going to find him, though? I mean, he can make himself look like anyone, that's the thing I could never wrap my head around. We can't just go up and question all the hot guys in New York. The only thing all his disguises have in common is that he never made himself resemble anyone ugly. But that still leaves a pretty large sample size."

He disguised himself as pretty boys so he could seduce all these girls, I thought glumly. What girl would say no to an out-of-this-world night with a supernatural man who looked like a movie star? Cory was going to find a lot more victims, if I couldn't figure out how to stop him. I still didn't know how he was doing it. But if he'd figured out a way to steal dopamine, he could do a lot of damage. And even if he wasn't killing his victims, they were suffering so much. And they might end up dead. Quinn was a serious suicide risk. I had to stop him.

"I know of someone who might be able to find him."

Eva's eyebrows raised. "Who?"

The Fairy Queen. She seemed to know everything in the Vale, and certainly knew what everyone was up to, with her ever larger network of spies. I sighed. All the more reason I was going to have to go home.

"I might need to go away for a little while."

"If you go anywhere, I'm coming too," said Eva. Her eyes lit up. She was looking at this as a great adventure.

"No, I can't risk your safety. You remember what happened last time."

She pinched her lip. "Some of it?"

"Well, okay, maybe you don't remember everything, but you almost got killed. I can't risk that again."

She frowned. "Look, this is all so new to me. It rips open everything I thought I knew was true. But if there's anything I can do, I want to help."

"I appreciate that, but I may have to figure out this one on my own. I need to go home."

"I don't understand."

"I need to go back to the Vale."

"Oh, your *other* home." There was a sadness in Eva's eyes as she seemed to realize that there was a part of my life I could never fully share with her, a place she could never fully go with me, even if I let her come. It was the tiniest wedge slipped into our friendship.

"Well, since I don't remember much of what happened last time, I'd be happy to take the risk and come with you again."

"I'd never forgive myself if you got hurt again. Plus, you just started your new job. Do you think Tamira would let you take that much time off from work?"

Eva frowned. "Probably not. And I wouldn't want to leave, with us right in the middle of such important experiments."

She was quiet for a while.

"Are you bringing Obadiah?" she asked.

"I don't want to. I mean, I *do* want to." I sighed. "But he'd be risking his life too, and I can't allow that."

Eva raised an eyebrow at me. "You know he's never going to be okay with you doing something risky without him being there to protect you. He loves you, Mab."

I flushed, feeling the throb of my heart in ears. "I know," I said softly.

I changed the subject because talking about Obadiah made me think of his hands trembling, and the way he tried to hide them in his pockets, and it made me too sad.

"Thanks for inviting me to your group," I said. "It's the best lead I have to figure out Cory's real identity and figure out what he did to Quinn and maybe others."

"Of course, no problem." Eva smiled at me, but I detected a slight hint of wariness in her eyes.

"You seem nervous. Do you not want me to come?"

"No, I do, it's just"—Eva twisted her hands—"maybe it's my own damage, but I guess I just feel intimidated about bringing you to our group. I mean, now that I know what you really are, that you're a *fairy*." She said the last word in a hushed, awed whisper. "Which I can still barely wrap my head around, by the way. I guess I thought maybe you'd be insulted by our group, that you'd think it's silly or something. That you'd judge me. I mean, sometimes I worry that we're all just playacting, and now I know that you . . . you're the real thing."

I slid my hand across the countertop and held hers.

"You guys are the real thing too, though," I said.

Eva blinked her long, dark lashed eyes, not seeming to understand.

"I mean, you summoned a fairy."

Eva laughed nervously. "Yeah. I guess we did." She paused. "There were times I questioned if my own spiritual beliefs, practices, whatever you want to call

them, were bullshit. I believed, but I didn't *really* believe. And then this man appeared in our circle. This
not a man. I guess it makes me believe that anything
is possible." Eva shook her head. "I don't know what
to think anymore."

I wished I had something comforting to say to her.
Her understanding of the world was being ripped
apart, and all I could do was stand there in awkward
sympathy and then offer her a hug.

"Do you think the members of your group would
be willing to let me interview them?" I asked at last.
"I'm afraid there might be a lot more girls like Quinn
out there, given how many people Cory may have
dated. I'd like to try to track his network, find out
how many people might be at risk."

"I think they'll talk, if you tell them why you're
there. A lot of them are understandably leery of
opening up to an outsider. We've had a few report-
ers approach Tiffany. They were all trying to run
some lurid tabloid story, like 'Oooh, black magic!'"
She made a face. "But they'll see that your intentions
are to help. And they're scared too. We've noticed
there've been a few absences from the group lately,
long-standing members who suddenly stopped
showing up. It's possible they're Cory's victims.
And Tiffany said one of the girls has been really depressed. She tried to kill herself. Before tonight, I
thought it was all coincidence. I never thought to
trace it back to Cory. But now that we know"—she

shivered—"we've got to alert everyone, and stop whoever is behind this."

"Do you think they'll believe me, if I tell them not to trust Cory? If I tell them I'm a fairy too?"

Eva nodded. "A few months ago I would have said no. But after what we all saw in that ritual, I think they'd believe just about anything now."

CHAPTER 5

I was lucky that the full moon, and hence Eva's group's next ritual, was only a few days away. We took the subway to a part of Brooklyn I wasn't familiar with, near the canal—an ugly, forgotten wasteland of ship-yards and warehouses, perfumed by an ever present sewage-stench that now was slowly metamorphosing into Brooklyn's next trendy neighborhood. It had a way to go before its transformation was complete, however, and it was still more pupa than butterfly. Eva and I walked for a long time down an unnerv-ingly dark street past boarded-up warehouses, chain-link fences and empty lots, with the occasional loft or trendy bar like fireflies blinking out of the dark.

I kept looking behind me as we walked down the poorly lit and empty street, our footfalls echoing against the concrete. There were too few people out. I didn't feel safe here. We continued walking, down a steep hill, the pungent odor of the canal growing stronger, till Eva pointed to a warehouse that appeared to be no different from any of the others. In fact, it seemed to be abandoned.

"This is it," she said, then saw the dubious look on my face. She shrugged. "The space was cheap," she said by way of explanation, and I nodded; it was an explanation all New Yorkers understood. We'd all live in shipping crates if the rent was reasonable.

She buzzed the door.

"Hello?" a female voice answered.

Eva leaned in close to the dirty speaker. "The grain is reaped in silence," she whispered. Then she turned to me. "It's the pass phrase."

"You guys have a secret pass phrase?"

"Yeah, I guess it's kind of dorky, but . . ."

"No, I think it's cool." I felt slightly giddy, as if I was about to be inducted into a secret society. For a moment I wondered if we'd open up the door to this seemingly abandoned warehouse and it would turn out to be an opulent villa on the inside where everyone was wearing masks and was either in long robes or totally naked, like in that movie. But something in my gut told me the warehouse would just be a warehouse, filled with a couple of twenty-somethings cobbling together bits of different old traditions, seeking some kind of meaning in a meaningless age.

A female voice spoke through the tinny buzzer again. There was nothing mystical about her tone.

"Come right up," she called cheerfully.

She buzzed the door and we entered, walking gingerly up an old, rickety flight of stairs.

Eva led me to the top floor. It was warm up here, and not terribly well ventilated, the building being one of those barely legal residentials that had never really earned their C of O.

At the top of the stairs was an enormous green velvet curtain, like the kind that would be strung across a stage. Eva pulled the heavy, tasseled rope, and it slowly swung open, revealing the loft space behind.

It didn't resemble anything out of a movie, but it was beautiful in its own way, because a couple of kids, with no budget and no skills but boundless enthusiasm, had obviously put a lot of time and care into making it so. The walls had been painted a deep sky blue, and there was a paper moon hung up in one corner that made me think of the old Tin Pan Alley ballad. Someone had brought in some secondhand sofas and armchairs. There were low coffee tables scattered with little tea-light candles, and the whole room smelled thickly of incense, Florida water and sage.

A girl approached us: twenty-something, tall and striking, with natural coal-black hair and eerily pale skin. She was wearing a purple velvet dress that looked like something one might wear to a Renaissance festival. She held herself with a grace and confidence that one usually didn't see in girls our age. If her luminous skin didn't make her appear so young, she had the presence of someone middle-aged or beyond. There was something hypnotic about her bright green eyes that made me want to keep staring at her.

"Tiffany," Eva called out, and the two girls embraced each other. Tiffany greeted me with a cheerful grin that dispelled her mysterious allure but made me feel welcome.

"You must be Mab," she said, going to shake my hand, and then deciding midshake to envelope me in a hearty bear hug. "I've heard so much about you. All good things." She winked at me.

"Eva tells me wonderful things about you guys. Thank you for letting me come."

"Of course," she said magnanimously. "Our doors are always open. Sorry about the password. It's just . . . we were having a lot of gawkers—guys who thought all we do is dance naked around a bonfire. I mean, not that we don't do that too—" She threw back her head and laughed, a warm, genuine cackle that made me instantly like her. "They were terribly disappointed when I treated them to a two-hour lecture on the epigraphic evidence of the Eleusinian Mysteries instead." She laughed again. "I don't think they'll be bothering us anymore."

She led us over to another girl, a heavyset blonde who was greeting the people entering the large room with a smoldering bundle of silvery dried sage leaves in her hand.

"Get yourself saged first—we can talk later," said

Tiffany, and she returned to the crowd to welcome the other guests.

The girl with the smoking sage bundle approached me.

I smiled at her hesitantly.

"Um, I'm sorry. I don't really know what to do here."

"Nothing to do. Just be," she said cheerfully. "Close your eyes, and let go of all the stress you walked in here with."

I closed my eyes as I was bid, and took a long slow inhale, breathing in the smoke that smelled of memories of summer bonfires and Eva's little bedroom altar. I tried to shake off all the worry that was clinging to me: Obadiah's trembling hands, Quinn's soulless eyes, all those children trapped in a sleep of death in their cocoons and the weight of trying to fix it all. I let out a long exhale as I felt rather than saw the girl slowly waving the warm wand of smoking sage inches over my body. When I opened my eyes again, I realized I did feel more relaxed.

"Blessed be." She smiled at me.

"Um, yeah, you too." I smiled back. I had no idea what I was doing here, but these people seemed nice. It touched me how warmly and openly they'd welcomed me, an outsider, into their group. They were trusting me, or rather, they were trusting Eva, and she was trusting me. I didn't want to let them down.

Once she was finished, we rejoined Tiffany. The

loft space was filling up. People were milling around, sitting on the sofas in groups of twos or threes and chatting. Clearly there was a social aspect as well as a spiritual one to this group.

Tiffany motioned us over to a well-worn love seat in the corner.

"Eva told me you work for a private detective," she said to me, and I nodded. "We'd appreciate your help. I'm really concerned about what's been going on recently, and, well, we can't exactly go to the NYPD about it. They'd never believe us." She looked from me over to Eva. "You told her already? About the ritual where Cory appeared?"

Eva nodded.

Tiffany's warm, green eyes were suddenly so focused and intent it made my breath catch in my throat.

"Do you really believe all this?" she asked me. "About Cory?"

Looking her right in the eye, I nodded.

Her brow pinched. I didn't think she was convinced.

I took a deep breath. Should I tell her the truth? Eva trusted her. And if these people really believed in magic, maybe they would believe me? "I believe what Eva told me about Cory because let's just say where Cory came from, that's where I come from too."

Tiffany's eyes widened. She exhaled in a slow whoosh.

"Wow," she said at last. "Well. We are honored by your presence."

Her voice had changed in character, and I realized she was talking to me as a fairy, as if she was greeting some kind of deity. I figured I needed to put a stop to that before she offered me oaten cakes, a bowl of cream and a place by the hearth.

I put up my hand. "Look," I said, "for all intents and purposes, I'm as human as any of you are. I'm a changeling. A fairy is something I *used* to be, not something I am anymore. I lost all those powers years ago. So you don't have to talk to me like that."

"Got it," she said. And she was back to her warm, grinning self.

"But to answer your question, yes," I said. "I believe. I believe because I've experienced."

Tiffany's eyes were serious. "I feel you there. I realize now maybe I never really believed, until I saw what I witnessed that night."

Eva, who had been silent all this time, her feet propped up on the coffee table, spoke up. "I thought as the High Priestess, if any of us really believed, you did?"

Tiffany shook her head. "I tried," she said. "I did the rituals, I chanted the chants, but I guess at the end of the day, I thought all our summoning and songs were just lovely metaphors. It's not that I didn't believe in some kind of spiritual *something*. It's just I didn't think a being would *literally* appear in our circle."

I studied Tiffany's face. Her eyes held an inner light, shining in the twinkle from the dozens of flickering candles from the coffee table, and I could see how much all of this meant to her. Here she'd been invoking the names of spirits and deities for years, and then one night it had *worked*: one had shown up. It was the confirmation of her faith. But she was in danger. All the people here tonight were. Fairies weren't necessarily good. They weren't even *usually* good.

"This being you summoned, that calls himself 'Cory'—I'm afraid he's dangerous," I said to her. "I wouldn't trust him."

Tiffany looked up at me and I could see in her eyes that she'd had the same fears.

"I understand that now. I didn't realize it then, when he first came."

Her eyes were far away as she recalled the memory, her hands twisting through the green fringe of the sofa. "We were in shock, ecstatic, when he appeared. People were screaming, fainting. No one had ever dreamed it would really happen. But there he was. One moment the circle was empty and the next moment he just appeared out of the incense smoke, this beautiful, beautiful man . . ."

"I'm sure it must have been incredible," I said. "But I've known a lot of the Fey; I've lived amongst them. You can't trust them."

"Yeah, I see that now," she said quietly. "It didn't surprise me when a couple of the girls in the group became his lovers. I mean, here's this being from another world, who happens to look gorgeous—who wouldn't want to be with that? The thing that surprised me, though, and honestly was the first sign that made me question him, was whom he chose to be his lovers. It's not that I'm jealous he didn't choose me. I'll admit, I flirted with him, and I was hurt when he never returned any of it. But it was okay. He was free to not choose me."

"I would have chosen you, if I were him," Eva said, and Tiffany playfully hit her on the arm.

"But what I didn't understand," Tiffany continued, "was why hadn't he chosen any of the other priestesses? Nicole and Liz, they've dedicated themselves to the fairies; they've been making offerings to the Fey for over a decade, and when they met him, they were so honored. They just wanted to learn about him and the world that he came from. They're really beautiful, strong, amazing women. But he never went for anyone like that. He always went for the new girls."

"Like Quinn Sheffield?" I asked.

Tiffany nodded. "Yeah. I'm not knocking her. I remember when she came. She was sweet; she seemed like she was genuinely seeking something. But she was young, and she seemed really insecure. All the girls he went for were like that. The ones on the periphery. The ones who were still all uncomfortable and giggly about the ritual nudity. The ones who, I hate to say, seemed weak."

"The ones nobody would miss?" I said.

And with a devastated expression on her face, Tiffany nodded.

"I noticed Quinn stopped showing up to the large rituals a few months back. Some of our other new members, who'd been Cory's lover, did too. I didn't question it at first. A lot of new people drop out. They haven't made the commitment to it. But I saw one of them again, this girl Lauren, and she looked terrible. She was always smiling before, and the last time I saw her, she didn't smile at all. Her eyes were just vacant, half-dead. I asked her if she was still seeing Cory, and all of a sudden she started crying, and asked me not to speak of him again."

The look on Tiffany's face was pained, guilty. "Cory didn't show up at last month's ritual. And honestly, at this point I'm not sure I'd want him to come back. But even if he's not here, he could still be out there. He could still be involved in these other people's lives. From what Eva told me about Quinn, that's scary. She's in danger. She could, goddess forbid, you know . . ."

I knew the words Tiffany didn't want to say: "kill herself."

"I feel responsible for all this," Tiffany said, and I saw a weight of guilt in her eyes that I knew well, because I felt it myself. "I mean, I started this group. All these people are ultimately here because of me. They trusted me, and I let someone into this space that hurt them."

"It's not your fault," I said softly. "Whoever it was could have come into this world anyway."

Tiffany nodded, but she looked unconvinced, her own guilt clearly not assuaged.

"But I'm the one who summoned him," she said quietly.

"If he comes to the ritual tonight," I said, "I'd like to question him. I think I know the right questions to ask. We'll find out who is behind this. We'll figure out how to stop whatever he's doing to these girls."

I tried to sound more confident than I felt. I didn't know if I'd be able to see the fairy behind the human disguise or how I'd make him give up whatever it was he was doing to these young women. But still, it was the best lead I had. Tiffany seemed heartened.

"He hasn't come the last two rituals," she said. "But maybe if you're here . . ." Her voice trailed off, a hopeful look in her eyes. "Thank you for coming," she said. "We appreciate your help."

She glanced at the pocket watch clipped to her dress. "It's almost time for the ritual. I can't guarantee he'll show up, but we can try it."

Tiffany hopped off the love seat and began to assemble the ragtag group of people who had been milling around the room. It was a fairly diverse group, I noticed, looking around at the faces that were now making a circle. Though the average participant seemed to be a twenty-something-year-old white girl, there were men as well as women, as well as those to whom such labels needn't apply, and different races, different ages. What all these people must have had in common is that they'd come here as seekers.

When I looked over at Tiffany, she was holding one of those Tibetan singing bowls, and with a practiced hand, she drew a long, sweet, ringing note from it. It had a hypnotic effect on the crowd. All the chatting conversations stilled, and everyone gathered around to form a circle in the center of the room as the note continued to reverberate through the space.

Tiffany spoke into the silence that engulfed the crowd.

"Thank you all for coming," she said, smiling at the assembled faces. "We will now begin the ritual. Please turn off all your phones and electronic devices . . ." She then proceeded to do a perfect impression of an annoying cell phone ring with her mouth, and everyone laughed. The mood lightened, but became serious again when she held up her hand.

Tiffany's voice sounded different as it rang out above the audience, and I could see why she was a leader here. Her presence made us all stand up straighter, stop chatting and be *present*.

"The ritual will now begin. Close your eyes."

I did as I was bid.

She asked us to feel our feet touching the floor, touching the earth, way down deep below New York City. Together we took a long, slow inhale and exhale, and tension I didn't know I was carrying around slipped from my body like a leaded vest shrugged off. I felt light but grounded. Eva whispered in my ear that this was the warm-up before the real ritual would begin.

The sound of a drum made me open my eyes, and I saw that a trio of drummers had assembled inside the circle, beating on skin drums and a battered djembe. The beat was steady, rhythmic, like a beating heart.

"We will now perform the Mystery play," Tiffany announced.

Somehow I knew she wasn't talking about one of those silly murder mystery dinner theaters. This was Mystery with a capital *M*, like the sacred festival theater of Ancient Greece. I waited, wondering what I'd gotten myself into as several people entered the circle. They were dressed in an eclectic assortment of robes and flowing garments, with staves in their hands and crowns of leaves on their heads. Their clothing was like something out of a low-budget high school production of *A Midsummer Night's Dream*, but the looks on their faces as they entered the ring were deadly serious. The robes and crowns and sticks meant something to the wearers, and the cynical part of my brain shut up and listened.

A girl in a white dress, knotted with a golden tasseled rope that seemed like it had once held a curtain, stepped forward into the circle.

Tiffany spoke. "This is Kore, queen of summer. Her reign has ended. Soon she must go back to the underworld."

"Welcome, Kore," someone cried out, and the whole circle responded, "Kore, Kore!"

The girl playing Kore began to walk along the perimeter of the circle, stooping down to pick up several long stemmed red roses that someone had scattered across the floor. I looked over towards Tiffany, but she had disappeared from the circle, the place she'd occupied filled in by others. Kore continued "picking" these flowers as the crowd began to move in time to the drums, a slow rhythmic dance, and sang, "Hail Kore, queen of summer, your reign has ended, go in peace."

Then suddenly, a figure dressed in long black robes, wearing a mask decorated with black crow's feathers, broke through and entered the circle. It was impossible to tell whether the wearer was male or female.

The masked one began to slowly stalk the perimeter of the circle, following Kore as she blithely gathered her flowers. All around me the people began to chant: "Hail Hades, the unseen one, ruler of the underworld, come to take fair Kore home."

At that, the masked Hades seized Kore. She dropped her bundle of flowers, scattering them across the floor. But she made no move to resist, and it was she who extended her hand, and took Hades' black glove, linking arms with the god of the underworld. They walked together, hand in hand, kicking away the rose petals from before their feet, walking to the perimeter of the circle, where two chairs draped in black had been set up, and took their seats. One of the drummers scurried over and placed transparent black veils over both their heads, shrouding them.

"Hail King and Queen of the Underworld," someone cried out, and the crowd echoed them.

The heavyset blonde girl who had saged me entered the circle, now wearing a red robe and holding a husk of corn.

"Where is my daughter? Where is fair Kore?" She went around the ring, asking each of us, and I didn't know if I was supposed to shout out, "Over there, under the veil!" or not. But she went on walking, round and round in a circle, as if lost. When she went by me, I could see real tears glistening on her cheeks.

A young man spoke up from the circle. "We will help you return her to the Light. Please teach us your gifts in return: how to grow the seed into the plant, how to make the barren earth bear fruit, how to make something out of nothing."

The circle of people all began to dance and sing, and the refrain of the song was the password I'd heard Eva say at the door:

"The grain is reaped in silence. The grain is reaped in silence."

Suddenly, the drumming and the singing stopped, and someone killed the lights. We all stood there in the darkness together, silent, and I closed my eyes, breathing into the stillness.

Then the lights came back on. The blond girl, "Demeter," walked over to the two chairs, where

Kore and Hades sat enthroned, and lifted up the veil from her daughter. The two embraced each other. But Hades drew something out from under the veil and gave it to Kore. She placed it in her mouth, then pulled the veil over herself again. Demeter sank back into the circle, dropping and scattering her sheaves of wheat upon the ground, while the crowd chanted, "Hail and welcome, King and Queen of Winter!"

The girl in the white dress rose from her throne. She came around to each of us, a wooden bowl in her hands. I could see when she drew near me that it was filled with glistening, red, pomegranate seeds. She made a motion to each of us to take one. As she offered up the blood-red droplets of fruit, I could hear my mother's voice in my head, saying how any human who ate something from another world would be bound there, and for a moment, I hesitated as she offered the seed to me. But something deep within made me open my lips, and she placed the red seed on my tongue. I chewed it thoughtfully, savoring its bitter burst of sweetness.

Next, to my surprise, Eva entered the ring. I hadn't known she was actively taking part in the group ritual tonight; I wondered if she'd kept it from me as a surprise. When she addressed the crowd, her eyes were bright and her voice, loud and steady, held a confidence I'd seldom heard from her: "We bid farewell to Kore as the maiden of summer and welcome her as the Queen of Winter. We thank the mother Demeter for teaching us these rites, and trusting in the knowledge of the return. Like the pomegranate seed that draws Kore back to the underworld, we will always be drawn back into the silence of the heart."

The crowd began to dance and chant: "The grain is reaped in silence, the grain is reaped in silence," and this time, I joined the chant with them.

Eva spoke again.

"Kore and Hades will remain enthroned as our oracles. Our friends have entered a trance state, and are now not speaking, but being spoken through. If any of you has something you wish to ask, you may speak with them."

Two lines began to form, one leading to the white-clad Kore, the other to the black-clad Hades, as people left the circle, one by one. They knelt beside each of the oracles and whispered in their ears. Through the veils that covered their faces, I saw Kore and Hades were whispering something back.

Eva nudged me. "Do you want to go?"

Honestly, I wasn't sure. I wasn't sure I believed. But I had nothing to lose, I supposed. And so I got up awkwardly, and walked over. I hesitated for a moment about which line to join, looking back and forth between the two, light and dark sitting side by side like the two halves of a yin yang. Kore was more approachable. Hades I couldn't see through the feath-ered mask; I wasn't a hundred percent sure if it was Tiffany under there or someone else. At last, I chose the mystery of the oracle clad all in black, and walked over to stand in line, the little voice in my head telling me all the while that this was silly. But I was curious, and there was something sincere about their vibe, which made me inclined to think this was the genuine article, if there was such a thing.

At last it was my turn.

Feeling shy and awkward, I squatted on the floor next to the chair. Silently, Hades motioned me closer. I scooted forward across the hard floorboards. I was so close that I could hear Hades breathing under the veil. It had to be Tiffany. Her face was covered by the raven feather mask, and over that had been laid a translucent black gauze veil since she became the oracle, but I could still see her eyes, two bright glimmers amidst all the darkness. She didn't look at me. She was staring straight ahead but it was like she wasn't seeing the room. Her gaze was fixed on something simultaneously here and far away.

"Speak, my child," she whispered.

I gulped nervously, but she waited.

"Um, I've never done this before," I started. I felt silly and stupid, and like I should just leave this line, leave all these nice people to their slightly odd but nonthreatening way of spending a Saturday evening, and go home to my apartment with a good book and a glass of wine.

But then Hades looked at me.

"Your heart is full of questions, I can feel. Ask."

I gulped at that. It was true; I was full of questions, questions I could barely articulate to myself sometimes.

"I'm trying to find someone," I said. "The one who hurt Quinn Sheffield, and maybe others. He was here."

Why was I telling Tiffany what she already knew? But somehow, it didn't feel like Tiffany. When she spoke, she didn't *sound* like Tiffany anymore either, and a shiver tingled through me.

"You have not yet asked your true question," she said in that not-her voice.

I realized what I'd said before wasn't really a question, more of a comment. I tried again.

"Who is he?" I said. "And how do I find him?"

I couldn't believe I had just said all that. What was I expecting? That this girl draped in black Halloween gauze and feathers would somehow psychically know the answer to all these questions? I didn't believe that.

I looked up at her. I could see her eyes through the darkly translucent fabric.

They were staring right at me.

My breath caught in my throat as I realized her eyes were *glowing*.

Tiffany's eyes were glowing a strange, otherworldly light beneath the veil.

What the . . . ?

"Ask the question again," she said in a voice that was not-her voice. "Say what you wish to know clearly and I will answer."

I gulped.

"I wish to know the real identity of the fairy known as Cory."

When she spoke, I didn't see her lips move under the gauze.

I felt like she was talking directly to my soul.

"He is already known to you," she said.

My heart froze at her words.

"What do you mean?" I asked.

But the oracle was silent.

I guess that wasn't the kind of question she answered.

What did she mean I knew him already? My mind whirled frantically through all the male Fey I knew. There was really only Obadiah . . . and it couldn't be him.

I could feel the people behind me in line growing impatient.

I asked the oracle another question, my heart still hammering nervously.

"Where do I find him?"

"You do not have to look far to find him. But you must go home. You have dallied too long here already."

I stared at her open-mouthed, waiting to see if she had more to say.

But her eyes were distant now; she was no longer seeing me.

She placed her hand on my forehead and muttered a blessing I couldn't quite hear. I knew my time was up, and I had to leave now.

I got up, my legs shaking from squatting on the

floor before her chair for so long, my mind and heart shaken from the eerie sight of those glowing eyes.

Cory was someone I already knew? Who could that possibly be?

Of course, the cynical part of my brain chided me, I was assuming that Tiffany was telling the truth, that she really had an ability to know these things. And yet, the way she'd looked at me, the way her eyes had glowed that otherworldly blue, the way she'd spoken in that voice not her own—she *knew*. She had become a *real* oracle.

I shivered.

I stepped back into the circle, but I had more questions than answers.

I was very quiet as the people began filing back in from their lines and slowly reforming the circle.

Tiffany appeared in the circle again. But she was wearing her purple dress now. Her face was glowing, but in her own hearty, joyful way—whatever I'd glimpsed under the black gauze veil was gone. "Place your intention at the center of our circle," Tiffany instructed us. "Our hearts are open, our hearths are open, we welcome all beings with good intent who wish to visit us."

Tiffany's voice called out above the chanting and the drums.

"If there is a spirit of Nature who is Good, who wishes to bless us with their presence, let them enter our circle."

"Let it come," cried the crowd.

And I cried out too, somehow not feeling afraid anymore.

This was how the group had summoned Cory last time, I thought as the circle of people began to move in a kind of walk-dance around the drummers, in time to the beat. Feet drummed on the wooden floor, echoing the rhythm, making me feel it deep within my bones. My heart was beating fast. Would he come tonight? Would I recognize him when I saw him? Was this what the oracle meant?

High and clear above the crowd, Tiffany began to sing.

She didn't have a trained, or particularly melodious, voice, but she sang from the heart, and I found myself tingling with goose bumps and wiping my eyes with my fists as I listened to her.

"Let it come," she was singing, over and over again.

"Let it come," the crowd echoed back their own chant.

I wasn't sure who or what we were letting enter our midst, but I found myself singing too, along with the rest of them.

I couldn't help but think, as I watched it all, that if you took away the drum, and the candles, the paper moon and the Ren fair wardrobes, it wasn't all that different than the way *I* used to do magic when I was fairy: a quieting of the mind, a focusing of intent, the singing repetition of the spell that let the self dissolve and something new be created out of the emptiness. These humans might have blood in their veins and not Elixir, but otherwise, our practices weren't that different. Maybe that was why their magic worked. And it had worked, hadn't it? They'd manifested a fairy in their midst. Of course, he'd chosen to come too. But still, I couldn't be dismissive anymore of the power these humans wielded. For better or worse, they were *for real*. And all of a sudden I realized why I'd always been so cynical about Eva's group, because deep inside, I *missed* magic. I missed the ability to manifest things just with my intention, to feel the quickening in my soul. And groups like this, they were too close to that, too unbearably close. Except *not*, because to these nice people magic was just a metaphor. Until it wasn't. Until something or someone showed up in their circle. Kore or *Cory*. Was the similarity in their names just a coincidence?

"Place your intention at the center of this circle," Tiffany was saying. "We create it, and it creates us."

"Let it come," the group and I chanted.

Tiffany's voice rang out through the crowd.

"Out of the darkness and void, it becomes."

"Let it come," we all chanted. My body began to rock and sway of its own accord as we moved rhythmically around in a circle. The drumbeat and Tiffany's voice had a hypnotic effect. But what moved me most was these people's sincerity. They really were open to whatever showed up.

"We dissolve into the empty space, where the manifestation has begun."

"Let it come," the people sang.

"Let us be still and welcome it inside ourselves."

The drumming stopped, and we all stood still and silent. I could almost hear the intentions of the strangers whose hands I held as everyone's awareness rested at the center of the circle. I swore I could feel something manifest.

But when I opened my eyes, the center of our circle was empty, apart from Tiffany, and the three drummers, their heads bowed reverently over their tabors.

"He didn't come," I heard a girl next to me whisper, the disappointment clearly written on her face.

"He who visited us before has chosen not to visit us tonight," Tiffany said.

But *she* did not seem disappointed.

"It was not meant to be," she said to the crowd. "But the power of our presence is never wasted. We created something good tonight, even if it's something we cannot see."

I found myself nodding. We had created something. I'd come in here so tense and scared and stressed over everything going on lately, and now I felt calm, peaceful, heartened, rejuvenated. I understood why Eva came here.

Tiffany led us in the same grounding exercise to close as she had at the opening. We held hands, gave a shout of gratitude to the powers of the unseen and then it was over.

Everyone went back to milling around and chatting, though when I looked into these strangers' faces, I could see that they were refreshed, heartened.

I found Tiffany, her eyes bright, cheeks flushed.

"That was you," I said, "under the mask, as Hades?"

Tiffany smiled at me, neither confirming nor denying.

"What did you mean by what you said?"

"I don't remember anything I say when I'm in the trance. People sometimes tell me afterwards they found what I said helpful. I hope so. I have no control over it. It speaks through me. I just try not to get in the way."

"So you have no memory of telling me that Cory is someone I've already met, that I have to go home to find him?"

Tiffany shook her head, and I could tell by one look in her very-normal-now eyes that she wasn't lying. "I don't. But if that's what it told you . . ."

". . . I should listen?" I finished for her.

The crowd of people were beginning to disperse, slowly heading for the exits. Several stopped to say thank you to Tiffany and hug her goodbye. At last she turned back to me. "I know some people are probably disappointed that Cory didn't show in the circle tonight. But I think it was for the best."

I nodded. "I guess it makes sense. I mean, you said,

'We welcome all beings with *good* intent who wish to visit us.' Sounds like Cory didn't have good intent."

Tiffany's face grew pale. She seemed struck by my words.

"You know, I never thought about it," she said slowly. "When I did the ritual months ago where he first appeared, I said, 'We welcome the deities within our midst.' I never specified *good*. I should have been more specific."

"Always be specific, particularly with fairies," I said as I hugged her goodbye.

CHAPTER 6

After we said goodbye to Tiffany and the rest of the group and exited into the dark, quiet street, I reached for my phone, which I'd had turned off during the ritual. I noticed there was a text from Obadiah:

There was a little emergency at the club. Not to worry, Reuben and I are handling it. But I'll probably have to stay here tonight. Don't wait up for me. I love you. XO.

Whenever Obadiah said, "Don't worry," it made me very worried.

"What's going on?" Eva asked me.

"Obadiah," I said. "Something's wrong. I know he was having some issues with some of his customers," I said, stopping myself a split second before I said "werewolves." "Do you mind? I want to give him a call before we get on the train."

I stood under the haloed circle of a streetlight and called him. The phone rang and rang and went to voicemail. I sent him a text as well, and waited. No answer. At last I tried the club's landline.

Reuben answered. He sounded harried.

"Oh hi, Mab." His normally slow Southern drawl was sped up with nervous energy. "No time to talk, things are a little crazy round here tonight. Obadiah told me in case you called to say he's sorry he can't come to the phone. Dealing with a situation. But he also told me to tell you not to worry. Everything's fine."

"Everything is obviously not fine. Will you tell me what's going on?"

There was a silence on the other end of the phone.

"Let me get Obadiah; let him talk to you."

I waited.

I could hear a lot of background noise on the line. It was a cacophony in there, and it wasn't music. There were loud crashes, bangs and a screaming, howling sort of sound that made me shiver. What was going on?

"Oh hi, Mab, love, did you get my text?" It was Obadiah's voice on the line. "Sorry I can't come over tonight."

"Will you tell me what's going on? The more you tell me not to worry, the more I'm going to worry."

There was silence on the line, and then at last Obadiah spoke.

"It's the werewolves. One of them is . . . it's a long story. But we've got it under control."

I heard a large crash and a shrieking yelp, and then Obadiah cursed.

"It doesn't sound very under control," I said.

Obadiah sighed. "It will be."

"Will you let me come over? Maybe I can help?"

"No!" he almost shouted. "No, there's no need for that. I'll call you in the morning."

"I'm coming over," I said with finality.

"Mab," he protested, but I cut him off.

"I'll see you in twenty minutes."

"*Mab.*"

"I love you." I made kissy noises into the phone.

"Love you too, but, Mab . . ."

"See you soon, babe." I hung up.

I turned to Eva. "Something's up. I need to go over there."

She nodded, understanding.

We walked down into the subway together. I hugged Eva goodbye at our stop and then continued on to Obadiah's.

When I walked up to his whitewashed brick building, I could hear the shouting from outside.

There was a handwritten sign in the window apologizing for being closed for the evening; it was, after all, Saturday night. The sign said there had been an "emergency leak." That sounded like a lie. The only thing that appeared to be leaking from the very walls of the old building was uncontained werewolf fury.

I paused nervously at the door. Obadiah had told

me not to come. Was it safe inside? I was on friendly terms with Obadiah's werewolf bouncer, Reuben, and on a smile and wave basis with most of his Wolfmen customers by now, but that didn't mean they weren't dangerous. Then again, I looked up at the moon, shining over the rooftops of Brooklyn: it wasn't full. Wasn't anywhere close, just a crescent sliver. I'd be fine.

I dug the key Obadiah had given me out of my purse, and unlocked the door. It was one thing when he'd given me a key to his apartment, but when he gave me a key to the club, that was when I knew things were serious.

As I opened the door, five of the biggest, most hulking, yellow-toothed, scary-looking Wolfmen I'd ever seen in my life turned to glare at me. More Wolfmen moved in from along the walls.

"You've got to be kidding me," one of them snarled. "Well, if it isn't the daughter of the Queen Bitch herself?"

"Um . . . hi," I said.

"How dare you speak to my girlfriend like that." Obadiah strode out of the back room and through the crowd. The werewolf who spoke was almost twice his size, yet he slunk back at the look of fury on Obadiah's face. I'd never seen Obadiah that angry before. It was a terrifying and almost majestic sight as he drew himself up to his full height, his dark eyes blazing fire.

"Mab," he cried as our eyes met, "you shouldn't

have come. Please, go home. I'll take care of these . . ." He grumbled something low and insulting about his Wolfmen clientele.

"Will you please just tell me what's going on?" I said. All the werewolves were still staring at me. It was making me more and more uncomfortable. Maybe I really should leave? If all of them decided to rush me right now, Obadiah couldn't fight them all off. I caught Reuben's eye in the corner, looking sympathetic and helpless. The three of us would be completely outnumbered.

"What's going on," the big Wolfman said, "is the fucking Fairy Queen has royally screwed us."

"I don't know what you guys are talking about," I said as all the pairs of angry yellow eyes glared at me. "But I'm on your side, okay? The Queen screws everyone; that's what she does. Whatever this is, I can tell you, I've got nothing to do with it. So will you please tell me what's . . ."

We were interrupted by a loud crash and a high-pitched yelp, like a hurt dog. I realized the sound was coming from upstairs, where Obadiah kept a secret store of magical goods to sell to his supernatural clientele. What was going on in there?

Obadiah rubbed his brow. "Reuben, can you go in there and check on him? Make sure he's not hurting himself. And please, try not to let him destroy the entire shop, will you?"

"Right, boss." Reuben trotted away towards the hidden door behind Obadiah's bar.

"What's happening in there? What do you mean he's destroying your shop?"

Obadiah sighed in exasperation. "One of the Wolfmen, his name is Blake, who belongs to these *gentlemen's* pack," said Obadiah, "was not able to change back into human form after the last full moon."

"Oh my god," I said as the reality of what he was saying hit me. "You mean he's still in . . . ?"

"Yes," said Obadiah.

"And he's in your back room right now?"

"Yes."

"But you've got so many glass vials in there."

"Yes." Obadiah sighed. "And witches' crystal balls, and Sanguinari crystal blood flutes, and some priceless Elvish manuscripts, which he's probably urinating on at this very moment. I really can't think about it right now."

We heard another howl from the storeroom, and then the cajoling sound of Reuben's voice, followed by a crash. Clearly his efforts weren't working.

"You're sure Reuben's safe up there?" I said.

Obadiah nodded. "He's got body armor on. And he knows how to handle a Were. He'll be okay." Obadiah pressed his lips into a thin, hard line. "There's no other option. I can't have Blake running around here loose on the dance floor. He could hurt someone before we can figure out how to get him to change back."

"But he's going to destroy your store." I shot dagger looks at the hulking Wolfmen, furious at how they were abusing Obadiah's hospitality.

"The werewolves insisted on bringing Blake here so I could see him like this, see how bad it is," Obadiah said to me. "They want me to fix this. As if I could." He shook his head. "I guess that's what I get for using Elixir to fix everyone's problems for so many years. Everyone comes to me whenever they're in a bind."

One of the werewolves interrupted us. It was the same one who'd spoken before—clearly he was the Alpha here. He sauntered over from where he'd been leaning up against Obadiah's marble-topped bar.

"Blake isn't the first of our kind who has had a problem lately," the Alpha said abruptly. "For months, several of our members have been having the opposite problem—they were *unable* to change. And it comes down to Elixir."

"What do you mean?" I asked. Honestly, I didn't know much about werewolf culture. The fairies and the Wolfmen had very little do with each other, each of them sadly looking down on the other's kind.

"We do the ritual of the change in the Vale," he explained. "We drink from the Elixir streams. That's what makes us change forms. Did you know that?"

I shook my head.

"We drink from the streams to activate the change, and then when the night is done, we drink from the streams again in order to change back," the Alpha said. "Only lately, it hasn't been working."

"Because the Elixir streams are diluted," one of the Wolfmen cried out from the back of the room. "It's like drinking fucking tap water."

"Calm down, Jed," snarled the Alpha, but he nodded in agreement to what the pissed-off Were had said. "That does about sum it up, though. Something has changed about the streams of late. We'd heard there was a drought that was affecting the fairies, but we'd paid it no mind. It hadn't affected us. But now it does. Some of the older Wolfmen weren't able to change at the moonrise ritual. I guess there wasn't enough Elixir for them. And then Blake. He's a young pup; I guess he needs more Elixir to change back than those of us who are more experienced. So he didn't."

"And it's all because of the fucking Fairy Queen," yelled a young Wolfman.

The Alpha put up his hand for silence again, and begrudgingly, the one who had spoken out of turn was quiet. But I could feel all of the werewolves glaring at me.

Was this what my mother had been talking about on the knife, was this what she meant by "it's getting worse"? Could it be that there wasn't just a drought of Elixir anymore, but that what Elixir there was wasn't as strong as it used to be? That wouldn't just affect the Wolfmen; that would affect all of us. But the fact was, I knew less about what was going on than my mother did. Who was I to play diplomat here?

"I'm sorry to hear you've been having this problem," I said to them. "That sounds awful. But if you don't mind me asking, why do you think my mother is behind it? She's been dealing with the ill effects of the Elixir drought herself. I know for a fact that she's making it better, even if I don't approve of her methods." I scowled, and Obadiah squeezed my hand. "It's the Vale itself that's failing. It isn't any one individual's fault. It affects all of us."

But the Alpha shook his head. "I know the Queen is concerned with the drought too—that's just it. I get it; everybody cares about their own pack, and everyone else's pack can go fuck off. That's how the world works—human world or the Vale, it don't matter. But that's why I've begun to suspect, and my Wolfmen agree with me"—there were enthusiastic nods from the crowd—"the Queen is stealing our Elixir. She doesn't care about us. She cares about the fairies."

"But where's the proof?" I asked.

"The proof is our pup Blake is in full Were form tearin' up Obadiah's store at this very moment. Somebody's been stealing our Elixir and my bet's on the Queen."

I was silent. It was tough to argue with him about it because he very well could be right.

"The Queen is violating our treaty," he continued. "We had a treaty that said that the fairies would never use the Elixir streams in our territory. They've got Elixir in their veins; all we've got are the Elixir streams that run through the heart of the Central Forest. The last Fairy Queen signed a treaty with us that said the fairies would always leave our streams alone. If this Queen violated our treaty, we view that as a declaration of war."

"Now hold on," Obadiah and I said together, but

our voices were lost over the bellicose roar that had erupted from the crowd. My stomach tightened. These furious Wolfmen *wanted* a war, and a war breaking out between the Fey and the Wolfmen was the last thing the Vale needed. We were just barely surviving in peacetime, as our world mysteriously deteriorated. I wasn't sure the Vale could even handle the stress of such a conflict. This was bad. Very, very bad. I cast a panicked look at Obadiah.

"I understand how grievous things are, but please, don't do anything rash that could ultimately hurt your own people as much as it hurts the fairies. The Vale is in a very delicate state right now. If our land gets destroyed, you lose your forests to run in, just like we lose our House Trees. It would be the end of the fairies and the werewolves both."

Obadiah smiled at me; he thought I'd spoken well.

The Alpha smiled too, but I didn't think it was to acknowledge the rationality of the point I'd just made. There was something sly in the way he grinned, showing one yellow canine. He was just pausing before dropping the inevitable bomb.

"I have considered this," he said slowly. "There is an alternative. I know we can't blame every regular fairy for the crimes of their Queen. I'm sure there's plenty of fairies that just want to live in their tree houses and pick flowers or whatever the hell your kind do. There's one thing that would eliminate the problem without going to war."

"Yes?" I said.

"We have a coup and we kill this Fairy Queen."

An image of my mother's face flashed before my mind, and a tenderness I didn't know I felt for her welled up in me, stinging my eyes. I understood why they hated her. Sometimes I did too. The Queen had committed horrible crimes; there were things I'd never forgive her for. But she was my mother, and she was doing the best she could. I wasn't going to let them kill her. She'd promised me she'd stop kidnapping the children. She was open to reason. She didn't deserve to die.

"No, please, you need to reconsider," I started to say, but my voice was lost in the din of cheering werewolves. I could tell by the look in the Alpha's eyes that my appeals were not working.

"Why are you on her side anyway?" the Alpha asked me. "Rumor I heard was that she castrated your magic powers and shunted you off to the human world. Don't know if I'd be so quick to defend someone who did that to me," he said.

I bit my lip, stifling the anger that flared at his words. "I know what she did. And why she did it," I said quietly, realizing this Wolfman Alpha could have very well been among the assassins that my mother had put me in the human world to protect me from.

"If the current Queen is out of the picture, though," mused the Alpha, "we'd be willing to work with you. We have no interest in ending the fairies' line; we just want our streams back, to protect our way of life. We could make a new treaty, you and I."

He thought I actually wanted to be the next Fairy Queen—as if I cared about power like that, as if I was like him.

"She's my mother," I said flatly. "And I'm not going to let you kill her over a groundless accusation. You have no proof that the Queen is behind what's been happening to your pack."

As if to demonstrate evidence of proof, Blake gave an anguished howl, followed by a crash and a string of muffled curses from Reuben. The Alpha shot me a satisfied look, crossing his arms over his chest.

Obadiah spoke up, trying a different tactic. "The Queen is aware your packs hate her. Her security is insane. You'd never get into the palace."

"Ah," said the Alpha, grinning, "but that's where you're wrong. The rules of the game have changed now. Now we've got a member in our pack who can be in full werewolf form outside of the moon. The Queen's not expecting that. She thinks she's safe from any Wolfmen threat till the next full moon. So do her guards. A Wolfman with the full strength of his powers will rip right through whatever defenses they've got set up. They won't even know what hit 'em."

What he was saying was terrifying, because I could easily see it being true. It would be the ultimate surprise attack. The Queen would never expect a fully grown Werewolf to be able to storm into her palace at any time, no longer restricted by the moon's phases. The drought had weakened the once-immortal Fey. They really could kill her.

I had to do something to stop this.

"Please don't act on this yet," I said, looking up pleadingly into the hard-set eyes of the enormous Alpha. "Let me talk to her. Let me see if she's actually behind this. Let us see if there's something we can do."

"Why the hell should I wait around for that? My boys are ready to end this immediately."

I stared up at the Alpha, his arms crossed tightly in front of his chest. His posture was grim, uncompromising, but the expression in his eyes gave me pause. There was fear there, and it was just the crack in the door I was searching for.

Standing up on my tiptoes, I whispered in his ear.

"I know you can't compromise in front of your pack. But please consider: a war with the fairies will decimate you, just like it will decimate us. It won't bring back the Elixir; all it will do is decrease your numbers in the slaughter. And that's the very thing the Fairy Queen would want."

I pulled away from him. His jaw was still clenched in anger, but I saw a brief flicker of understanding in his eyes; he knew I was right.

"You've got until the next full moon to make our streams come back. Beyond that, I make no promises," he growled at me, too low for anyone else to hear, and then sauntered off to join the rest of his pack.

I walked over to Obadiah, who gestured for me to take a seat at one of the empty tables by the side of the bar.

"He gave us till the next full moon," I said to Obadiah. "I can't let them kill her."

"No, you can't. We'll figure out a way to stop this. They're all riled up and hotheaded right now. They'll calm down."

"Not if the same thing starts happening to more of their pack."

"Do you think your mom might be behind it?" he asked, his voice low. "I mean, between you and me?"

I sighed. "I have no idea. I wouldn't put it past her. I know she's desperate for any source of Elixir. And I did make her promise she wouldn't take it out of any more kids."

Oh crap, the promise I'd made her make to me—was this its unintended consequence? She wasn't kidnapping children and extracting Elixir from them anymore, so she'd begun stealing from the Wolfmen's streams? She had to get it from somewhere, or the fairies would die. I put my head in my hands. It was looking more and more likely that my mother was really at fault here. I supposed taking away a fully grown man's ability to turn into a werewolf was a lot more ethical than stealing the life energy of kids. Though that probably made no difference to the werewolves.

I rubbed my brow. The whole thing was a mess. And if I didn't do something, they were definitely going to kill my mother.

As we sat there in silence, our hands interlocked across the table, we heard another howl, scream and crash from the upstairs room, an auditory reminder of how bad things still were.

"I need to go up there," Obadiah said.

"Why isn't their Alpha in there right now? Why is poor Reuben having to deal with this?"

"Because Reuben's their wolf-whisperer," Obadiah said. "It's his role in the pack to keep a rogue Werewolf calm. He's been trained for it."

"It doesn't sound like he's doing a very good job," I said as the sound of another crash came from the storeroom.

"These are extraordinary circumstances. The Alpha can't leave the rest of the pack alone, even for a few minutes. He needs to watch over the group, keep them calm. Believe me, that's a big job in and of itself. I know the crowd probably seems pretty rowdy to you right now, but trust me, he's keeping them under control. If he wasn't there, they'd be rioting and killing."

But fear crystalized in my gut. "I know you need to check on the back room. But he's in full Were form. He could hurt you."

"Blake won't hurt me. He was always a nice kid."

"He may have been a nice kid, but now he's a werewolf," I protested. "Let Reuben handle him." But I wasn't sure if Reuben could get control of him. Was it even possible to control a full-on werewolf?

"I'll wear body armor," he said, clearly hearing the worry in my thoughts and trying to mollify it. "Reuben lent me an extra set. We're roughly the same size. I've got it behind the bar."

Obadiah walked over behind the gleaming marble counter and picked up a large cardboard box. He began taking the pieces out and showing them to me as he put them on. I guess he thought it would ease my mind, but it was only making me more nervous. There was a hulking black vest-like thing that covered the whole torso and would protect all the vital organs, and long protectors for the limbs that were attached with strips of Velcro. There was a black helmet too.

I frowned. "Do they have a suit that's my size? I'd like to come with you."

"Mab, I appreciate the support, but no, they don't. One, I don't think there are any four-foot-eleven Wolfmen," he said. "And two, I could never put you in harm's way like that."

"But you'd put yourself in harm's way?" I countered.

"I'll be fine. I'm just going in there to check on him, then I'll come right back out. Reuben is doing the long-term babysitting."

I sighed, but I could tell I wasn't going to change his mind.

"Let me walk with you up the stairs at least. I want to be able to hear what's going on in there. If I hear you scream, I'll run and get their Alpha."

Obadiah tapped on the eyes of the carved wooden gargoyle in the back of the bar to unlock the secret door.

"If you insist," he said. "But whatever you do, do not open the door to the back room."

"Right," I said.

I opened my arms and pressed him to me, reaching up to kiss him hard on the mouth. "Please be careful," I said. "Promise?"

"I promise," he whispered.

And then he opened the door to the room and closed it quickly behind him.

I stood outside the closed door.

This close up, I could hear the terrified squeaking and squawking of the animal familiars in their cages. Poor things—the bars were probably protecting them, but I bet the werewolf had been trying to eat them.

I heard Reuben's voice call out.

"Boss, you shouldn't be in here. It's not safe."

"Relax, I've got body armor on. How is he?" Obadiah replied.

There was a low growl from the Were.

"Not good," said Reuben. "I can't seem to calm him down. He's just so scared."

"Understood. Oh boy . . ." Obadiah's voice trailed off. I could only assume he was surveying the level of damage the frightened Werewolf had caused. I pressed my ear to the door to be able to hear what he said next.

"It's like a tornado ripped through here."

"You okay, boss?" I heard Reuben ask.

"I'll be fine," said Obadiah, though his voice didn't sound fine. "It's just shock."

And then there was a terrifying, guttural howl from the werewolf. And then a thud.

My heart stopped.

"Boss?" I heard Reuben cry out. "Boss? Obadiah?"

My fingers itched for the door handle, but I stopped myself, hearing Obadiah's words in my mind: *Whatever you do, do not open the door.*

"Boss, are you okay? Obadiah, talk to me, say something!"

"Reuben," I shouted through the door, praying he could hear me. "I'm right outside. What did the werewolf do? Should I get the Alpha? Should I call 911?"

"Mab," Reuben called back, "I don't know. It wasn't Blake. Blake's over there on the other side of the room by the birdcages. He didn't touch him, I swear it. Obadiah just collapsed, on his own. Say something to me, Obadiah, say something," he begged.

I couldn't help it. I just couldn't.

I threw open the door.

The scene of chaos and destruction took my breath away. It did indeed look like the scene of a natural disaster. There was broken glass everywhere. Shelves had been ripped out of the floor and torn to splinters, their contents strewn all over. And there was blood smeared on the floor, on the bar top, on the walls.

Obadiah was lying on the floor.

I rushed over to him. He wasn't moving.

"Obadiah!"

"Mab, no," Reuben screamed.

The werewolf was lunging for me. His eyes glowed a bloodthirsty red.

Reuben caught him in a tackle, pinning him down.

"Mab, I can't hold him like this very long. You have to get out of here."

"What happened to Obadiah? What's all this blood? If that thing did this . . ."

"It's not his blood," Reuben was shouting, wrestling with the salivating werewolf. "Blake got into the Sanguinari's snack packs. He broke their vials of animal blood and smeared it all over the place."

Obadiah wasn't injured? But he also wasn't moving. Was he breathing?

I pressed my face close to his. I could feel the gentle warmth of his breath coming in and out. He was alive.

"What happened to him?"

"I don't know. He was really pale and then he just hit the ground. You've got to get out of here. I can't hold Blake back much longer."

I linked my arms under Obadiah's shoulders and began to drag his limp body out into the hall. It was slow going. He was even heavier with all that body armor. But inch by inch we got there.

I shut the door behind us, collapsing onto the floor next to Obadiah, breathing hard.

I reached in my pocket for my phone to call an ambulance, horrible flashbacks of the last time we'd had to call 911 from this club running through my mind.

As I started to enter the numbers, I looked down at Obadiah.

His eyes had opened.

"Mab?" he gasped softly.

"You're awake. I'm calling 911."

"Don't." He touched my hand.

"Of course I should. What just happened in there? Something happened. You're not okay."

"I'm fine," he said weakly, and I shot him a look.

"You're not fine."

"I'm fine," he repeated. "I just blacked out. It's rather embarrassing." He frowned.

"It's the Elixir sickness," I said, my voice shaking. "It made you black out."

"Nah, it's not that. Probably just the shock of seeing all the damage to the store."

The sight of that devastation would've been enough to fell anyone, but it wasn't just that.

"I'm so sorry about what he did to your place," I said.

But Obadiah waved his hand dismissively. "Don't think about it. I'm trying not to. That's what insurance is for." He smiled wanly.

"You don't have insurance, though, do you?"

"Trifle difficult to fill out paperwork when your birth certificate says 1708." He laughed, a high-pitched strangled snorting noise that showed me he really was in shock.

"Don't worry," he said with false lightness, "I can always get a loan from the Sanguinari mafia."

"You will *not* borrow money from them," I said, aghast. "Do you know what they do to anyone who doesn't pay on time? Now come on, let's get you downstairs, and I'm going to call the paramedics."

Obadiah shook his head from where he lay across the floor of the landing. "Don't call anyone. I'm fine."

"Did the werewolf bite you, even a scratch? We should get it checked out. What if that thing had tetanus or rabies or something?"

"Blake didn't hurt me. And don't call the paramedics. They're not going to be able to do anything."

"But . . ."

"What are we going to say when they ask what happened? Tell them there was a werewolf, that there *is* a werewolf, loose above the club? I don't think that would go over well."

I nodded, glumly acknowledging that he was right.

"I still want you to get checked out by a doctor, though. We don't have to tell them the werewolf part of the story."

"A doctor can't fix what's wrong with me."

I put my head in my hands, because I knew he was right. It reminded me of Quinn, that despair in her voice when she'd said no professional could help her, and I'd wanted so badly to contradict her but knew I'd be lying.

What was wrong with Obadiah was Elixir sickness.

The first symptom of the Thirst was shaking. The second was weakness.

"Oh god," I said, barely breathing.

"I'm fine," he said again, sitting up, as if to show me he was okay.

"No," I whispered. "You're not fine. The Thirst is progressing."

CHAPTER 7

Reggie closed the office early the Friday before Labor Day, and I decided to take the train out with Obadiah and have dinner with my folks in Grover Heights, New Jersey. I had planned to spend the whole holiday weekend with them, but I couldn't if I was going to use it to go back and check out the situation in the Vale, so this was my compromise. I had told Obadiah he didn't have to come. He was still dealing with the werewolf, and the overwhelming cleanup of his upstairs storeroom, and though he insisted he didn't need my help, that the werewolf clan was pitching in to assist him, I still felt bad. But it wasn't just that. Part of me was afraid to face a family dinner at my parents' house with Obadiah's hands potentially shaking under the table. It would just get my parents worried, and they couldn't even know the real cause.

It wasn't the first time Obadiah had met my parents. That had happened months before, and hadn't been nearly as nerve-wracking as I anticipated. After eight months of dating, my folks had accepted Obadiah as a part of my life now. My mom had started referring to our visits as "the kids are coming to stay," as if Obadiah was now their other grown-up child. I think they liked him. Sometimes my dad made a crack about how much older than me Obadiah was, and I always flushed with shame at the half joke. They thought Obadiah was thirty-three to my twenty-three. They didn't know he was really three hundred and eight. But ultimately, I could see in my parents' eyes that they saw Obadiah made me happy, and that touched me. I wished my other mother, the Fairy Queen, could understand that.

My parents met us at the train station in Grover Heights.

As we joined them in their aging Toyota, it occurred to me how much older my parents looked. It had been less than three months since I'd seen them last, so it wasn't that. It was a subtle, almost imperceptible shift. My hands noted how my father felt a little frailer as I hugged him. My mom's voice was bubbly and cheerful as she took my hand, but her eyes seemed tired. I felt bad about how little I'd visited lately.

Grover Heights was just as I remembered it: the shining chrome diner; the dying main street with its mostly closed-up shops; the various churches; the red-brick school with its sign proudly proclaiming a blue-ribbon award for excellence; the rolling green hills of suburban houses. It was just on the edge of being too far from New York City for a person to commute, though there were still many who did, and the quaint old-fashioned train station was always packed at 5:00 a.m.

Obadiah and Dad talked baseball scores, while Mom asked me all about my newest case with Reggie as we drove the winding, forested back roads to the house.

We pulled up in front of their modest, split-level home, with its single oak tree in the front yard, from which my childhood swing still dangled, hardly used anymore. It always looked small to me these days when I visited it, nothing like the sprawling house and the enormous tree I remembered playing in as a little girl.

It still smelled the same, though, when Mom opened the glass all-weather door. That distinctive aroma of old-house always brought memories back. I used to find the smell of the house comforting when I'd come home on winter breaks from college. But somehow right now it just made me feel sad.

"I'll let you guys get settled upstairs," Mom said as we trudged up the plush, carpeted steps. "Your father booked us dinner reservations for seven o'clock at Mr. Giuseppe's. I know how much you like that place."

It had been my favorite Italian restaurant when I was ten, but I didn't contradict her. We made our way up to my old room.

Obadiah and I sat down on my childhood bed, still covered with the purple, floral comforter I remembered from high school, and I gently closed the door, so my folks couldn't overhear us.

We looked at each other in silence for a while inside my childhood room.

This place never changed. It was like walking inside of a time capsule. The door was covered in stickers, the bookcases were full of paperback fantasy novels and the stuffed animals on the windowsill had been cleaned and dusted but never removed. I was glad of that. It was the one constant in my world. And I knew there was a time—not now, but someday and probably not as far off as I liked—where I was going to have to say goodbye to this room, to my parents, to my entire human life forever, when I took up the mantle of Fairy Queen.

"Thanks for coming out here with me," I said to Obadiah. "I know Grover Heights isn't exactly an exciting vacation destination. But I really wanted to see them."

"Of course," he said. "And don't thank me. You were the one who was trying to talk me *out* of coming here. I told you it would be fine."

"Yeah, I guess it is a good time for a visit. Since I might be going away for a little while."

Obadiah stopped and stared at me.

It was the first time I was telling him of the decision I'd already made in my heart.

"Wait, you're not thinking of doing what I think you are, are you?"

"It won't be for long, but I don't have a choice. I have to go back and see the Queen."

"No, you don't. If you're worried about that knife, I think it was a ploy from the Queen to try to get your attention. She's needy. She wants you back. I get it—she's your mother," he said in a low whisper, so my human mother downstairs couldn't hear. "But you don't have to let her run your life. You go back when you want to, and not before."

"That's not why I'm thinking of going back," I said. "I'm worried about you. Your Thirst symptoms are progressing."

He opened his mouth to protest, but I cut him off.

"Passing out is a symptom of the Thirst. You need to get some Elixir. If you're worried about the ethical implications of getting it from the kids, I'll find a natural Elixir stream that hasn't gone dry yet. And don't worry, I'll go to the ones on the southern tip of Manahatta. I won't mess with the Wolfmen's territory. But seriously, you're not well. You need something."

"I don't need any Elixir. And you don't need to do this."

I could tell there was no way I was going to win Obadiah over talking about his own needs. The only way he'd think the trip was a good idea was if it was about helping someone else.

"Look, I also told you about Cory. He's still at large

out there. I need to find out who he is, and how to stop him. I'm sure the Queen knows. She keeps tabs on everyone in the Vale. I'm not sure she's behind Cory, just like we're not sure if she's the one who's really diluting the Wolfmen's Elixir streams, but the only way we're going to get any answers is if I go there and talk to her."

"I'm worried about you going back to the Vale by yourself and chasing some rogue, potentially dangerous fairy. I want to come with you."

"You can't; you've still got a werewolf locked up in your store."

Obadiah frowned. "Reuben is caring for him. Blake's gotten a little calmer since you saw him last."

I raised a doubtful eyebrow.

"I still would like to come with you."

"You'd be putting yourself at risk. The Queen hasn't accepted you in my life the way my human parents have. Look," I said, trying to keep my voice down for the sake of my parents and shout at him at the same time. It turned into sort of a hiss. "I appreciate that you want to help, but my mom almost *killed* you last time. If you came back, she'd just try to kill you again. Even if I make her promise not to, she'll find some way to weasel out of her promise. She always does. I don't want you risking your life!"

"Well, I don't want you risking yours!"

We stared at each other, at an impasse. His hands were cocked on his hips, mine were crossed tightly over my chest. The dozen or so My Little Ponies on the shelf above our heads stared down at us, their overlarge eyes looking thoughtful. I didn't want this turning into our first major fight, but it seemed like it was going that way.

"Listen, I don't mean to get so angry. It's just because"—he ran a hand through his dark curls in frustration—"I'm just worried about you. Because I love you."

He sat down on the bed, and I sat down next to him. We were silent for a long time. I lay my head against his chest.

"I know. I love you too, and I'm worried about *you*."

I could hear my parents' voices from downstairs, though I couldn't make out what they were saying. I wondered if they'd heard us arguing. I tried to think of a compromise.

"If you insist on coming," I said at last, "can you stay in the Central Forest, away from the Fairy Queen? When I meet with her, I'll do that on my own."

Obadiah frowned. "I'd prefer to come with you, but if that's the only way you're going to agree to things, I suppose I'll have to live with it." He sighed. "I'm glad at least I'm coming."

I kissed him on the cheek. "Eva wanted to come too. She wants to help, but I told her no. I'm too scared of what could happen to her."

"I agree. I've at least been in the Vale many times before, so I know what to expect. Eva only had that one trip and she doesn't remember most of it. She's fully human. It would be too dangerous for her.

"What are you going to tell your parents? And Reggie?" he asked.

"I'll tell my parents I can't stay the rest of Labor Day weekend, that I have to go back to the city to work."

"And then hope your parents and Reggie don't talk to each other?" said Obadiah, raising a brow.

"They don't have each other's numbers. They wouldn't track each other down to get in touch unless it's a real emergency. And it's only four days."

I felt bad lying to them both, but I didn't see another way. What I was telling my parents was closer to the truth; I did have a lot of work to do. And as for Reggie, he'd never understand, but my trip to the Vale wasn't just about helping Obadiah; it was about helping Quinn too.

I called Reggie before we left for dinner. He sounded harried.

"Brenda Sheffield has been calling nonstop," he said. "Asking us if we've found anything helpful for her daughter. I've been telling her these things take time, but she keeps calling." There was a moment of silence and a strange noise that might have been Reggie chewing on his pencil. "I kind of wish you'd planted a spy cam. Then at least we would have had something to give her."

I flushed, feeling the weight of his disappointment

with me. It was the first time I'd heard Reggie sound disappointed in the way I'd handled something.

"I didn't think it was a good idea. She was just starting to open up to me. If she found out I was filming her against her will, that door would close permanently; I'd never gain her trust back."

There was another pause and then Reggie said, "You're right. I see your point. The mother's just stressing me out, is all. Between you and me I'm this close to just dropping this case. The kid needs a shrink, not a P.I. I don't think we're going to win this one. I think we should just give her a refund and drop it."

"No, we can't quit yet."

I looked over and saw that Obadiah's and my parents' heads had raised at the sudden loudness in my voice.

"I have an idea I'm working on," I said. "I don't know if it'll pan out, but I have to give it a try. One last try. I want to talk to her again after the holiday weekend."

"Sure. I'm glad we're off for a few days. I think it would be good for you to have some free time. I always say when you get stuck, it's good to take a break and get away from things for a while."

Get away for a while. He had no idea how true his words were. It bothered me that Reggie was writing off this case as unsolvable. I was going to find Cory, dammit, find out who he really was. And get to the root of what was really wrong with Quinn. Now that Tiffany had told me how many other girls there might be, it wasn't just Quinn's case anymore either. It was everyone Cory had touched. Reggie might be ready to write it off, but I wasn't giving up so easily.

My folks drove us back to the Grover Heights train station later that night. Mom pressed a Ziploc bag of her organic, gluten-free cookies into our hands. Obadiah managed to act excited about them, and I appreciated his effort. We'd had them before. They were as hard as hockey pucks and had a strange aftertaste of Stevia; the only one who seemed to genuinely enjoy them was Reggie. But I tucked them into my purse and told her we'd have one on the train. The whistle blasted, and it was time for us to go up onto the platform.

But I found myself lingering as I hugged my mom goodbye.

"What's the matter, Mabily?" she asked me. She always knew, instinctively, when something was wrong.

"Nothing," I said, forcing a smile, and turned to hug my dad.

I didn't know why a lump was forming in my throat. I wasn't going back to the Vale forever. I was just going back for a few days. I'd be back here with my folks for Thanksgiving, if not Columbus Day. So why did I feel like I might be hugging my human parents goodbye for the last time? I swallowed the lump in my throat, telling myself I was being melo-dramatic.

That night, we sat together on my bed in the apart-ment, plotting how we were going to transition to the next world. As terrifying as the plummet in the Times Square New Year's Eve ball had been, I missed it compared to this. There was no other way—we would have to use the Vale Cleaver.

Obadiah frowned, his forehead wrinkling. I could tell he was remembering the time when he had stabbed himself with this same knife, as the Queen's prisoner.

"You've never had to stab yourself with the Vale Cleaver to travel to another world before, have you?" he asked me.

Mutely, I shook my head.

"I wouldn't wish those moments on my worst enemy. You think you're going to die. Intellectually, you know it can make you disappear from this world and pop into the next, but you're still stabbing a knife into your own heart. It's terrifying."

"I'll be okay," I said, though in my heart I was ter-rified too. I was really going to have to stab myself. Would I have the guts to? Or would I chicken out at the last second? And god forbid, what if we were wrong about the Vale Cleaver? What if somehow it wasn't real? Obadiah had almost picked the knife's identical twin; I could too, and then I'd be dead. I felt bad voicing these fears to Obadiah, though. I didn't want to make him more worried than he already was.

"How is all this going to work?" Obadiah asked me, getting up to pace. "I mean, how are we both going to be able to use the same Vale knife? When I stabbed myself with it last time, I came to in the next world with the knife still in my hand. And it stayed in the human world with me. Well, until it disappeared from my back room. I'd been trying to hold on to it for you, in case you ever needed to go home. I guess your mother wanted it back." He rolled his eyes. "But the point is, for you to use the knife, I would need to somehow pass it back to you, otherwise it's going to transfer over to the Vale with me."

This problem had occurred to me too.

"That's why I have to go first," I said. "In case it doesn't work. If only one of us is able to get through, it should be me."

"That's exactly what I'm trying to avoid," Obadiah shouted in exasperation. "We just had this conversation at your parents' house. I don't want you to go alone."

"I'll be fine," I muttered. "But since you're worried and I know you want to come too, I'll try to drop the knife after I use it, okay? Then you can grab it?"

I didn't know if that was going to work and neither did he.

Obadiah crossed his arms over his chest. He didn't like the sound of this one bit, I could tell.

"I don't want you taking this risk," he said quietly.

I stepped right in front of him, stopping him short in his pacing. I raised my hands to cradle both sides of his face.

"I love you," I whispered, "but I need to do this. Please, let me do what I need to do."

He looked away from me, swallowing hard. I could tell it took a lot of effort, but at last he nodded. "Do what you must."

There was something so old-fashioned about the phrasing that it made me pause in what I was about to say. Sometimes I forgot how much older Obadiah was than me, and I didn't mean ten human years. Counting my fairy life before I'd become a changeling, I was closer to fifty, but Obadiah had passed more than three centuries. He never reminded me of that fact, never made me feel like anything less than an equal. And yet, the gap of years was there, like a tiny crack in how well we could ever fully understand each other.

"Thank you for trusting me," I said at last, and he pressed me to his chest so hard that I could barely breathe. I embraced him back as hard as I could. He held me like he could somehow keep me here.

At last we let go. I walked over to my bed and picked up the knife that I'd been sleeping with under my pillow since it had appeared. I hated to touch it. It was so eerily warm, like skin, pulsing, almost vibrating with an alien life. This thing was ancient, powerful. I didn't fully understand how it worked, but I was going to use it. That scared me, far more than

I wanted to admit to Obadiah. I looked down at the stone blade. How the hell was I going to stab myself with that? I didn't know if I could do it, or if I would flinch at the last second, just before it pierced my skin?

But Cory was still at large. He was going to suck all the joy from every woman he touched unless I could stop him, and the only way I could get any answers about his real identity was by going home and seeing my mother. If I didn't convince the Wolfmen the Queen wasn't behind the depletion of their Elixir streams, they were going to murder her. And what did the message on the knife really mean, that things were "worse"? I had to find out. This wasn't just about me and Obadiah.

I held up the knife in one palm. With the other, I squeezed Obadiah's hand.

"Wish me luck," I said with forced cheerfulness.

Obadiah's face was stricken. "My love, I'm already praying as hard as I can, even though I'm not sure I still believe in God." His voice was shaking. "Stay safe. Do you have any idea how precious you are to me?"

"You'll join me in just a few seconds," I said, making a promise I wasn't sure I could keep.

I let go of him and held the knife with both hands, pointing it towards my chest.

Terror took hold of me. A deep survival instinct screamed in my ears how stupid this was.

I began to move the knife towards my skin, then stopped.

I couldn't do it.

What was I going to do if I didn't have enough courage?

I could feel Obadiah watching me. I couldn't bear the concerned look on his face.

I closed my eyes, blocking out the sight of his tenderness, steeling myself for what I was about to do.

I took a deep, sharp inhale and, with a wild yell for courage, plunged the knife into my sternum.

Pain exploded through my chest. I tried to scream, but I couldn't. It was like all the breath had been knocked out of me. I felt like I was drowning in an ocean of pain. Everything was going black. And then a thought of pure panic rose in my mind:

I'd used the wrong knife.

I'd used the knife that looked like the Vale Cleaver, instead of the Vale Cleaver itself.

I'd really stabbed myself. And now I was going to die.

My whole body was burning, the entire surface of my skin from the tips of my fingers to the roots of my hair, all the way down to my feet. Was this what it felt like to die? I'd stabbed myself in the heart, and now I was dying quickly. Would Obadiah realize I was dying? I couldn't even scream for help. Would he think to call 911? Would an ambulance even be able to get here in time?

We didn't have a plan for if I used the wrong knife.

Betrayal buzzed through the haze of agony.

It couldn't be. Why would the Fairy Queen want to kill me? I was her daughter.

But what if the Queen herself had gotten confused and sent the wrong one? They looked identical.

It could have been an accident.

Or someone else had tricked her? Someone had switched the knives on my mother in an attempt to kill me?

Pain was wiping out my ability to think.

Waves of darkness were closing over me. I was going to faint.

Through the agony, I heard a voice. It was shouting something, over and over. What was it? It was a deep male voice. It was Obadiah's voice. What was he saying?

And then I heard him plain and clear.

"Drop the knife," he was screaming. "Drop the knife."

The knife. I was vaguely aware that I was clenching it still between both hands; the pain had locked my fingers in a vise around the hilt. I tried to loosen their grasp, but my hands were numb. Then suddenly the knife was wrested from my grasp. Air tumbled back into my lungs, and I screamed, plummeting into a depthless abyss.

The first thing I was aware of was the cool scent of pine needles and the slow whooshing sounds of water.

I was definitely not in my room. I was outside. There were twigs poking my back, and the air had the intoxicating smell of Elixir. It had worked. I was in the Vale. My eyes popped open to see Obadiah prostrate beside me, groaning. I rolled over to throw my arms around him, squealing with joy that we were both alive.

"You got through too!" I cried.

The knife was lying beside him, glinting in the brown leaves. It was the real knife.

"I managed to get the knife from you," Obadiah said, sitting up and smiling. "Though I almost didn't. Your fingers were like a vise. I had to pry it from your hands. You were halfway in and out of the worlds. You dropped it just at the last second before you disappeared."

I sat up and hugged him, not knowing if I was crying or laughing. I was making strange gasping, snorting sounds in shock as my brain and my body caught up to one another.

"Mab, try to be quieter, love. We don't know where we are," Obadiah whispered, but he held me tight, and I could tell he was just as ecstatic and relieved as I was that we had both survived. He picked up the Vale knife and put it in his pocket. I wondered if he could still feel its awful sensation through his jeans. I was glad he'd volunteered to hold it. I couldn't bear to touch that thing again.

I sat up, looking at the columns of trees that surrounded us. They were enormous, too big to wrap your arms around, but I could see no doors or windows. These weren't House Trees. We had to be in the Central Forest, the only place the Queen couldn't see with her spying network of pixies.

"You should stay here," I said to Obadiah. "I'll go to the Queen's palace alone."

"Mab." He cupped my hip to him, drawing me close. He was worried, but this was my fight.

"The Queen, um, my mom, won't let harm come to me. You're less safe than I am here in the Vale. You keep the knife. If any of her henchmen come after you, just use it. You'll pop back into the human world and they won't be able to get you."

"But what about you?"

"I'll be with the Queen. She can travel between the worlds as often as she wants. I'll be fine."

Obadiah looked stern. He didn't want to agree to this, but I wasn't giving an inch.

"I've got to do this. Whether you're happy about it or not."

He frowned. "Just stay safe, promise?"

"I promise."

I rose to my feet as he helped me up, brushing the leaves and twigs from my hair and clothing. We both stood facing each other, and I stood up on my tiptoes, kissing him full and hard on the mouth. He responded eagerly, his skin smelling of Elixir and the forest. It was with great reluctance that I pulled back at last.

"Get yourself to your safe house. Promise me you'll stay hidden?"

He nodded.

And with one last kiss goodbye, I set off to meet the Fairy Queen.

the Fairy Queen.

CHAPTER 8

I received an utterly different reception at the palace this time around. With all the Queen's goblin guards and elf butlers practically falling over themselves to serve me, like it was some sort of brownnosing competition, as if everyone wanted to win favor with the Queen by kissing up to her daughter. It made me grossly uncomfortable. "No, I don't want any refreshments; no, you don't need to take my jacket, I want to keep it; no, no, no Elixir please," I kept saying. "Just take me to the Queen."

At last I was led into the Great Hall. Memories from the last time I'd been here assaulted me as the huge double doors swung open. I'd run out these doors in blinding, angry tears when the Fairy Queen, whom I'd always thought was evil, who'd taken my magic powers from me and exiled me to the human world, told me that she was my mother, and that she'd tricked me into becoming a changeling for my own good. I still couldn't forgive her all her human captives, but she was my mother, and we were tied together in this life for better or worse.

I saw a figure hunched over at the far end of the room. It had to be my mother. She was turned away from me, clad in an ever-shifting iridescent blue dress that was made of fluttering butterflies. The hideous goblin Korvus Korax was crouched beside her, whispering something in her ear.

She must have heard my footfalls on the gleaming agate floor, because she turned around and I had to stifle a gasp. I clapped my hands over my mouth without meaning to.

She looked terrible. Her face was haggard—bone white skin, gaunt, with dark sagging purple circles beneath her eyes. She was so much thinner than when I'd last seen her; the fluttering butterflies masked it, but maybe that was why she'd worn this gown. She was clutching a cane. It was encrusted with gems, but still, it was a *cane*. She could fly; why was she leaning on a cane?

"Mother . . . ?"

She rushed towards me, hobbling on her cane, the butterfly wings shimmering rainbows as she walked.

I kept waiting for her to put on her glamour. In the past, she always did within seconds of seeing me when I caught her off guard. But her face continued to look the same. Was it a sign she felt comfortable with me, comfortable enough that she'd let me see her old? I wanted to believe that. That would have comforted me. It would mean she really considered me her daughter, not just her successor. That we were family; because you didn't care how you looked around family. But the Queen wasn't like that. There was a haunted expression of shame in her eyes as she approached me, and my gut twisted. She *wanted* to use her glamour, I realized, but for some reason, she *couldn't*. Was this what she'd meant by things were getting worse?

Guilt stabbed me that I had been away for so long.

"Mother? What's wrong?" I asked.

"I'm fine, my darling. Come closer, let me embrace you. It is so good of you to visit me. I didn't know you would come back so soon."

Tentatively, I walked closer, and steeling myself, I reached through the butterflies that tickled my skin, and gave her a hug. Her body was so frail beneath the swirling, living dress of wings that I could feel her bones beneath.

"Mother, no offense, but you look terrible. What's going on?"

She let out a long sigh.

"Leave us," she said to Korvus. He seemed very unhappy to have been so unceremoniously dismissed, but he nodded at me politely and shuffled out of the room. I breathed a heavy sigh of relief as I heard the door close behind him. I didn't think I'd ever be comfortable around him. He had only been following my mother's orders, but he *was* the goblin who'd grabbed the little girl I'd been switched with out of her crib, and ignored my screams for help when I'd realized I was stuck as a changeling. He might be polite, but I could tell he still hated that I'd returned when he thought he'd gotten rid of me all those years ago. I was the wedge between him and the Queen. There wasn't a lot of love lost between us on either side.

The other courtiers who were still loitering around the edges of the hall, trying to unobtrusively eavesdrop, filed out too. My mother sat down upon her great stone chair, carved with the likenesses of past Fairy Queens. There was a blank space at the bottom, a gap, reminding me of the mantle of power I'd been reluctant to have put on my shoulders.

"What's going on?" I asked again. "You look really unwell."

I sat down on the stool beside her, realizing as I did that the perch I sat on was probably usually occupied by Korvus. She extended her hand, taking mine and squeezing it. Her fingers were ice cold.

"I'm so glad you came, Mab. I didn't want to force you, you know. But it is such a delight to see you."

Her eyes were shining, even if her face looked horrible.

"It's fortunate you've arrived. It's time now."

I looked up at her, not understanding.

"It's time for you to take my place. For you to assume the throne."

I stepped back from her, vehemently shaking my head.

"You did promise me you would, dearest, when you begged me to save Obadiah's life."

I glared at her, furious. And in that moment I understood why all the old stories warned against making promises with fairies. They'd always find a way to trap you. But the Queen had trapped me once. I wasn't going to let her trap me again.

"I promised I'd do it. I never promised I'd do it *immediately*. What am I supposed to do about my human life? My human parents? Obadiah? Eva? Reggie? Where would they think I've gone? What do I tell them? I can't just leave. I need time to make a transition like that."

The Queen frowned.

"But we don't have time. The drought . . ."

I stared down at the floor, fuming at how she was trying to manipulate me.

"Look at me, Mab," she said, and reluctantly I raised my eyes to her haggard face.

"You see it—what the drought has done to me."

I gulped, nodding. There was no denying how awful she looked. I knew the drought was bad; I just never thought it would affect the Queen, and affect her so quickly. She seemed so all-powerful.

As if reading my thoughts, she said, "The drought affects all of us, but I suppose it affects me most of all. The more powerful you are, the more you're dependent on Elixir. My body feels the depletion in our atmosphere. Even drinking Elixir doesn't help me anymore, because my reserves are so low."

My mother was succumbing to the Elixir Thirst. Suddenly all her symptoms made a terrifying sense: the cane, the weakness. But that meant . . .

She looked down at me, and there was something tender in her voice when she spoke.

"I love you too much to lie to you, Mab." A shadow of shame passed over her face. "Well, not anymore. I won't *candy coat* it for you, as the humans say." She took a deep breath, her forehead pinched. "I'm dying, my dearest."

"No!" I grabbed her hand, staring wildly up into her eyes. She couldn't die. She was still young, by fairy standards. We'd just barely begun to get to know each other. And now she was going to die? I couldn't let this happen. There had to be some way to get her the Elixir she needed.

Panic took hold of me like a spreading frost in my stomach. If she died, that would mean I had to take over the throne. She was right; we didn't have time. Becoming Fairy Queen had always seemed like something so far into the future as to be almost theoretical. But if the Queen was sickening so quickly, it could be soon. How was I going to take over the care of the realm? I could barely manage my human life. And what would happen to my human life if I was forced to become Queen? How could I ever explain to my parents, Obadiah, Eva, Reggie, everyone I knew, where I had gone?

"Don't grieve for me, Mab," she said. "I've had a good long life. Seven hundred years. Even many of the vampires would be envious. Of course, once I expected to live forever, but I suppose those days are over for most fairies now. I am at peace. I found you again." She squeezed my hand. I squeezed hers back, but my vision was blurring.

"I may have found peace for myself, but I haven't found peace for our realm, and that troubles me. I can't leave the kingdom in its current state; it's why I am so grateful you've returned."

She lowered her voice, leaning into me. "I have to do something about Korvus. He's been my right hand since I had to send you to the human realm. He was a good adviser for a time; it was he who was the architect of the Elixir producing program." She must have seen the look on my face because she frowned. "I know you don't approve, but it bought us decades. He has been good to me politically, personally. But I've relied on him too much." There was genuine fear in her expression. "He thinks he should be the next leader, the next Fairy King. A goblin king." She scowled at the very idea. "He'd be a disaster. He likes power too much. I know I've been accused of being a dictator, but Korvus would be an evil dictator. I can't let him take over from me; I can't let that happen to the Vale. But if you don't take the throne when I leave it, he'll seize power. I know it's what he's already planning. I can see it in his eyes. Wait, he's coming."

The Queen suddenly stiffened and was silent as a door cracked open. Korvus appeared.

"Did you need me, Your Majesty? I couldn't hear what you were saying, but you sounded upset."

I couldn't read him well enough to tell if he was lying about not eavesdropping.

"I'm fine, Korvus," my mother said imperiously. "I asked you to leave me be."

He looked insulted, but gave a courtly nod and bid us both goodbye before shutting the door behind him.

"You have to take the throne. I didn't want to pressure you into it, but I didn't know how quickly I'd succumb to the Elixir Thirst. I know you've been *hesitant* to take up this role. But I'm afraid we don't have time to waste anymore."

"I can't."

The words sprang out of my mouth before I had time to think about it and hold them back. Up until this point I'd been vacillating, but now I knew with a certainty I'd never known before: I did not want to be Queen. It didn't mean I didn't want to help fix everything that was wrong with the Vale. But I wasn't ready to take up my mother's mantle of power. And as bad as I felt for her, I wasn't going to let her illness pressure me into it.

My mother stared at me, not understanding.

"No," I said again. "I love you, and I'm so sorry, but I can't."

I couldn't become the new Fairy Queen. I loved my mother—did I love my mother? I hardly knew her, but she *was* my mother, and I cared for her. And yet, I couldn't do what she did: kill innocents for the good of the realm. And my human life—I couldn't just give all that up.

"There has to be more time. Can you just drink more Elixir?" I was ashamed at the thought. More Elixir meant more children suffering.

My mother looked at me sadly. "I've tried that, my darling. It doesn't seem to matter how much I take anymore. My body isn't absorbing the Elixir. The Thirst has progressed too far." Her voice trailed off.

"Is the Elixir not as strong as it used to be? Is diluted somehow?" I asked, thinking of the wolf currently in Obadiah's storeroom.

"I don't think it's that. You see, Elixir has two parts. One we can manufacture from the children to bolster our supply, but the other part comes from within us, analogous to your human DNA. Once the Thirst has begun to attack that . . ."

The two parts of Elixir: the X-factor and the Y-factor, I thought, thinking of Eva's lab. The Queen could steal dopamine, but she couldn't fix an underlying problem with her fairy DNA. My mother was really going to die. And I didn't even know how to feel about it. If it were my human mother, I shuddered to even think; I'd be balling my eyes out right now. But this strange, remote Queen, this majestic, Machiavellian fairy—my birth mother—I didn't even know how to feel about her.

But I didn't want her to die.

"I tried to delay. I tried to not tell you, but now there's no more time . . ."

"There has to be something we can do," I said, twisting my fingers together. "I wish there was something I could do to help." But I had nothing. The look in my mother's eyes said she'd resigned herself to her death in a way I could not.

"There is something you can do to help," she said. "You can rule."

"But I can't."

"Mab, you will make a good Queen. If we start your training now . . ."

"I don't want to be Queen!"

I hadn't meant to yell at her, but the words came flying out my mouth. Every little fairy girl dreamed of being Queen. The other orphans and I had taken turns wearing acorn crowns and mantles made of leaves and made each other monarch for the after-noon, but being Queen for a lifetime, for eternity perhaps, was nothing like that. It wasn't a game any-more. It was hell. I would have enemies plotting to kill me for as long as I lived. And the children the Queen was using to manufacture Elixir . . . I could never, ever kidnap and kill anyone like that. But if I didn't, all the fairies would die and it would be on my head.

"Let Korvus do it, if he wants it so badly," I said, and then instantly blushed fever-hot in guilt. Let Korvus rule, so he could kill kids and I could feel like it wouldn't be my fault. But it would, because I hadn't stopped him.

"I can't let Korvus take power. A monarchy in his hands would be a catastrophe. He has no scruples."

"Scruples? Spoken from someone who kills *children*?"

"I know you don't approve of my methods, but I do what I have to do. I don't *enjoy* doing this to them, Mab. I have nightmares each night." Her bone white chin trembled. "I do what I must. Korvus is different. Korvus *likes* the experiments. He enjoys what we do to the Shadow children. He feels nothing when he hears them scream."

I shuddered.

"And even if you think I've gone too far, he would go farther. Korvus stops at nothing in pursuit of his goals. *Nothing*. He wants to increase the program, take even more children. He's desperate to find a solution to the Elixir drought as soon as possible. You know the goblins don't need Elixir like we do; that's not his motive. If he offers the fairy populace a chance at survival, they'll follow him anywhere. That's why he was so eager to help me with my experiments. I see it now. I thought he was just loyal to me, but I was blind."

There was fear in her dark rimmed eyes. "I've created a monster. He must be stopped."

I nodded.

When she spoke again, some of her fear and anger seemed to soften. "I'm making it sound like he's entirely evil, and that is perhaps unfair of me. I know you find the captive program abhorrent, Mab, but the truth is, if Korvus hadn't proposed that idea, and helped me carry it out, every fairy in the Vale could have died from Elixir sickness years ago, and over time the Vale would disintegrate. Korvus has taken many lives—too many—but he's also saved many lives. We can't forget that."

"There's got to be someone else who isn't Korvus, but who isn't me either."

"But I want you to be my successor." She took my hands and held them in her ice cold fingers. "I may not have been there for you before. But I'm here now. Let me be here. Let me train you to be Queen. Grant me that one final wish."

Her last words stung, but I shook my head. "I can't."

"But you're a fairy; you're the heir to the fairy throne."

"No," I whispered. "You made me human."

I looked up at my mother's face, and instantly turned away. I couldn't bear the heartbreak in her eyes. "I need to think about all of this, okay?"

Her face brightened. "Yes, of course, think about it."

She had taken "maybe" to mean "yes."

I sighed. "How does it even work, for me to become a fairy again? I tried that 'return' spell you taught me, dozens and dozens of times, as a child, trying to regain my old form. It never worked. You obviously taught me a fake spell. So how could I really become a fairy again?"

I wasn't ready to do it, but I still was curious.

My mother blushed, the faintest pink coming over her porcelain white cheeks. "I didn't teach you a *fake* spell, dearest. I just neglected to mention one essential part."

"And that is?"

"The return spell only works in the Vale, just like the changeling spell only works in the human world."

"So you made it so I'd have to find my way home in order to transform back into a fairy?"

Solemnly, the Queen nodded. "If you did the spell again here, it would work. You'd regain your old form."

A mixture of excitement and dread flooded through me at her words. I could become a fairy again, right here, right now, if I wanted to.

But did I want to?

For so many years, it was all I'd ever wanted.

And now with it suddenly possible, I felt paralyzed.

"I need some time," I said, and I pulled away from her hands.

I wasn't ready. I wasn't ready to give up the human life I'd come to love. And I couldn't live in the human world as a fairy. But that reminded me . . .

This whole conversation, this devastating news, had distracted me from the original reason I'd come here. But I wasn't going to leave without at least getting some answers.

"Your Maj . . . Mom. There's something I wanted to ask you."

"Anything."

"There's a fairy who's been in the human world—
but not a changeling." I told her briefly about Quinn,
and Eva's ritual group. The Queen frowned.

"I don't know who it is, but I think he's stealing
X-factor—I mean, the human component of Elixir—
directly from living people."

The Queen's frowned deepened. "I didn't think
that was possible," she said. "But perhaps . . ."

"Who could it be? I figured I'd ask you. I mean,
you keep tabs on everyone."

The Queen's mouth softened. "That's my job," she
said, though I could hear a hint of pride in her voice.
"And soon it will be yours."

I sighed. I had no desire to be master of the Queen's
network of spies. "But who is it?"

"I don't know."

I raised an eyebrow at her.

"I don't know everything, darling, despite the fact
that so much of the populace is convinced that I do."

"You must have some idea, though."

She shook her head. "There are very few who
know about our Elixir manufacturing program.
There are very few who really understand what
Elixir even consists of, that it has different parts, and
that some of them are shared with humans. I told you
because you're my daughter, but this is secret knowledge. The only one who knows everything that I
know is Korvus, really."

Korvus. Cory. Why hadn't I thought of it before?

But of course I hadn't recognized him; all the men were so beautiful, and Korvus was one of the most hideous creatures I'd ever seen. But he could make himself look like anyone he wanted. He'd once made himself into a perfect copy of Eva's ex-boyfriend, Ramsey. Of course he'd picked beautiful disguises. I felt ill. I had to find him. But would he talk to me if I confronted him directly? Probably not. I'd have to do it surreptitiously.

"Where does Korvus live?" I asked my mother, trying to sound nonchalant. "Does he live here in the palace with you?"

She shook her head. "He stays with me during the day, but at night he goes back to his own set of apartments, where we set up the laboratory. It's deep within the earth. I think he feels more comfortable there. I think all the light in the Quartz Spires bothers him. He is a goblin after all. They like the dark."

"Could you show me where his apartments are? I'd like to talk to him," I said, though I had no intention of going to Korvus' rooms during the night when he was there. That would be totally counterproductive. Obadiah and I would have to go during the day, when he'd be busy at court with the Queen. We'd have to sneak in and see what evidence of Korvus' rogue transformations we could find. Only then would we know for sure it was him behind the mysterious men that had such a grievous effect on Quinn.

"If you want to talk to him, you don't have to go visit him—you can talk to him now. He's right outside." She gestured towards the door through which Korvus had departed.

"No, that's alright," I said quickly. "I'll talk to him later. I need some time to think about everything. I want to be alone."

I wanted to leave at once to start talking over all these ideas with Obadiah, but one glance back at the Queen made me pause. What was I doing? She looked so ill, so frail.

"Please don't rush off again, my dear," she said lightly, taking my hand. There was no lightness in her eyes. "Take a stroll with me round the garden. We've spent so little time together."

I acquiesced. We walked out through the double doors at the back end of the hall, onto a loggia of sorts made from gleaming crystal. Fantastical plants bloomed to our left and right: towering topiaries, twining orchids and bluebells that actually rang. The Queen extended her arm to me, and awkwardly I took it, less as a gesture of affection and more out of worry that I might actually have to hold her up. Was she well enough to walk? But she seemed to perk up a bit in the fresh air. Perhaps it was the hint of Elixir on the breeze that revived her.

The Elixir breeze reminded me of my promise to the Wolfmen. "Mother, if I may ask you a frank question?"

She nodded uncomfortably.

I didn't know if she'd answer me honestly, but I figured it was best to ask her about the werewolves'

Elixir first, before divulging that they were plotting to kill her.

"Have you been stealing the Wolfmen's Elixir?"

She looked affronted. "No, of course not. There's a treaty."

I raised an eyebrow. "You would never break that treaty?"

She shook her head. "There would be a civil war between the Wolfmen and the Fey. We can't have that. Their Elixir streams are drying up on their own."

"So you're not diluting their streams?"

"No. Why would you think that?"

I looked her straight in the eye and she stared back at me. I believed that she was telling me the truth. It wasn't like the Queen had a great track record of being honest with me. But I knew she trusted me. Something in my gut told me that she was being genuine.

"The Wolfmen think you are," I explained. "Their abilities have been affected recently. They think you're behind it."

"I'm not."

"I believe you," I said, and my mother smiled at me gratefully. "But they think you are. And if something doesn't change, they're going to try to assassinate you."

"Lovely," said the Queen. "That's just what I need right now. Well, we have a few weeks till the full moon. I'll tell Korvus; we'll have time to prepare ourselves."

"But that's the problem," I said. "Part of the weakening of their Elixir is that some of their members can't change out of Werewolf form once they're in it. They're in full Were form all the time now, even when the moon isn't full."

"Noted," said the Queen. She sounded exhausted at the very thought. "I'll be on my guard."

She was silent for a long moment and when she spoke at last her voice was very quiet, very tender.

"Thank you for looking out for me, Mab. You didn't have to tell me that."

I squirmed uncomfortably, realizing the full impact of what I'd done: potentially saving the Fairy Queen's life at the expense of the Wolfmen. Was that for the best? Maybe Manahatta would be run better by Wolfmen. Who was I to know? But I couldn't let her die. The Queen had showed me that she was trying.

We walked farther down the garden path in the sun-dappled shade, through a loggia whose columns were carved into the likenesses of past Fairy Queens.

My mother turned to me. "I'm so glad we're able to spend this time together. Even if I don't have much left. Whatever time remains to me, I hope I can spend it with you."

My stomach clenched at her words.

Whatever conversations I'd ever wanted my mother and me to have, I had to start them now. And there was one question that had been burning in my heart, ever since she first revealed to me that she was my mother. I'd been waiting for the right moment to ask. And now I was afraid I couldn't wait anymore.

"Mom, I know you're my birth mother, but . . . who was my father?"

I held my breath as the words left my lips. I was so afraid to know the answer to this question. Her face looked stricken. For a second, I regretted asking.

"We don't speak of him," she said, her voice so soft as to be barely audible.

I started to say something in reply, then stopped. Her eyes were so full of sadness, and she was so sick, so frail, I felt cruel pressing her to talk about something that clearly pained her. But we didn't have all the time in the world anymore. We might not have much time at all. I couldn't wait for the perfect moment to have this conversation with her. I had to put forth all the questions I'd ever wanted to ask her now, while I still could.

"Look," I whispered, "I don't want to make you talk about things you'd rather not talk about. But I need to know. I have a right to know."

She turned to me, suddenly so very, very old.

"I know," she said gently. "You do. But it would do you no good."

I wasn't going to let her end the conversation like this.

"Please tell me. Let me make the decision for myself. I'd like to meet him at least."

She turned away from me, and I realized she was crying.

I felt awful. Listening to her sobs and being able to do nothing but fish around in my purse and find only an already used tissue.

"I would have loved for you to meet him," she said quietly. "But he's gone."

A soft sound of defeat escaped my throat and I looked down at the ground, feeling so incredibly disappointed. I didn't know what I had been seeking in my birth father, but the knowledge that I'd never, ever get to meet him, because he was dead, was a blow.

"When did he . . . ?" I started to ask.

My mother cut me off. "When you were still within my womb. He never met you."

At least she hadn't been keeping him from me. It was a small consolation.

"Will you tell me what he was like?" I asked.

"He was beautiful," she said, smiling to herself. "Kind. *Good*." Then her face darkened. "Too good for this world, I suppose. Anyway, it doesn't matter now; he's forever lost to us."

"Of course it matters," I piped up, and slowly she raised her shaking fingers and tenderly stroked the top of my head.

"He would have been very proud of you," she said softly. Then the old mask of reserve spread over her face. "I'd rather not speak of him. It pains me, even after all this time, that I couldn't save him. Let's go back to the palace, shall we, Mab? I think I need to sit down."

"Of course." I reluctantly slipped my hand into the cold, trembling crook of her arm.

We began to walk back towards the Great Hall.

"You must be famished, my darling." The Queen smiled at me. "I will have my servants prepare a feast for you. Come. We can talk more later."

"It's alright. I had dinner before I came."

"You don't want to eat?" the Queen asked, crest-fallen, and I felt a trifle guilty. Fairies didn't need food for sustenance, so my mother didn't have any sense of how often humans really needed to eat. She offered me food every chance she could. There was something sweet about it. But I was still afraid to par-take of her magical banquets—all it had taken to trap Persephone was a single pomegranate seed.

I told the Queen I had to go. She looked disap-pointed, and in truth, part of me was loath to leave too. But now that I suspected Korvus was behind what was happening to Quinn and the other girls, I had to take action. Plus, if the Queen wasn't the one stealing from the werewolves' Elixir streams, my bet was again on Korvus. Before I left, I asked my mother how to find Korvus' dwelling, and she drew me a map on a bit of bark parchment, carving lines into the soft wood with her razor-sharp fingernails.

"I'll be back," I said to her as we hugged goodbye awkwardly. She felt so frail in my arms.

She nodded, but something in her eyes said she didn't believe me.

"Just think about what I told you, about being Queen," she said, her eyes boring into mine. "It's your choice, Mab. But please, consider."

"I'll think about it."

I left her standing there amidst the shining Quartz Spires of the loggia, feeling heavy at heart. When I got to the double doors and turned around to look back at her over my shoulder, I saw Korvus coming towards her, walking quickly, his long robes bobbing in his wake. He was clearly anxious to be back with his Queen. I increased my pace. What if the Queen innocently mentioned something to Korvus about me saying I wanted to talk to him? What if she told him offhand she'd given me his address? If I wanted to spy on his dwelling, I needed to hurry, just in case.

CHAPTER 9

I walked as quickly as I could out of the palace and onto the road that would lead me back to Obadiah's safe house. It would be a long way, though, and I cursed the time as I walked as quickly as I could. The longer it took for me to get back to Obadiah, the less time we'd have on our spying errand. I had just left the last of the Quartz Spires behind and entered a grove of House Trees when I heard a rustle in the leaves behind me. I whirled around.

But then I heard a voice whisper, "Over here."

I looked behind me.

Obadiah was standing in the shadow of one of the trees.

I leaped off the path and into his arms. He raised a finger to his lips, and then lowered it so I could kiss him.

"You shouldn't be this close to the palace," I chided him.

"I didn't want you to have to walk all that way by yourself."

I shook my head, but in truth I was glad he was there. It would save us time on our errand to Korvus', considering his dwelling was much closer to the palace than to Obadiah's secret hideout.

"We need to break into Korvus' apartments. I'm pretty sure he's the fairy masquerading as Cory, but I'd like proof. He's busy with the Queen right now. Hopefully she won't tell him I asked for his address. Going while he's at work will be our best chance." I showed Obadiah the Queen's map.

"Then let's go. The sooner we're both out of here, the safer we'll be."

We set off, following the line on the Queen's map, which turned into a little pebble path off the shining Broad Way.

"The map shows it as the tenth House Tree on the right-hand side," I said. "This has to be it."

I pointed at the unassuming door in the small, gnarled tree before us. Korvus' tree was shaped very much like him: short, squat and ugly. The tree wasn't big enough to house any rooms. It must just be a vestibule to the real house underground.

"How are we going to get in, though?" I asked. "We've got a map, but no way through the door. I'm sure he has protective wards on it or something."

"I wouldn't be so sure. Goblins aren't innate magic users. He wouldn't use a spell if a simple lock would do. Luckily, I happen to be an excellent lock picker."

Obadiah produced a penknife with a mother of pearl inlaid handle from his pocket. It looked old and well used.

"Pardon me while I give this a try."

He squatted down to be eye level with the door handle and gingerly fished his knife blade in and around the lock, his brow tensed in concentration. I leaned up against the trunk, watching the path to make sure no one was coming. But the path was deserted. Obadiah continued to work. I heard him curse under his breath.

"Shouldn't have thought it would be easy," he said with a grimace. "Certain kinds of locks are much harder to pick than others. I would need better tools than this knife to get in there. Unfortunately, that's all I brought with me. I'd have to go back to the human world to get my kit."

"And we don't have that much time."

I squatted down next to him.

"What about this?" I pulled the Vale Cleaver out of my pocket. The hilt pulsed beneath my hand.

"That wouldn't work. That blade is even bigger than my penknife, and my penknife is already too large."

"I don't mean to pick the lock with, silly. This blade is magic; it opens things. I know we don't want to open up another world, but what would happen if we gave just a little prick to that door?"

"We could try it," Obadiah said.

"I guess it can't hurt, right?" I said doubtfully. I could create some kind of portal in Korvus' door. I could destroy his house, and then he'd definitely know we'd been here. My mother would protect me from Korvus' wrath. However, despite his malevolence, I felt guilty at the possibility of potentially destroying his home.

I stared off through the trees. If we didn't act soon, he'd come back and we'd lose our chance to spy.

"Come on, let's try it," I said to Obadiah, and taking the pulsing knife in my fingers, I gave the door the slightest prick, just enough to draw one bead of blood if the wood had been flesh. There was a rending crack, and for a second, I was terrified that we'd broken Korvus' door, but instead it merely swung open, neither hinge nor lock harmed.

I grinned up at Obadiah, hardly believing our luck.

"Well, in we go, then?" I said, and he squeezed my hand.

The tree was indeed only a vestibule, and it culminated in a staircase that spiraled down into the darkness of the earth. Luckily it was well lit with Perpetual Candles. As we descended, moving from light to light along the wall, it occurred to me that even these most mundane of magical items had been manufactured with Elixir; we were totally dependent on the stuff. At last we came to the base of the stairs, where an arched doorway led to what appeared to be a study. I motioned Obadiah silently to go inside.

I tiptoed as I crossed the threshold, not that there was any sign of anyone other than us being here. I felt guilty sneaking around like this. It made me feel low, ashamed. But I knew we could never trust Korvus to give us a straight answer. One didn't rise as far as he had in twenty-three years without being crafty and manipulative. Spying was the only way we were going to find out anything real.

The room was illuminated by more Perpetual Candles. It was stuffy and dank down here, absent of windows, but maybe that didn't bother an underground-living goblin like Korvus. I could see a desk, covered by a mess of papers. For such an efficient administrator I'd expected Korvus to be neat and organized, but his desk was even messier than mine. One wall of the study was covered in floor-to-ceiling bookshelves, the contents looking crumbling and old. But the other wall was full of shelves of identical glass vials. There were labels beneath them. I walked closer so I could read them.

Here the labels were neat and precise. Beneath each vial was a name and a number, written in the harsh block letters of the goblin language, and a thumbnail-sized picture.

"You can read Goblin, right?" I said to Obadiah. "I'm a little rusty. What do these say?"

Obadiah peered at the labels.

"Kyle Stevenson," he read. "BD: 2/16/89. BP: Columbus, OH. Employer: Modell's. GF: Tricia Hartly." He frowned. "It looks like there's more but it's been crossed out." He picked up the next vial.

"Jacob Humphrey. BD: unknown. Freshman NYU circa 2015. Part-time barista Starbucks 14th St. / University Place."

He picked up another vial.

"Deshawn Washington. BP: Bronx, NY. Age: late twenties."

There was something inside each vial, I realized, peering closer: a single strand of blond hair, a curly strand of black hair, what appeared to be a fingernail clipping, an eyelash. They were all suspended in some sort of liquid, a shade too dark and cloudy to be Elixir.

And then my eyes fell on a familiar face.

"Ramsey Cunningham. Age: late twenties. Employer: Union Jack's New and Used. GF: Eva Morales."

"That's Eva's ex-boyfriend," I whispered. "The one Korvus impersonated. Oh my god—all of these guys are his different identities."

"Are Quinn's men here?" Obadiah asked.

I bit my lip. "Let's search."

We scanned the shelves of vials. It took a long time, squinting at all the photos pasted onto the shelves above each glass tube. All the handsome men started to look alike after a while. But then I saw it: one of the faces Quinn had sent me. Obadiah spotted another. I assumed all of Korvus' disguises were unsuspecting mortals. They probably had no idea of the things he'd done while wearing their stolen likenesses.

"Well, now we know for sure it was him," I said quietly.

"So what do you want to do now?" Obadiah asked. "I mean, we have proof, but not proof Reggie or the NYPD would ever believe. Do you want to steal the vials? Confront him with them? See if we can get him to talk?"

"No, I'd rather not have him know we were here. I need to find out what he's doing with these girls he's seducing. I mean, he's stealing their X-factor for Elixir, but how? We should search his desk, see if we can find anything about his plans."

We walked over to the mess of papers.

"If I were a megalomaniac, where would I hide my evil plans?" Obadiah mused, eying the stacks. There were so many piles of papers, notebooks and journals; I didn't know how we were going to sort through it all.

"I guess just start at the top and keep going down, like an archaeological dig." I sighed.

As I made my way over to the desk, I looked up at the drawings pinned over it. I realized on closer inspection that they were all portraits of the Queen. Korvus was a fairly decent artist. He lacked professional skill, and yet, there was a tender attention to detail in the sketches. He'd caught a hint of a genuine smile at the corner of her mouth that no official portrait artist had been able to capture. I thought I'd been the only one to ever see it, but perhaps Korvus had too. He'd known her for a very long time. Perhaps he knew her better than anyone else did?

"Look at these," I said to Obadiah. "Who knew he could draw like that? They're all of the Queen."

"I guess that's your favorite subject when you're such a brownnoser," Obadiah scoffed, but I shook my head.

"I think they're rather lovely."

Studying them, he bobbed his head in eventual agreement.

Wishing I'd brought gloves, I turned to one of the notebooks on the desk and gingerly flipped it open. This one contained text, written in a scrawling handwriting. I couldn't read Goblin runes very well, but at least it was text. I stared at the scratchy letters, trying to put them together. I was about to ask for Obadiah's help with the translation when the meaning sprang forth at me.

Slamming the book shut, I turned away. I was blushing again, but it was a different kind of shame this time. I felt ashamed of myself.

It was a poem. *A love poem.* And it was addressed to my mother.

"Obadiah, we should go," I whispered. "This was a mistake."

"What is it?" He caught my hand. "What did you just read?"

I handed him the notebook.

"He wrote this about my mother."

Obadiah took the book from my hand.

He read silently, a faint flush of color coming to his cheeks. I could tell he felt the same way. We had pried into something that was absolutely none of our business.

"Good god," he whispered, closing the notebook. "He's in love with her."

We looked at each other.

"I don't think she has any idea," I said.

"Probably not. She would probably never return his feelings if she did. Fairies hate goblins."

"She thinks he's just power-hungry," I said softly, feeling almost bad for Korvus. I'd never seen him in such a light before. I'd always just dismissed him as an ambitious schemer. "She thinks all he wants is the throne. But what if what he really wants is her?"

Korvus was a ruthless goblin who had kidnapped and killed kids, and was now sexually manipulating adult women, stealing their joy and derailing their lives. How could someone like that love anyone? And yet, his plan of stealing X-factor from living humans to manufacture Elixir made sense in light of what I'd just read. It wasn't just to win over popular support of the Fey and make himself king. He was trying to save my mother's life.

If he wasn't such a bastard, I would have felt sorry for him.

"We should go," I whispered to Obadiah again.

"Not so fast," a voice croaked from behind us, and

I jumped. "Good thing I decided to come home early from my work today, wasn't it?"

Obadiah and I whirled around.

There, facing us, looking understandably furious, was Korvus. His hideous face was red, veins bulging from his gnarled neck.

"Korvus, I can explain," I said, but what was I thinking? I couldn't explain. He knew exactly what we were doing here.

"If you weren't your mother's daughter and she didn't have her Eyes trained on us, I'd kill you right now for this," he said.

I gulped. But then I stood up straight and tall and faced him. He might have a sad, unrequited crush on my mom, but what he'd done was wrong.

I looked him right in the eye, even though Obadiah clutched my hand in a silent warning to be careful. I pretended that I wasn't afraid.

"Listen," I said with mock confidence, "I know it was you behind all those men in the human world, the ones that seduced Quinn Sheffield."

"Well," he said, "if you're going to disguise yourself, you might as well make yourself *pretty*."

"What you did to Quinn was despicable. And how many other girls?"

"Oh, there were several. There'll be more too."

"This stops now," I hissed at him.

"Why?" he said.

"Because I will tell the Queen. I'm her daughter; you piss me off, you piss her off."

For the very first time I saw Korvus flinch. It was my wedge, my opening. He didn't care what I thought of him, but he did care what my mother thought.

"You need to give those girls back whatever you took from them."

"I can't give it back. Once you extract such things from a human, you can't return it. It doesn't work that way."

Something in his eyes told me he was telling the truth. My hope deflated. Was there nothing to be done for Quinn or the other girls he'd done this to? Could there never be healing?

"You're despicable." The words flew out of my mouth in my anger.

He rested his hand on his hip. "Despicable? Any more despicable than kidnapping and killing human children to accomplish the same end?"

"That was your fault too!" I yelled at him. But he was right. The alternative was taking the kids. Was it better? I thought of Quinn, lying in listless despair in her bed. She wished she were dead. But she wasn't. The Queen's captives would never wake up from their enchanted sleep. My confidence faltered.

"Not so black and white anymore, is it?" Korvus' eyes sparkled with derision.

"They're both wrong," I said at last. "And they both need to stop."

"And then all the fairies will die. Including your mother." He looked straight at me, his features softer somehow. "Your mother is dying, Mab," he said quietly.

"I noticed," I whispered.

"Well, some of us find that unacceptable. Some of us are willing to do whatever it takes to save her." Korvus' passion turned to anger, and his eyes were cold. "Maybe you don't care if your mother dies," he shouted at me, "maybe you're willing to just do nothing and let her suffer till the sickness takes over, but I'm NOT. I'm going to save her."

I swallowed hard at a lump in my throat. Damn him, I couldn't hate him for that. It was what I wanted too.

"I don't want my mother to die either," I said. "But there has to be another way, other than destroying the lives of all those women."

"Seducing human girls and stealing their Elixir wasn't my first plan, you know. I looked for a solution within the Vale itself first."

"The Wolfmen's streams?" I asked.

"I figured they could still change even if I diluted their streams a little bit. The Queen needed that Elixir more than they did. But it wasn't enough. That's why I had to seek out alternative sources. I've found much better sources in the human world. And procuring it is certainly more enjoyable."

I scowled at him, resisting the urge to strike him across the face. Humans meant nothing to him. In his mind they were *sources*, not people.

Obadiah, who had been silent all this time, tapped his finger on the small of my back, a small signal to me, and I turned and looked up at him. His hand was on his knife. With the tiniest of movements, he threw his gaze towards Korvus. The meaning was plain. It whispered clear as words: *I could kill him right now, if you want me to.*

But I shook my head. The risk was too great. I might be furious at Korvus, but I couldn't let anger make me stupid.

"Leave. My. House," Korvus hissed.

I shot Obadiah a look, and we started to leave, walking backwards towards the opening of the study, keeping our eyes fixed on Korvus. I didn't trust him not to kill us enough to turn around. But when we got to the steep flight of stairs there was no choice. We had to run, and hope we were faster.

We bounded up the stairs, all the way to the top, till my lungs were burning. But we didn't stop there. The door slammed behind us, and we kept running, back to the main road.

The sunshine burned my eyes, wrongly bright after having been underground. The golden pave-stones of the road gleamed and I leaned up against the tree to catch my breath, panting. Obadiah leaned against the bark next to me.

"That went well," I said sarcastically, and he put his arm around me.

"Now at least we know for sure," he offered. "If it was me, I would have killed him."

"It's not like he wouldn't deserve it, but we can't kill him—not yet. We don't even know how many girls he's stolen from. There could be dozens more

Quinn Sheffields, hundreds. I don't know if he's telling the truth about not being able to fix the damage he did to those girls, but we have to try. We need to stop him from stealing from more women, but we also need to find out how many women he's already gotten to, who they are and where, so we can track them down. I don't think Korvus will talk to us, but if he's dead, we lose him as a source of information. And we need to know everything Korvus knows. We need to think this through."

Obadiah sighed.

"Let's get away from here," he said softly. "Somewhere where neither Korvus nor your mom can find us."

"Sounds like a good idea to me. We need to alert the werewolves too, let them know that it's not my mom who's stealing from their streams."

"I know where their camp is," Obadiah said. "It's not too far from my House Tree."

"Then let's go."

I reached out, interlacing my fingers in his, and we walked together into the forest. His hands didn't shake when I was holding them tight.

CHAPTER 10

We walked for a long way without speaking, and I didn't even pay attention to the path. I just wanted to get *away*, wherever that was. At last I saw it, up ahead: Obadiah's secret House Tree, the hideout I'd escaped to when my mother first broke the news to me of who I really was, the first place Obadiah and I had made love. I'd always have a fondness for this place, even though I'd spent one of the worst mornings of my life there, when I thought I'd lost him forever.

The House Tree looked much the same as I remembered it. Nothing much from the outside, no sign of a door. But Obadiah knocked his rhythmic pattern of raps upon the trunk, and the door cleverly disguised in the bark swung open. We stepped inside and began to climb the rough, uneven steps. When Obadiah opened the door to the little bedroom, everything was just like I remembered: the bed carved into the wall of the tree, covered by velvety soft wolf pelts, the wide plank floors fragrant with the smell of pine. The little clay fireplace was dark now, but I knew soon we'd have it cheerfully glowing.

I squeezed Obadiah's hand. "I remember the last time we were here."

He winked at me roguishly. "We could have a repeat of that, you know."

A little tingle ran through me at his words. "I'd like that."

I leaned up on my tiptoes and kissed him full and hard on the mouth, delighting in the scent of him, the surety of his arms, the scratch of his stubble on my lips. I wanted to forget about everything except the feel of Obadiah's body against mine.

He took off his leather coat and tossed it beside the bed. I did the same with my jacket.

I looked back and forth between Obadiah and the bed.

"As much as I want to be under the covers with you right now, there is one thing we should probably take care of first."

Obadiah raised an eyebrow.

"Telling your werewolf friends it's Korvus and not the Queen who's been stealing their Elixir. Because otherwise they could be storming the Queen's palace any moment now and it will be a bloodbath. I'm not sure I trust the Alpha to give me a month, like he promised me, as pissed off as they are. I don't want Reuben's friends to get killed any more than I want them killing my mother."

"You're right. I'll go to their camp. They'll spread the word to the packs in New York."

He rose from the bed and began to get dressed again.

Obadiah must have seen me buttoning my shirt.

"I can go by myself; you don't have to come," he said. "Stay here in bed. You'll be more comfortable. And as soon as I get back . . ." He winked at me knowingly, and I smiled, feeling warm inside. But I didn't want to wait.

"I'll come with you," I said, continuing to button my shirt. "I don't mind. And then we'll head back together."

"I think it's best if you don't come." He frowned.

"Why?"

Obadiah sighed. "They're *werewolves*." He paused, weighing his words. "They don't like fairies. And being your mother's daughter, I'm not sure they'd believe your 'proof' that she's not the cause of their problems. They might be more likely to listen if the information about Korvus comes from me—I'm sorry to say. I won't stay long—I'll come back as soon as I can."

At last I conceded.

"Take this at least," I said, handing him the Vale Cleaver I'd been carrying with me. "You never know when it might come in handy."

Reluctantly, he took it.

"There are some books under the bed," he mentioned as we said our goodbyes. "They're all in Faerie. Plus, there are some Elvish romances. You can read Elvish runes, right?"

I nodded. "As enjoyable as that sounds, hurry back, okay? I'll be worried about you."

He touched his fingers to my cheek, then kissed me. "I promise I'll be back soon."

I stood in the doorway for a long time after he'd left, still feeling his lips on mine.

At last I walked over to the bed, curled up under the warmth of the wolf skins and waited.

After a long time of reading deliciously lurid elven romances, I realized it had grown dark outside the House Tree's round window.

How long had Obadiah been gone?

It felt like I'd waited a long time, but then again, there were no clocks in here. That was part of the house's charm. All I could do was wait.

So I lay there, listening to the sap whoosh through the walls of the tree like a beating heart, and trying not to think about my fears.

The events of the last few days kept going through my mind. We had to stop Korvus from getting at more women, but even if we did, it wouldn't help the untold number of women he'd already hurt. Meanwhile, my mother was going to die without a cure for her Elixir Thirst. And Obadiah needed Elixir too.

He might not be as far gone as the Queen was, but if something didn't change, that day was coming. Dammit it, where was he?

These worries running over and over in my brain were like great stones slowly grinding me down, and I felt exhausted. I closed my eyes, letting my head fall back into the pillow of pelts. A restless sleep overtook me. I didn't know how long I was out for. I heard faint sounds from outside the House Tree that stirred me. It sounded like fighting, but it could just as easily have been from my dreams.

I woke with a start. Obadiah was standing over me, his clothes covered in bits of broken leaves and dirt.

"You're back." I leaped up out of bed and into his arms.

For a moment, he stiffened, then he threw his hands around me, pressing me hard against him.

I closed my eyes, breathing in the smell of him. His natural scent had been replaced by the smell of the forest.

"I was worried about you," I whispered. "What took you so long? How did the meeting with the werewolves go?"

"Ah, it went all right, I suppose," he said. "I'm sorry it took me a while. I'll have to go back again tomorrow."

"That's all right." I kissed his cheek.

I threaded my hands through his hair and he

kissed me full and hard on the mouth. His lips were hungry, demanding. There was an urgency there, a need, and I flushed with pleasure at his obvious desire for me.

His fingers traced down my cheek, trailing deliciously across my neck, then down to my waist. He placed his hands possessively in the back pockets of my jeans and pushed me up against the wall of the tree. I could hear the pulse of the sap throbbing, just like my own hot, excited heart, as he continued to kiss me, raising my wrists up above my head, leaving my whole body deliciously vulnerable to the whims of his tongue and teeth.

He was slowly sliding my shirt up over my head, then unzipping my jeans. I shivered as the cold night air hit my bare skin, before he pressed against me. Seconds later, his own shirt was off, and he leaned forward, pushing me back onto the bed, so that I sprawled out across the soft pelts. He loomed over me, his eyes sparkling dominantly. I smiled up at him. So it was going to be like *that*, was it? That sounded just perfect right about now.

His hands pinning mine against the wolf-carved headboard, he looked down at me, and an expression I couldn't read crossed his face. But a moment later it was gone, and his mouth was roving over my body, whiting out all the worries from my mind.

It had always been good with Obadiah, ever since the first time, but we'd been dating for eight months now, and we'd fallen into our tender routines. But something was different tonight. There was a fierceness, a longing, I hadn't seen in a while, and I liked it. I didn't want tender and sweet tonight; I wanted not to think. When I looked up into his eyes, I almost didn't recognize him. I could imagine what those maidens in Greek myths must have felt like, being ravaged by a god.

When it was over, I lay panting beside him, sweat trickling down my stomach, wondering what had just happened. It had all been so sudden, so intense, I still felt like I was in a daze. I rolled over on my side to look at Obadiah. He was lying quite still, staring up at the ceiling, and he seemed startled when I put my arm around him. I nuzzled my head against his chest, and slowly his stiff shoulders relaxed.

"Good night, my love," I whispered, nuzzling my cheek into his chest.

"Good night," he whispered back. When I looked up into his eyes, there was something deeply sad in them. He lay still for a moment, not touching me, then slowly picked up one of the wolf skins and laid it over my shoulders.

I was about to ask what was wrong, what that look had been, but he had turned his body to face the wall of the tree. He was probably exhausted, I thought, from his long negotiations with the werewolves, and what we had just done. I'd talk to him tomorrow, I told myself. I turned over onto my side, laying my arm across Obadiah, stroking his chest, but he didn't respond. He must have already been lost in sleep.

CHAPTER 11

The first rays of dawn woke me, coming through the curtainless quartz window set into the tree. I yawned and stretched, slowly opening my eyes. Obadiah had gotten out of bed, and was standing at the window, his backside gloriously naked in the rosy morning light.

He turned towards to me at the sound of my yawn.

"Good, you're awake. Come, get dressed, we have to go."

"Where?" I asked sleepily, rubbing my eyes. I wanted to stay in bed with Obadiah, maybe fall asleep again under the warm pelts. I wasn't ready to face the day yet.

"I told the werewolves we'd meet them at dawn."

I sat up in bed.

"So you want me to come with you this time? We didn't have time to talk about how the negotiations went last night. Did they understand? What was their reaction?"

"Good, I think," said Obadiah, though he frowned. "But they still want to meet with you. Come on, let's get dressed. We're already late."

I scrambled out of bed, gathering up and putting on my clothes from last night. As I did, I cast a glance at Obadiah, buttoning the tiny buttons of his crisp, white shirt.

Something suddenly occurred to me.

"Obadiah, your hands have stopped shaking."

He looked up at me, his brow furrowed, as if confused.

"Last night I don't remember you having the tremors once," I said. "And you haven't had any this morning, have you?"

He shook his head.

"I don't think you had nightmares last night either. At least, I didn't hear you."

"I don't think I did," he said quickly. "I don't think I dreamed of anything."

I grabbed his hands, bouncing with excitement.

"So you're feeling better?" I asked.

He shrugged nonchalantly. "I feel alright."

"But the Elixir symptoms, they're gone?"

"Yes. I suppose they are."

"Oh my god, that's great. I wonder if it's because we've been in the Vale. There's Elixir in the water here, in the air; that's why you can smell it. Maybe there's enough of it in the atmosphere that you're absorbing it, getting enough just from the environment?"

"It must be."

"I don't want to get your hopes up, or get my hopes up, but this is the best sign we've had in a while." I smiled at him, and tentatively he smiled back.

I put my arms around him.

"Well, fingers crossed that this sticks around," I said.

My mind was whirling with the possibilities. Was Obadiah's "cure," if it was that, dependent on him staying in the Vale? He'd be pissed if that turned out to be the case. Obadiah hated it here. To him it would always be associated with his capture.

"Mab, we have to go now. You know you can't be late for Wolfmen; it's an honor thing with them."

I nodded, and threw on the rest of my clothes. Together we ran down the winding flight of stairs.

We walked a long way through the woods in silence, the leaves crunching under our feet, till we reached an unfamiliar House Tree.

"This is it," Obadiah said briskly.

I stared at the trunk.

"This isn't where I remember the werewolf camp being."

"Ah, well, that's not surprising. The rebels change their location frequently. It's how they stay one step ahead of the Queen's spies."

The bark of the tree was a greenish gray, sloughing off in places. It looked sickly. Perhaps it was already succumbing to the Elixir drought and the werewolves would have to find a new meeting place soon, even without the Queen's discovery. There was something foreboding about the gnarled trunk, mottled and molting, and I felt suddenly ill at ease. Obadiah knocked in a rhythmic pattern on the bark of the tree and a small door swung open. There was only a yawning blackness inside.

"Come," he said.

We stepped through the small door together.

I blinked in the dark, trying to adjust my eyes to the lack of light inside. The forest had been dim, but this was pitch-black. I couldn't have seen Obadiah if he'd been waving his hands right in front of my face.

"Couldn't they have gotten some Perpetual Candles or something?" I muttered, reaching out to grab Obadiah's hand so I didn't trip.

"Werewolves can see in the dark, remember?"

"Well, humans have no night vision at all," I muttered, clinging on to him. "Don't let me trip. Can you see?"

"I can see enough."

It must have been the Selkie in him. I'd once been able to see in the dark too, before I'd lost my powers.

I clung to his hand and let him lead me like a blind person down a long hallway. I could tell it was sloping. We were going deeper underground.

At last we came to a stop. With my free hand I reached out and touched something. It felt like the back of a large chair.

"Have a seat," Obadiah said, "and I'll go see about some light."

I hoisted myself up and took a seat on the big chair.

Something lashed itself over my arms and I screamed.

"Obadiah, what the . . . ? It's a trap!"

Something lashed itself over my feet too.

I screamed, then the lights came on: green phosphorescent torches.

I stared around in horror.

The room looked like a laboratory. The walls were lined in shelves of glass vials, with labels I couldn't read. The script appeared to be Goblin. There was also a rack of terrifying surgical instruments gleaming in the greenish light. I looked down at my hands and saw they were bound to the chair with straps, and that the straps were locked. There was no way I could break myself out of that.

"Obadiah!" I cried out. Where was he? Had whoever had captured me captured him too?

From somewhere nearby I heard an anguished cry.

And then I saw Obadiah looming over me.

"Obadiah, thank god you're free. Get me out of this thing; we have to get out of here!" I cried, panicked.

But Obadiah only smiled, a terrifying smile. And then he raised his hand. He was holding one of the surgical knives.

Was I dreaming? Was this some kind of horrible

nightmare? I blinked my eyes, trying to convince myself I was still asleep, that I could wake up, and Obadiah would be lying beside me under the wolf-skin pelts of the House Tree. I blinked once, twice. My eyes were open, and he was still standing over me holding the knife.

"I've been waiting for this for a long time, Mabily Jones," he said.

I heard that voice again, screaming. It was a man's voice—I could tell that much—a gut-wrenching, ago-nizing cry.

I craned my neck as far as I could through the bonds in the direction of the voice.

There was another room, next to this one, with another chair. Someone was strapped to it, writhing against the bonds. He wrenched free of a gag over his mouth and cried out, the voice unmistakable. "Mab, no!"

It was Obadiah.

But Obadiah was also standing over me holding the knife.

Had I gone mad?

"Mab, that's not me. It's him," Obadiah's voice was screaming.

Obadiah smiled his terrifying smile over me.

"Yes, it's me," he said, and my stomach turned to ice.

CHAPTER 12

I stared wildly up into Obadiah's face, the knife glinting between us in the sterile light. A wave of terror rocked me, and I felt like I was going to vomit. *No, it couldn't be.*

But it was.

"Korvus?" I said, my voice shaking.

He smiled.

Hot tears filled my eyes. I couldn't see. It couldn't be. He looked *exactly* like Obadiah. How had he fooled me?

And then a thought even more horrifying than Korvus standing over me with a knife occurred to me. Memories of last night filled me: Obadiah's body arching over me, except it hadn't been. I couldn't bear to think that. I leaned over the side of the chair as far as I could with the bonds and vomited.

Korvus jumped out of the way, cursing at me, but

I kept throwing up, roiling from the anguish, praying that what I knew was true wasn't true.

How had I not known?

Oh my god, how had I not known?

Korvus just grinned his sickly grin.

"It was certainly a lovely evening we spent together, wasn't it?"

"Shut up!" I cried out, trying to punch or kick him, but the bonds wouldn't let me.

"I enjoyed myself immensely."

"Shut up!" I was screaming and crying, snot running down my face, my mouth full of bile.

"Oh come on, Mabily, you enjoyed yourself too: don't lie to me and tell me you didn't."

And then to my horror, he began to do an impression of my voice in intimate moments of pleasure.

I wanted to plug my ears, but my hands were tied. I tried to bite his hand, but the restraints stopped me.

I wanted to die.

I kept praying this was some sort of sick nightmare and I would wake up. Please, let me wake up. And Obadiah, the real Obadiah, would be by my side, rubbing my back and telling me it was all just a dream.

I kept blinking my eyes, but he was still standing there over me with his sick grin and his knife. And I wanted to die, because it was true. I had willingly slept with him. I hadn't known. I'd thought it was Obadiah. Oh god, I'd had no idea it wasn't Obadiah.

And Obadiah, the real Obadiah, was lying in the next room, screaming from behind his gag, crying out for me. Could he hear my conversation with Korvus right now? Could he hear what Korvus was saying? How could I tell him what had happened? How could I tell him how Korvus had deceived me?

I leaned over the chair and vomited again.

I looked up at Korvus, radiating hate from my eyes, wishing I could cut him with the sheer force of my rage.

"How could you? How could you do this? Why?" I asked, more a cry of the soul than a question.

He paused, cocking his head to the side as if considering. "Why? You broke into my house. I saw your fingerprints on all my notebooks. You pried your dirty fingers inside everything I hold dear. So maybe I wanted to do the same to you. But that's not the real reason I took you captive, or your friend Obadiah either. I have far more pragmatic reasons for that."

My heart was pounding in my ears, my stomach roiling, and all I could think of was Obadiah tied to his chair in the next room. I could hear him screaming my name over and over again. He couldn't see me. His bonds wouldn't let him turn his head. He could probably just hear me when I screamed, like I could hear him. And as I listened, his anguish twisted in my heart like a knife. How could I tell him I hadn't known? That I'd thought it was him, Obadiah, my love? How would he ever forgive me?

I could never forgive myself.

"You're the key to the Elixir drought," Korvus said.

I stared at him, not understanding.

"I realized it recently," he went on. "That's why I came to the human world, and seduced your roommate, so she'd take me home with her, and I could plant the Vale Cleaver in your room."

"That was you?" I gasped. "I thought my mom sent the message."

"Of course you did. I was banking on that. Because it would make you come back."

Suddenly it all made a terrifying sense: the presence of "Cory" the morning the knife had appeared, and why the Queen seemed surprised to see me.

"But why?" I cried. "What do you want from me?"

"Don't you see? You're the world's only changeling, both human and fairy at once."

I still stared at him, dull hatred replacing any thoughts. I didn't know where he was going with this and I didn't care.

"Haven't you wondered why you never experienced the Elixir Thirst, even though you didn't touch the stuff for years?"

"Because I'm human," I said.

"Yes, that's right, you're human, but you're also a fairy. And the combination keeps you safe. Somehow the taint of humanity preserves the fragile Elixir in your blood, and it keeps it from evaporating. It's why the Fey have been able to use the dopamine they steal from children to keep themselves alive. But it's even better with you, because your fairy nature and your human nature have been bound together by being a changeling; the two live symbiotically. You don't need to look for the cure, Mabily Jones, you *are* the cure."

I stared at him, not able to breathe. I'd had Elixir in my body all along? Then why couldn't I do magic? But maybe it was just that the potential for magic was waiting within me, manufactured in my very cells. My body made Elixir. I might not be able to do magic myself, but I was the universal donor for those who needed Elixir. It would have been a wonderful thought, if Korvus wasn't standing over me with a knife.

"And once I find a way to harvest it from you, I can give it to your mother and she will be saved."

"No, you can't. I want to help her too, but can you get it from me and keep me alive?" I knew Korvus didn't care about my life, so I argued, "If you kill me, my mother will never forgive you. She will hate you forever."

"She already hates me," Korvus muttered, and I saw a flicker of despair in his eyes. "I can't make her love me. But I can save her. And she never has to know it was I who led to your demise. I've already framed your werewolf friends for your murder. Then she'll come after them in a rage and that will be one more pesky problem I don't have to deal with anymore. But I digress."

"I want to help my mother get well too—but if you think killing me is going to help her . . ,"

"I don't need to kill you now. As you say, that

would be foolish, to endanger my most precious resource before I have determined the best method for the extraction. I want to keep you alive as long as possible, so that you can feed your mother. She won't come searching for you, no one will, if I convince them you're dead. However, I do have your friend Obadiah to experiment on. The Queen told me he's half Fey. His body does what yours does, only on a much smaller scale. I'll determine what the best method of extraction is from him, whether it's blood, spinal fluid, brain cells. And if he dies in the process, well, he's not so rare and precious as you. There are other half Fey. I'm willing to wager him."

No, he couldn't do that to Obadiah. I couldn't let him.

I writhed against the bonds, as if I could escape, as if I could do something, anything, to stop him.

CHAPTER 13

Korvus left me, walking into the next room. My heart sank. He was going into the room where Obadiah was. He was going to torture him with his experiments. If I didn't stop him, he was going to kill him.

Korvus closed the door behind him, leaving me alone in the room. I wrenched against the bonds, but they didn't budge. There would be no fighting my way out of this. It wasn't even that I lacked the brute strength to free my arms and legs from the straps. There was probably magic involved in the way he'd tied me down.

Think, I told myself through my haze of fear. I had to stop panicking.

I struggled in frustration against the bonds. I could hear Obadiah's screams coming from the next room, and my eyes blurred with tears. *Your panicking will do him no good*, I told myself. *You have to think your way out of this.*

The only way I could escape magic bonds like this was if I had magic myself.

The Queen had told me I could change back into a fairy again, if I did the spell while I was in the Vale. If that was true, I'd have magic at my disposal—I could break free of these bonds and free myself and Obadiah. But then I'd be a fairy . . . What would that mean? Would I be able to become human again? Get my human life back?

I didn't have a choice though. If I stayed here bound and helpless like this, I was probably going to die, and Obadiah was definitely going to die.

I had to try it.

I closed my eyes and whispered to the Elixir potential inside me. *Please*, I begged. *Let me become who I really am.*

I began to sing the spell I distantly remembered from twenty-three years ago. I sang it softly, almost under my breath, so that Korvus couldn't hear me from the next room. I stumbled through the words, butchering them, my human tongue unaccustomed to the delicate syllables of Faerie. I was unable to sing in the Fey octaves, but I didn't stop. I kept singing. I could feel a tingling in the base of my spine, like a limb waking up from having been asleep. *Come on*, I thought. A strange energetic rush filled me, a quickening of the soul. Did that mean it was working? I didn't know, so I didn't stop. Was my body dissolving into Feydust at this very moment, reforming into my fairy self? I was too afraid to open my eyes and find out.

Vaguely I heard a noise, a subtle clinking, turning into a fast staccato rattle. I cracked open one eye. One of the vials in Korvus' library of identities was beginning to shiver and jump, while all the other remained stationary. Was that vial mine? I shut my eyes and kept singing the spell.

I could smell Elixir in the air, the scent of a coming thunderstorm. It was working.

Korvus must have heard the clinking vials, because he called out through the wall. "You'd better not be trying anything or, believe me, I will hurt you."

You already have hurt me, you sonofabitch, I thought, white-hot rage burning through me.

My anger pulsed through the spell, and that subtle tingle of magic I'd begun to feel at the tip of my spine turned into something else: a wave of pure, raw power. It jolted through me, more force than I could control, and I almost lost my grip on the old chant. What was happening? I'd never done magic *angry* before, I realized. My own rage was fueling the spell, spiraling it out of control.

I felt like fire was bursting out of my heart. I screamed in agony. I couldn't help it; I wasn't doing the spell anymore. It was being done *through* me, as magic tossed my body like a storm.

I opened my eyes as the door burst open and Korvus ran into the room. He must have heard me screaming.

"You little bitch," he cried, lunging for me. But I kept singing the spell.

The moment he touched me, there was an explosion. Light burst forth from my body, a blast shook the room. Korvus was thrown up into the air. He crashed against the wall and it crumbled around him, burying him in rumble.

Light, real natural light, was pouring in from the outside.

I blinked as the dust settled around me and looked down at my body. It was shimmering. Light poured from my skin, and when I glanced down at the manacles I saw they'd all been snapped. They had been built for a human; they couldn't contain the wild kinetic energy of a fairy.

I ran my shimmering fingers down my arm and felt it shiver like mist at my touch. It had worked.

My body felt so unnaturally light. I didn't realize how accustomed I'd grown to my dense, heavy, human form. I felt like I was going to float away. I started to cry and my tears smelled like Elixir.

But I didn't have time to feel all the emotions that were flooding through me. I looked down at the pile of rubble. Korvus was under there. Was he dead?

I didn't know. But I had to get out of here. And I had to get Obadiah out.

I flew over the pile of wreckage and into the next room. The door had been blown off its hinges. There was nothing to stop me.

My sudden rush of joy at my lack of gravity stopped as soon as I saw Obadiah tied to the chair.

He looked like hell. There were deep purple bruises and crusts of dried blood all over his face. One of his eyes was swollen shut. There was a dried trail of blood on his arm, where Korvus had obviously been trying to extract vital fluids from him.

When I entered, his eyes widened in awe.

"Who are you?" he gasped.

Of course he didn't recognize me. Obadiah had never seen me as a fairy. I could see the shimmer of my body reflected in his eyes. His mouth was open in awe and I realized how transcendentally beautiful I must appear to him now.

"Are you an angel?" he said, his voice raspy and weak. "Did I die?"

"Obadiah, it's me," I whispered.

He seemed confused.

"It's Mab. I'm in fairy form."

His eyes widened for a moment, and then he screamed, "How dare you, Korvus! How dare you make yourself look like her? When I get out of these bonds, I will tear you apart, piece by piece."

"It's really me," I said. "I've come to get you out."

I reached to undo his bond but he jerked away from me.

"Don't you dare touch me again."

"Obadiah, it's not a trick. It's not Korvus, it's me. Please believe me," I begged, but I knew my words were futile. There was no way he'd believe me. How could he, after we'd both been so deceived?

My heart stung as he recoiled from my outstretched hands. I couldn't bear this. But what could I do? An idea occurred to me. I flew back into the other room. The pile of rubble was still there; there had been no movement. Had I really killed Korvus? I didn't know, and I wasn't digging through the layers of stone to find out. I flew towards the cases of vials still in the walls. A few had shattered in the blast, but they were mostly intact. I began to search frantically. I didn't know if I was right about this, but there was a chance.

There was a chance Korvus had a vial that was me.

Luckily the vials were sorted alphabetically and by year.

And I found "Mabily Jones."

The Queen said I could only change back into a human again if I was in the human world. But Korvus had his doppleganger spells. He could make himself look like anyone, and it wasn't just a surface glamour. When he took on a person's form, he *was* that person. Maybe if I could use his vial to become my human self again, Obadiah would believe it was really me?

I stared at the vial. Had he stolen a sample from the infant Mabily when we'd switched, or had he taken this more recently from my Shadow? There was no way to know; there was no date on the vial.

Could I beat Korvus at his own game? Use his own

library of identities to do a doppelganger spell, and transform myself back into *myself*?

The taste I'd just had of my old magic had been thrilling, but Obadiah would never believe me if I didn't look like myself, and I had to be human if I was going back to the human world.

I took the vial. I had no idea how Korvus did his doppelganger spells, but on a whim, I opened it. I dipped my pinky finger into the strange liquid. There was no way it could be made of Elixir—it didn't look right; it didn't smell right. It must be some sort of potion that Korvus drank in order to change into the desired form.

Closing my eyes, and praying I was doing the right thing, I swallowed it.

Pain and nausea rained down on me and instantly I regretted what I had done. Why hadn't I just stayed a fairy? But it was too late now. Contact with my human self was already beginning to turn me back. The discomfort of human skin came crawling back over me. My flesh felt heavy, dense. For a few brief moments, I'd been free of it. Now mortality hung heavy on my shoulders again.

"Mab!" Obadiah cried out. He had seen me.

I ran back into the room with Obadiah and began undoing all his bonds.

"Mab, are you all right? Where's Korvus? Did he hurt you? I'll kill him."

"He might already be dead," I said. I couldn't bring myself to answer his other question. I forced myself to focus on undoing the rest of his bonds. It stopped me from thinking. Being a fairy seemed like a distant memory, and the great weight of everything I had to tell Obadiah crushed me down.

"Mab, what happened?"

"I can't talk about it right now. We have to get you free."

There was so much love in his eyes when he looked at me I had to turn away. I couldn't bear it, not after what I'd done. I couldn't think about that. I had to get him out, before Korvus crawled out of the rubble.

"I'm so glad you're alive," he kept saying.

"We don't have much time," I said breathlessly. "He could still be alive under there. We just have to get you out of here."

I had released his last bond.

He rose up slowly, moving stiffly with his wounds.

As soon as he was on his feet, he moved to embrace me. But I shrank back from his touch.

"Mab?" He looked down at me, hurt.

I couldn't answer him. The lump was in my throat again.

I turned towards the other room, and that's when I saw it: a tremble of movement from the rubble.

I turned back to Obadiah. "Run."

"But . . ."

"Just run!"

"Where are we going?" he asked in a whisper.

"You're not coming with me," I whispered back.

"We need to go in opposite directions. Korvus will follow me, not you, since I'm key to his plans. I'll go to my mother's palace. He won't dare hurt me there."

"But, Mab . . ."

"Just go," I cried.

But Obadiah just stood there.

In exasperation, knowing it was the only thing that would get him to move, I started running myself.

I sprinted up the stairs.

Obadiah ran after me.

In the distance, I heard a sound. It must be Korvus, but I didn't look back, didn't stop running. Obadiah didn't either.

We ran up the stairs that seemed to go on and on forever, till my lungs burned and I tasted something metallic in my mouth, but still I didn't stop. There was no time. At last we got to the door, and wrenching it open, we found ourselves in blinding sunlight.

"Go to the woods," I said to Obadiah. "I'm going to the palace."

"But, Mab . . ."

"Just go!" I cried.

"Take this with you at least, will you?" Obadiah pressed his folded knife into my palm. I stuffed it into my pocket. And then I ran, ran in the direction of the road I knew would take me back to my mother's home. With all my being, I wanted to look back, to see Obadiah one more time. Would it be the last time? But I couldn't. I listened for sounds he was running too. At last I heard his footsteps receding. I relaxed a little, but kept up a quick pace. I ran till I reached the main road, its gilded stones blurring together through my tears.

There were other creatures there, fairies and Wolfmen and Sanguinari. They stared at me curiously, but I paid them no heed. I slowed down to a jog, though. Korvus wouldn't attack me here; there would be too many witnesses. I prayed that Obadiah had gotten himself to the relative safety of the Central Forest. But the best thing I had done to protect him was not being with him, I told myself. Korvus would come after me if he came after either of us. I was keeping him safe, I told myself. So why was I still crying?

I ran until every last muscle was screaming.

At last I saw the Quartz Spires in the distance. I was almost there. If I told the Queen what happened, she would capture Korvus and kill him. Then Obadiah would be safe. But I couldn't think about that right now. All I could focus on was going one more step, getting closer and closer to the spires before my body could go no further.

I collapsed in front of the gate.

CHAPTER 14

I don't remember what happened after that. One of the goblin guards must have recognized me and carried me inside the Queen's palace.

When I came to, I was lying down on a flat, very soft surface, the soft, ticklish texture of pussy willows beneath my skin. An elven butler was attempting to force some liquid and some kind of food into me, but I kept refusing him.

And then I saw the Queen, my mother, gazing down at me.

"Mab," she cried. "Oh my darling, what happened to you?"

What happened to me? I thought, her voice echoing in my ears. *How could I ever explain?*

I just lay there, staring up at her.

At last I said, "Korvus Korax tried to kill me."

That was part of the truth anyway.

The Queen's face went totally white. Then it went red with fury.

If she'd shouted, it wouldn't have been half as terrifying. It was the way she said, utterly calmly but with complete resolve: "I will kill him for this."

"Mom, I think . . ."

But suddenly the Queen was a whir of motion, shouting things to her subordinates, and she rushed off, the feathers of her gown scratching against the floor. She was heading to her room of Eyes. She was going to find him and fulfill her promise. If he was still alive, he wouldn't be for much longer. I watched her, her back straighter, her eyes bright with channeled rage. For a moment, her righteous anger had made her forget she was sick.

I stared at her in wonder.

I'd never seen her look more like a Queen.

"Mom, stop," I cried.

She whirled around to face me.

"Korvus told me something, when he had me in his lab," I gasped. "I think I might have a cure for you."

"Mab, don't worry about that right now. I'm going to find Korvus and make him pay for this."

But I could hear Korvus' voice echoing in my head. What if my body somehow did hold the cure for my mother's illness? And what if I didn't have to die to give it to her?

From where I lay, collapsed on the catkin sofa, I could see my mother talking to some figures I didn't recognize. I couldn't see their faces. They were swathed in cloaks that seemed to take on the texture of the wall behind them, like a chameleon's skin.

"Find him," I heard her say. "Take him alive, if you can, and bring him back. I want to deal with him personally."

"It is done, Your Majesty," said one of the figures in a voice that made me shiver.

And then they were gone.

My mother turned back to me.

"Rest, my darling. Don't trouble yourself about me."

"No, but, Mom, I have information. The spell you did to me . . ."

"You know I regret that."

"No, I think it may have done something you never intended. I'm *both* human and fairy—don't you see what that means?" I was babbling now, and my mother put her hand on my forehead as if I was a child to see if I had fever, but I kept talking. "I have X-factor and Y-factor within my body, the fairy DNA and the human DNA. I'm a hybrid of both. That's what's kept my Elixir alive. That's what Korvus wanted with me. He wanted me for my cure to save you. He's in love with you; he was trying to save your life."

I couldn't believe I had said that out loud, but the words tumbled out of my mouth before I could think about them.

My mother's face grew very pale again. She didn't say anything, but her hand that was holding mine clenched tight.

"Maybe there's a way I can give some of what I have to you? Maybe it's contagious? If I give you a transfusion of my blood . . ."

"I wouldn't want you doing anything that could hurt yourself. I don't want you taking any risks," the Queen said quickly, but I wasn't listening. This was the one thing I could do that might do some good. And focusing on helping my mom, I wasn't thinking about Korvus, or Obadiah, or the conversation we would have to have.

I pulled the knife Obadiah had given me out of my pocket with shaking fingers. There was no way to know if this would work, and I felt like one of the kids on the playground about to become schoolyard blood brothers. But it couldn't hurt to try it, could it?

Praying that I was right about this, I took the tip of the knife and made a tiny slit in my hand, wincing slightly at the pain.

"Mab, what are you doing?" the Queen cried out.

"Give me your hand."

She reached her palm out to me, not even asking why. My mother trusted me completely.

"This is going to sting a little. I hope I'm right about this."

I pricked her skin. She shivered at the touch of the blade.

But I pressed my hand against hers. We locked fingers, pressing together palm against palm.

I closed my eyes, and whispered inwardly to the Feydust and the human blood that mixed and fused in my veins, as if they were living creatures. *Come on*, I begged, *move from me to her.*

My mother's hand flinched in mine. I could see the change in her eyes. She had felt something.

"Mab," she started to say.

"If it works, I've given you some of what I have, a synthesis of fairy and human. But we can't get our hopes up yet. We have to see if it takes."

She nodded, her eyes still very big.

She trusted me. I wasn't sure if I deserved that trust.

Suddenly, I just felt exhausted. Had I given something to my mother? I felt drained, spent, depleted.

"Forgive me," I said, "but I'm so tired. I have to rest."

It had taken something out of me, to give that much, I realized. I collapsed back down on the too-soft bed, the urge to sleep sucking at me like an undertow. The last thing I felt was the touch of my mother's hand on my cheek, and I noticed it was warm this time, instead of icy cold.

CHAPTER 15

I woke up in a bed. An unfamiliar bed. Someone was softly shaking me awake, and I pulled strange coverlets over my head.

"Please just leave me alone," I muttered.

I didn't want to get up. I didn't want to face reality.

Dimly, through half-open eyes, I realized I was probably in my mother's bedchamber. I'd never seen it before. I could smell Elixir drifting over me, like the scent of a fresh breeze from an open window, permeating the room.

I huddled down under the blankets, wishing I could fall asleep again.

For a few hours I'd had a focus: escape from Korvus, save Obadiah, give my cure to the Queen. But now that that was over, the pain inside that had been paused so briefly came rushing back over me again.

I just wanted to sleep. Because I didn't want to think.

"Mab?" I heard a voice calling.

I rolled over, to face the crystal wall.

There was a hand on my shoulder.

My mother was standing over me. She was not using her cane. And her face . . . her eyes were shining, her skin had a healthy glow. She was still terrifyingly thin and frail; some things don't change overnight. But she looked so much better.

"I think it's working," she said to me, reaching out and taking my hands. For the first time in her eyes I saw something I'd never seen there before: hope.

I collapsed in relief against the softness of her bed.

"This changes everything," she whispered.

"I know."

I sat up in bed at last.

"Mab, Obadiah wants to see you. He's here in the palace."

I turned away, dread filling my stomach. I had to see him. I had to talk to him. But I couldn't. Not yet.

"I . . ." My voice trailed off, not being able to find the words for what I wanted to say. My mother touched my shoulder.

"You don't have to see him."

"I want to, but . . ."

"Whenever you're ready to, he said he'll be here. I prepared him a guest room, and my butler will bring him food and drink."

"Thank you," I said quietly.

"There's something else," she said, her face an un-readable mask. "I have something for you. You get to choose what I do with him."

Panic gripped me at the word "him." It had to be Korvus. She must have caught him and was holding him here in the palace. My body seized up beneath the blankets. I didn't want to see him. I didn't ever want to see him again.

"If you don't want to see him, I fully understand," my mother said, as if reading my mind. "I'll deal with him. I'll handle his punishment myself."

She was going to kill him, I realized, reading her words. Slowly I rose from the bed. I wasn't going to leave this to my mother. I had to face him myself.

I got up and followed my mother into a small an-techamber.

There at the other end of the room, bound from head to foot, staring back at me with sulking eyes, was Korvus.

His face was covered in bruises, one arm at an un-natural angle, a crust of blood across his brow.

I turned away; I didn't even want to look at him.

"Just say the word, Mab. Or if you'd rather do it yourself?"

She was giving me free rein to kill him, I realized. But I shrank away.

I hated Korvus with all my being, but I'd never killed anyone before. I didn't know if I could. We could lock him in prison for life, so that he could never hurt another girl again, and maybe that would finally make me able to sleep at night. But could I draw the knife and end his life? Should I?

"I can't," I said.

"I wanted to offer, but I would never have asked it of you. I'll do it."

"No," I cried. "Not yet . . ."

Korvus was watching both of us, his eyes dull, past caring what his fate was. But when he turned away from me and looked only at the Queen, there was a peace in his face. He'd gotten what he ultimately wanted, I realized; his beloved was going to live, was going to get well. It wasn't by his own hand, but I wasn't sure that mattered to him. He would die content, knowing his love was saved.

Stifling my repulsion at his presence, I walked over to him, trying to see his eyes.

He turned his head away, as far as he could with his bonds, his gaze fixed on the floor. He was trying his best not to look at me, but I persisted, and he must have felt the pressure of my eyes on him because at last he looked up. His expression was sullen at first, but there was more to it than that. There was guilt too.

A memory of him standing over me with the knife flashed through me, and I wanted to hit him. And if I was honest with myself, I wanted to kill him too. The thought of the night I'd unwittingly spent with him was crawling around like a bug in my insides. I wanted to have him out of my life forever. And I could do that. I had carte blanche. The Queen had sentenced him to death. No one would ever have to know I had done it. Obadiah would kill him, if he were here.

I thought of Quinn, lying on her bed in listless misery. And all those other girls—how many other girls?—that he'd seduced, deceived, sucked the life and joy out of. And all the kids, in death-like sleep inside their cocoons. And what he'd done to me. He deserved to die.

But could I really say the word to end someone's life? Could I live with myself?

A small, truthful voice in me whispered, *No.*

I kept pacing back and forth in front of him, while he remained utterly silent. My mother was silent too, waiting at the other side of the room. She was going to let this be my decision.

I looked him in the eyes, and all of a sudden I saw the fear there; he *was* afraid of death, and he knew at any moment I could give it to him. I'd be lying if I didn't admit that that power, the power to hold someone's life in my hand like the most delicate egg, didn't secretly elate me.

But I stopped myself. If I killed him or had him killed in this moment, what did that make me?

It made me no better than Korvus.

"This is what I propose," I said, a new strength in my voice as I turned towards my mother's disappointed face. "We punish Korvus to life imprisonment. Keep him somewhere very far away." *Where I don't have to look at him and have his face be a constant reminder of what happened,* a small, wounded part of me whispered.

"There's an island, far off in the Elixir Sea, where we keep prisoners. It's the most secure place we have."

I knew of the island she was talking about; it was the Vale's Alcatraz. No one had ever escaped it. Even someone has crafty as Korvus would be outmatched there.

"We'll send him off with the next tide," said the Queen.

"Good," I said quietly.

The Queen nodded. Her posture had grown straight, the confident mien back in her face. Now she looked like a Queen again.

She turned to Korvus, her voice like stone. "You are hereby sentenced to life in prison. If you ever attempt to escape, however, this pact is broken and you will be killed. You understand?"

"Yes, Your Majesty," Korvus said meekly.

I spoke up. "All the young women that you preyed upon . . . I want a list of names. If you don't comply, I'm not above using more drastic means to extract that information. You must rectify the damage you've done."

I didn't actually condone torture, but Korvus didn't need to know that.

"I will give you a list of every name. But . . . I'm not sure they can ever completely be restored to the way they were before."

I bit my lip; he'd said it before and I feared it was

true. But there had to be a solution. I wasn't giving up hope for Quinn, or for the others. Or for myself.

"Get me the names first. That's the first step. But we will fix this."

"I'll have my guards supervise Korvus and ensure that list gets made," the Queen said. "We'll be sending you away at sunset."

"Thank you," he said in a voice almost too quiet to hear.

"Just get me the list," I said. I watched the guards drag him away in the direction of the dungeons, as I imagined killing him a dozen different ways in my mind.

CHAPTER 16

After the guards took Korvus away, I lay down again on my mother's bed. I felt like I could sleep for a year. When I woke up a few hours later she was waiting by my side. Once that might have alarmed me, but now it was a comfort. I felt, if not better, at least hungry, and that was some sign of feeling alive. So I finally answered my mother's pleas and ate something.

She must have sent someone to the human world to fetch the dishes laid out on the table beside the bed, because it was real human food instead of just magicked confections of Elixir and air. My hands trembled as I sipped the soup and broke the crusty loaves of bread. There had been a time I'd been too scared to eat anything in the Vale, scared I'd be trapped forever amongst the fairies, but that was before I'd learned to trust my mother.

I looked over at her. She looked visibly healthier

than she did yesterday, a flush in her cheeks and a light in her eyes that I hadn't seen for a long time. It made me think—did every fairy suffering from the Elixir Thirst need a transfusion from me, or would the "cure" take root in my mother, make her able to pass along the human-tainted blood to other Fey, curing them too? Could the cure be spread like that?

"I'm feeling much better," my mother said, noticing my gaze, "thanks to your cure."

"I wonder if you could pass it on," I said. "We should try doing another transfer to heal the Elixir sickness, but this time from you. That way, we can see if it will take."

Her eyes held a sparkle in them as she looked at me. "I've already done it, my darling. While you were resting. One of the members of my court had begun to suffer from the Elixir sickness. I performed the same ritual you did for me. She's already healing. She's going to transfer it to someone else."

"Each fairy who receives a transfer can transfer it to someone else. The cure will spread exponentially," I said, my voice hushed with awe. This really did change everything.

"Yes. We will spread the cure throughout the Vale."

Through the haze of depression that still hung over me, I smiled. We sat together in silence as I finished my soup. There was a lot I still hadn't told my mother. I hadn't told her the full extent of what Korvus had done to me, and I felt like I could never tell her. My mother could sense that something was still wrong, something that even the joyful news of the Elixir cure couldn't fix, because she kept stroking my hand and trying to get me to eat more. The Queen had no sense of how much food a human being required, not requiring food herself. She kept refilling my bowl with stew, pushing more loaves of bread into my hands. It was touching.

But each time she asked about Korvus, I just shook my head. I wasn't ready. So I decided to try a new subject, one that had been weighing on my mind.

I squeezed her hand across the table. "I need you to promise me one thing," I said.

"Anything."

"If we've found an alternative means of saving the fairies, you have to release the kids."

She bowed her head. "I will. You have my word. If we can do this ourselves, we don't need them anymore."

A tension that had been coiled in my heart all these many months lifted at the thought, but I wasn't finished.

"And I don't just mean not kidnapping new kids. I mean every kid who is alive currently in the Vale needs to be freed."

The Queen opened her mouth as if to protest, but at last she said softly, "Agreed." She added quietly, "Some of them were taken a very long time ago."

I grimaced. "I know." It would be a huge problem. She was right; some of these kids were taken fifty, a hundred, two hundred years ago. They had no human lives to go back to. They would be furious when they found out how long they'd been asleep. The shock of it could make them go mad. How could they transition back into society, what kind of lives could they possibly live, all these lost boys and lost girls? But we would have to deal with that later. All I could do was make my mother promise they would be freed.

"What sort of records did you keep on these children?" I asked her. "Did you keep track of where they were from, who their parents were? Maybe there are some we could still return to their old lives."

"I can give you every record I have. Perhaps for some that would be possible. But there will be many for whom too much time has elapsed. Everyone they knew would be long dead. I'm sorry, Mab."

It was going to be a nightmare, and I shuddered at what the implications might be. But I thought of Obadiah. He'd come back after being held captive for two hundred years. And he'd turned out okay. Of course he'd been angry, of course he'd been bitter, but eventually he'd found peace. He'd built a life that brought together his past and his future. Maybe I was being overly optimistic, but maybe there was hope for these children? I wasn't sure I could survive an emotional shock like that, but Obadiah had, and if he could be so resilient, maybe these children could be too.

Thinking of Obadiah, my chest ached. I wanted to see him. I *needed* to see him. As soon as I finished with my mother and the children, I resolved to go visit his room.

Later that afternoon as we made our way down to the dungeons to visit the formerly hostaged children, the tiny spark of joy I'd felt began to flicker out. What would it be like for them, once they were released? How would we break it to them as to how much time had passed? It would be like that Robin Williams' movie *Awakenings*, and there was a reason that story turned inevitably tragic. You couldn't just throw something of that magnitude on someone without repercussions.

And yet that was exactly what we were going to do.

My heart was heavy with dread as we walked deeper and deeper into the earth. The thought of my Shadow, of her madness, of her fear of seeing the light, pressed down on me, and I had no answers.

"I've set up some House Trees for them," the Queen was saying as we made our way to the base of the stairs, "if they don't want, or are not able, to return to their human lives. They are welcome to remain here in the Vale."

I nodded.

"I also contacted your old bear nurse, Ursaline," the Queen added, and my heart leaped up. "She has significant experience as a foster parent, and I figured she could help them with their transition."

I felt slightly better about this whole arrangement, knowing that Ursaline would be there. Ursaline might be the only one who could give solace to children like these. I remembered how she used to comfort the fairy orphans in her care, the ones who'd been old enough to remember their parents. She'd be perfect.

As we walked down the low passage together, and stooped to crawl under the small arched door, I couldn't help but remember the last time Eva and I had come here. I'd felt so powerless then. But now I wasn't. Now I could do something to make it better.

Entering the cavernous room, I expected to see all those silent, still, little bodies again. But instead, the kids were rising up from their cocoons, yawning and stretching.

"I already started the spell to free them, before you came," said the Queen.

A few had climbed down from their stone bunks on the wall, and were skipping along the floor, pointing at the stalactites, giggling shyly at one another.

They looked happy.

They had no idea how long they'd been asleep.

They all stopped talking and froze when the Queen entered the room. Clearly they remembered her, and the memories weren't good. Some started to cry; others cowered, or tried to climb back into their shattered cocoons to fake being asleep.

I had to say something to calm their fear.

"Hello," I called out, and I felt their eyes shift from

the Queen to me. "We've come to get you out of here. You're free."

Small faces looked back and forth between the Queen and me. I could tell they weren't sure. I went on, trying to reassure them, but I didn't know what to say.

"You have a choice. If you want to go home, back to the human world, we'll try to arrange that. But . . ." My voice cracked. How could I possibly tell them that for some of them everyone they'd ever loved or even known was dead?

"Some of you have been asleep a very long time. Things may have changed a lot since you've been gone."

The little ones stared at me blankly, but I saw fear in the older children's eyes, and something darker too: the awakening of hate for the fairies who'd kept them here.

I continued. "If you'd like to stay here, though, you can live in freedom in the Vale. No one will ever take you captive again. We have homes for you. You can live together. Ursaline . . ." As if on cue at the sound of her name, my old bear nurse came lumbering through from another entrance at the far side of the room.

At first some of the kids screamed and ran at the sight of the enormous bear. I cried out over the din of their voices that she was an Animalia, that she was friendly, but I don't think they heard me.

But then some of the youngest children, barely

bigger than babies, too young to understand yet of what they should be afraid, crawled or toddled over with drooling smiles and began to pet and grab at Ursaline's long tendrils of fur. She responded by licking their downy heads and the little ones giggled.

"See?" I said. "She's safe. She's not an ordinary bear. Once you stay with her awhile, you'll learn to understand her speech." *I did.* "She'll take care of you."

The older ones began walking over, tentative, curious, extending their hands to stroke Ursaline's soft fur and receive a lick themselves.

"Ursaline will take you to the House Trees we've set up," said the Queen.

"You can stay there until you've figured out what you want to do. Or you can stay there forever," I added.

I watched them beginning to follow Ursaline like some enormous, bear pied piper, and I felt a pinch in my heart. Right now it was all new; they were still groggy from the sleep spell and still in shock. Perhaps some of them thought they were still dreaming. But one day, and soon, it would hit them: the reality that twenty, forty, sixty, a hundred, two hundred years had passed. And they would hate us.

"There's one more, Mab," said the Queen, and I turned to look where she was pointing.

Two goblin guards were leading my Shadow forward. She blinked and shaded her eyes from the light.

I turned my face away from her quickly, afraid

she would recognize me, afraid she would attack me again, and then instantly felt cowardly for trying to hide from her.

But she wasn't looking at me. She was staring at Ursaline, who was now carrying about a dozen laughing children on her back. I could almost see her thoughts in her pose, head tilted forward, body angled back, afraid but curious. The Queen gave a signal to the goblin guards and they loosened their hold on her. My Shadow stepped forward a few paces, towards Ursaline and the kids, her hands stretched out tentatively ahead of herself to guide her. Ursaline turned at her approach and sauntered over to her. Instantly, my Shadow recoiled in fear, but Ursaline lowered her head, her posture gentle, submissive. She licked the edge of my Shadow's hand and then I saw something I'd never seen before.

My Shadow smiled.

Hesitantly, she patted the old bear's fur.

Ursaline licked her cheek, and a strange sound came out of my Shadow.

Perhaps it was a laugh from someone who'd forgotten how.

Ursaline had a magical effect on people, I thought as I watched her. She had communicated something that words couldn't. Though one day my Shadow might learn to understand her speech as well,

Shadow was following after the other freed captives, who were making their way to the low door. Ursaline nudged them through with her nose, one by one. When it came to my Shadow's turn, she looked back over her shoulder, and her eyes connected with mine. She stared at me, a long, enigmatic look. And then she followed after Ursaline and disappeared into the passage.

I let out a long sigh.

Things were still a long, long way from being alright with my Shadow and these other children. But I looked at the empty cocoons lying like cast-off clothes along the rock wall, and I knew deep in my bones that we couldn't have let them stay asleep just because we didn't know how to handle them being awake.

"It's the first step," I said to my mother as we made our way back out of the cave.

"The first step in a long journey," she replied, and I nodded.

"But it's the first step towards doing the right thing."

We didn't say anything more as we climbed the stairs back up to the sun-filled towers. I think we were both too lost in thought.

"**W**ould you like to be present when the boat takes Korvus away?" my mother asked me.

I thought about it for a moment, frowning.

I was about to say no. I didn't want to see him again; I didn't want to *ever* see him again. And yet, something in my heart whispered *yes*. The thought of watching him sail away, disappear as a speck over the horizon, sounded like a kind of closure. It probably wouldn't give me closure; I was a long way from "over" what he'd done. But I liked the symbolism of the thing.

"I would," I told my mother.

The sun was sinking when we made our way down to the shore, dancing like a thousand sparkling diamonds on the waves. It seemed too beautiful a day for what was about to happen, but there was something triumphant about it, as if Nature had come out in all her glory to show she couldn't be stopped.

I took off my human shoes and wandered barefoot, like the Queen, over the hot sand down to where the waves lapped.

I could smell the tangy scent of the Great Elixir Sea, wild and peppery in the air.

The sea wasn't made of the same kind of Elixir as the streams.

You couldn't drink it. It was wild, uncontrollable magic. It could kill you as soon as quench you. The Fey had largely left it alone, since it couldn't cure the drought. But there was no denying how beautiful it was. The waves were calm, and when a beam of sunlight touched the surface you could almost see down into the alien world of the merfolk.

I stood silently, my mother by my side, listening to the song of the surf.

Several of the Queen's guards were standing on the beach, talking amongst themselves and milling around the sides of the boat that was to take Korvus away. But there was another figure there too, I noticed, a head taller than the rest of the group, and his deep voice barked over their high-pitched Faerie accents. When he turned towards us, I recognized him at once: it was the Alpha werewolf I'd met at Obadiah's club.

He strode towards us across the beach, his heavy boots sinking into the sand. There was a snarly expression of annoyance on his face as he walked awkwardly across the dunes; clearly the too bright, too hot, too beachy landscape made him ill at ease, used to as he was of the cool dim leafy forest. But it was merely annoyance, not anger; he looked significantly happier to see me than the last time we'd met.

As he approached my mother and me, he gave a curt nod. The Queen did the same. I noticed her expression was not warm, but it wasn't hostile either. They weren't friends, but they'd always been allies.

"I came to apologize," said the Alpha with great difficultly. "I know it wasn't you behind the theft of our Elixir. It was the goblin. I'm glad to hear he's being punished for his crimes. If it were me, I'd have killed him. Sets an example for the rest of the pack, you know."

"I know," I replied. "Believe me, I wanted to."

"When the Queen's guards raided Korvus Korax's laboratory, they found casks of Elixir he'd stolen from our streams. I must say, to your mother's credit, she honored our treaty and gave them back to us, replacing what was stolen. Blake has returned to his human form."

"Glad to hear it," I said.

"Think things are pretty much back to normal for us now. But the young pup does feel awfully guilty about what he did when he was stuck as a werewolf, how he tore up Obadiah's store. He promises he'll work for free until Obadiah's premises are returned to their original state."

"I'm sure Obadiah will appreciate that."

It would be a long, slow slog, but at least he'd have help.

"Well, I'd best get going. Just wanted to say that to you both. I know you fairy folks probably don't have the best opinion of my kind, but we don't believe in laying blame unjustly."

"Thank you. And as for opinions, I think you guys are alright." I smiled.

He nodded at us both again and departed, slowly moving across the dunes and back into the forest.

The Queen and I stood on the beach in silence until the ship was readied, and another set of guards came, escorting Korvus. They were the ones with the chameleon cloaks, now blending with the sand. Only their bare faces and hands prevented them from disappearing entirely. Korvus didn't appear to be fighting them as they moved him along. He didn't look in our direction, just stared out at the sea. The Queen approached the group and gestured for one of the guards to come speak with her privately. The two conversed in hushed tones for what seemed like a long time; likely they were working out all the details of how they would guard Korvus. I waited, shifting from foot to foot in the sand, but at last my mother came away, seeming satisfied.

"We're ready," she said, grim determination in her eyes.

I studied Korvus, bound hand and foot between the two sets of guards. The expression on his face as he squinted in the bright sun was unreadable. I wasn't sure if he was feeling anything at all as he gazed blankly out at the sea.

While the other guards loaded Korvus onto the boat, one of the guards approached me and explained what would happen. Korvus wasn't allowed to bring any equipment from his laboratory, or any other possessions. He was a goblin; he couldn't do magic from his own innate abilities like us. He needed all sorts of ingredients for his wizardry, and the guards outlined their plans to make sure he could never acquire what he needed, lest he transform himself into one of them and use that as the means to escape. The guards seemed like intelligent sorts, I thought as I listened to their carefully constructed plans. Hopefully they were up to the challenge of containing someone as crafty as Korvus. It was the risk we would have to take, if we were going to keep him in prison instead of executing him.

"Set sail," I called to the guards. And they did.

I watched his boat get smaller and smaller in the

distance, until it was just a tiny speck in the vastness of the sea, and then it disappeared. I walked back to my mother, and squeezed her hand.

"I hope I have no reason to ever have any dealings with him again," I said to my mother as we watched his boat vanish into the distance.

"You won't."

"You're not going to have your guards kill him when they get to the island, are you?"

"No, I promised you I wouldn't. And I keep my promises." She linked her arm in mine and we began to walk, the sound of the ocean singing in our ears. "You're going to be a good ruler, Mab. You'll do better than I ever did. You gave us the cure for the drought. Everyone in the Vale will love you; you became the answer to their most fervent prayers. You will start your reign with an enormous amount of goodwill."

I nodded, but my mind was elsewhere. I was still thinking about Korvus. I couldn't get him out of my mind, no more than I could the memory of what had happened between us out of my body.

We continued to walk along the shore. My mother was very quiet. She was looking past me, staring out at the sea. I noticed a tear glistening in the corner of her eye.

"Mom?" I asked.

She quickly wiped her eyes, and then smiled.

"I'm fine," she said gently. "It's just . . . this is the first time I've been down to the shore since . . ." She took a deep breath, as though steeling herself. "You asked me about your father. There is one thing I can tell you."

I waited, nervous about what she might be about to say.

"He drowned," she said quietly. "Here in the Great Elixir Sea. We can be killed by too much Elixir, just like we can die from not enough." She let out a long, weary sigh. "I wish I could tell you he died doing something noble and heroic, but in truth it was just a meaningless accident. He was noble and heroic in *life*, and that's what matters. We don't get to choose how we die. But the reason I'm telling you all this is I know you want *closure*."

My heart clenched in my throat; it was like she was reading my mind.

I was about to speak, but my mother went on.

"I understand that. I had them trawling this sea, day after day, week after week, year after year, trying to find him. But it's too big. It can't be done. His body was never found, and it probably never will be. Eventually I just had to accept I'd never get closure. But I've found peace within my heart, and you will too. Life doesn't give you closure. You make closure for yourself."

She opened her arms and I hugged her tight. For the first time, I felt like I was hugging my mom, my *real* mom. What she'd said comforted me. *And she only thought she was talking about my father.*

We had reached the Quartz Spires of the palace. I shaded my eyes, looking up at them, a thousand rainbows gleaming in the sun.

"Obadiah's still here in the palace, isn't he?" I asked.

The Queen nodded. "He's been waiting for you. He would have come with us to send Korvus off, if you'd have asked for him."

I cast my eyes down to the stones. "You've been talking to Obadiah?"

"I have. We had quite a long talk actually, while you were resting."

"Last time you two talked, you tried to kill him," I said, eying her.

The Queen looked ashamed. "I did. But I'm sorry. I won't ever try to hurt him again. I gave you my word. And as much as I was loath to admit it, I see he's good for you."

I smiled at her. "I'm glad you see that now."

I hugged her goodbye, and then headed down to the wing of guest rooms where she told me he was staying, my heartbeat quickening with every step.

CHAPTER 17

Obadiah turned the moment I opened the door handle, and our eyes met.

My breath caught in my throat, and I lowered my eyes, unable to meet his gaze.

"I've been waiting for you," he said. "Ever since you helped me escape Korvus. I didn't want to intrude while you were with the Queen; I figured you and your mother needed some time alone. And I wasn't going to force you to see me. But I'd been praying you'd come back, that I could just see you—talk to you."

Picking up the last shreds of my courage, I dared to look up into his eyes. *Did he know? Did he know what had happened between Korvus and me? Had he heard that conversation?* I had to say something, but I couldn't. I felt paralyzed.

"I should go back home to New York," I heard

my own voice say, but it didn't sound like me. The voice was hollow, numb. "The fairies will recover. They have the cure for the Elixir Thirst. My mother is going to free the kids. It's all good now. I'm done here. I'm going home."

"Okay, should we leave now or do you want to wait awhile?"

I faced him, stricken. He'd said "we." He was still expecting that everywhere we traveled, we went together, like a couple. He still wanted to be with me. I couldn't bear that.

"I meant I should go back to New York. You can come too, if you want. But"—the lump in my throat had grown so big I could barely swallow—"I can't see you anymore."

I didn't look at him, but I heard his sharp intake of breath. I felt his gaze on me, the weight of it.

"Mab, if this is about what happened with Korvus . . ."

Suddenly, I was sobbing. I couldn't stop myself anymore.

Obadiah put his hand on my shoulder, but I shrugged it off. I couldn't bear the tenderness of his touch.

I realized I had to speak. I couldn't avoid him forever. I couldn't avoid him at all. I had to tell him.

The moment I gave myself permission, the words poured out in a torrent.

"I'm so sorry," I gasped. "I had no idea. I thought it

was you. He looked just like you. His voice sounded like you. His skin smelled like you." I was sobbing, my voice breaking as the words tumbled out. "I should have known it was a spell, but it was so convincing. Obadiah, I . . ." I raised my eyes to his, my body trembling and shaking with the guilt that seemed as if any moment it would crush me. "I thought he was you, so I slept with . . ."

I couldn't bear to meet his gaze anymore, so I buried my head in my hands.

"I know," he whispered.

I looked up.

He was gazing at me. His eyes were sad, but they weren't angry.

"I heard your whole conversation, when he had us both tied up in his laboratory."

"You heard all that?" I gasped.

I should have known; if I had heard him screaming, he could hear us. Our voices had been softer, but he had his mother's selkie hearing.

"You heard *everything*?"

There was nothing I could hide now. He knew everything Korvus had done. I felt like I was going to be sick. I lowered my face to my hands again.

"I heard everything. It just about killed me, Mab."

"I'm so sorry." For the first time, I reached out; my hand connected with his and I squeezed it so tight I thought my fingers would go numb.

"Mab, you have nothing to apologize for. You said it yourself; you didn't know. You thought it was me."

"I should have known. I shouldn't have let myself get fooled by that."

"How would you have known? Anyone can be fooled by a spell. Anyone. How do you think the fairies kidnapped me when I was a child? One of them looked just like my mother; that's why I went with them. I thought she'd come back for me. Anyone can be fooled by magic."

"Still," I said. "I didn't want to hurt you."

"I know," he said quietly. "But when I said it killed me, Mab, it was because I knew he'd hurt you. Why do you think I wanted to stay and find him, and kill him? Because I wanted to hurt him for hurting you. The butler who's been bringing me meals told me about what you did, sparing him from execution, putting him in life imprisonment instead. That was noble. I never could have done that. I would have killed him. Tortured him, and made him suffer, made him pay for what he did, and then killed him."

"Killing Korvus wouldn't have made you feel better, or me either," I muttered into my hands.

"You're probably right," he acknowledged. "But still. I would have." He threw his hands up into the air helplessly. "I want to do something to make this better, and there's nothing, nothing, I can do!"

We were silent for a long moment, looking at each other.

"I'm sorry I didn't come to you sooner," I said. "I'm

sorry I avoided you. I just didn't know what to say. I thought you'd be angry at me."

Obadiah shook his head silently.

"I mean, I . . ." I swallowed hard, barely able to say the word. "I guess I cheated on you."

"It's not cheating if you think you're sleeping with your own boyfriend," Obadiah countered.

"But it ended up the same, didn't it?"

Obadiah studied my face silently for a moment; at last he spoke.

"Hell, Mab, I'm just glad you're alive. You shouldn't fault yourself for . . ."

"But I do," I cried.

He was silent for a long time.

"You're sure you're not mad at me?" I whispered.

"I'm not mad. I'm mad at Korvus; I want to murder him. But never you."

I didn't believe him.

How could he not be mad at me, when I was so mad at myself?

"You're hurting more than I could ever imagine." He reached out to me, and I met his hand, holding it, his fingers interlacing with mine. "But what's killing me is how you're pulling away from me right now because of this. Please, let me help make it better."

I sat down on the bed; he sat down next to me. Slowly, tentatively, I lay my head against his shoulder. I felt his sigh, a slow lowering of his chest against my cheek. He began to stroke my hair.

"I thought I was never going to see you again

when Korvus captured me. I thought he would kill us both. This sucks, Mab, but we're alive. We can go on. We can get past this."

"But it may take a while."

I tilted my head, looking up at him, and for the first time, I saw light in his eyes again.

"The first step, though, is that you have to forgive yourself."

I said nothing, staring down at the floor.

"If you can forgive that bastard Korvus, can't you forgive yourself?" he said.

Wiping my eyes, I nodded, then fell into his arms, letting him hold me at last, wondering why on earth I'd thought to deny myself his love.

We spent the night in my mother's guest room. The unfamiliar bed and sterile sheen of the polished agate floors was like being in a hotel, somewhere far from home. I laid down on the catkin coverlet in bone-deep exhaustion. Obadiah laid down next to me. He didn't touch me more than I wanted to be touched, just lay with his body pressed against my back, his arm arched protectively over me, chin against my shoulder. We lay there silently, and I found the constant presence of his body next to mine was more comforting than any words that could be said. At last I fell into a heavy sleep. When the pale blue light of dawn woke me early in the morning, Obadiah's arms were still around me.

The morning sun made me feel better. Not good, but able to function. I said goodbye to my mother, marveling at how rosy her cheeks looked. For the first time, I was leaving her without feeling guilty, because she was going to be all right. The next time I visited, it would be out of choice rather than necessity. The Queen and Obadiah bade each other, stiffly formal but not hostile, goodbye as well. I could tell my mother was trying to accept him, and it touched me to see her effort.

We walked outside into a little courtyard, where we would have a bit of privacy.

I looked over my shoulder to where my mother had disappeared behind the doors to the Great Hall. "I'm glad to see the Queen warming to you," I said. "Well, maybe not warming, but at least being more cordial."

"Yes, she is," Obadiah said as we walked along the garden path. "I would have been satisfied with her just not trying to kill me; it's been a delightful surprise." He cocked his head to the side thoughtfully. "I think it's just that she cares about you so much. We had a long talk yesterday, while you were sleeping."

"Really? What did you talk about?"

"She told me my hand shaking and the weakness will get better over time—it's not Elixir Thirst after all. She said it's just withdrawal symptoms that came from drinking Elixir as a halfling. Because I make my own Elixir, like Korvus said, I don't need to drink it—so it was like a drug to me. But once all the Elixir I drank is out of my system, all the symptoms should go away. Apparently it's a common problem that happens to half fairies; I didn't know, being the only one I've ever met."

"I'm so glad you're going to get well."

I threw my arms around him and he held me close.

When we pulled back, he pointed to the open clearing in the middle of the Queen's garden.

"This looks like as good a place as any to do the transfer and go back to the human world. Are you ready?"

I reached into my jacket pocket and pulled out the Vale Cleaver. The Queen had given it back to me; Korvus had taken it from Obadiah when he captured him, and her guards had taken it in turn from him when they raided his dwelling.

I turned the blade over in my hands, watching the way the shifting light glinted on the crescent moon handle and the smooth polished flat of the stone.

"I'm ready," I said to Obadiah.

He held tightly onto one of my hands as I raised the knife with the other. Hopefully the hand-contact would keep us together when I passed the ceremonial knife to him and we fell.

Looking down at the stone blade in my hands this time, I didn't feel so afraid.

It wasn't like I felt completely calm. I didn't think I'd ever get used to the feeling of safely stabbing myself with a six-inch knife, but my heart wasn't racing with the terror of the unknown anymore.

Closing my eyes, I thought of my fairy self. The memory was so fresh now.

I'll see you soon, I told her, *but right now, I need to go see my human friends.*

With a yell for courage, I plunged the blade into my heart.

Reality smacked me in the form of hard concrete and I opened my eyes, blinking. We were in Times Square, huddled together on the median. Obadiah was still squeezing my hand. I rose to my feet shakily.

"It worked," he said.

I patted my body, making sure I was still solid, then patted the sidewalk, making sure that this was real.

Taxi cabs swerved around us, yellow streaks with blaring horns, and Obadiah protectively edged me back towards the median.

"Come on, let's get you home," he said.

Taking his hand, we made our way shakily down the steps to the subway.

When Eva answered the door to our apartment, she didn't say anything. She just threw her arms around me, squeezing me so tight I could barely breathe. She held me for a minute or so, and when she let go and our eyes met, I saw that her lashes were wet.

"I was so worried about you," she whispered.

I felt a pang of guilt in my chest, feeling like I should have said a better goodbye before I left. I'd left her a note saying I had to go to the Vale for a few days and not to call my parents. But my phone hadn't worked down there. She'd probably been worried sick.

"I'm sorry. I shouldn't have done that to you."

She hugged me again.

"It's okay. You had to do what you had to do. I'm just glad you're home."

"Me too," I sighed.

Eva gave Obadiah a hug as well, reaching up on her tiptoes to wrap her arms around his neck. She'd accepted him as a part of my life, and truthfully I think she was glad there was someone else besides her now watching out for me.

"Well, I'm making breakfast; you guys want?" Eva asked, busying herself in the kitchen. We both said yes at the same time and smiled. We never said no to Eva's cooking. As Eva began to pull cooking implements from the cabinet, she cast a sidelong glance at me.

"You okay, Mab?"

"Okay" was such a relative term.

She must have heard my answer in my silence.

"You want to talk about it?"

"Later," I said, and she backed off, knowing I would eventually keep my word. "Let's eat first. I need a little bit of reality."

Obadiah and I helped Eva make one of her traditional Dominican breakfasts: mashed plantains, fried salami, queso frito and sunny-side-up eggs. The sizzling aroma in the kitchen, coupled with the scent of Eva's sweet, strong coffee, was close to heaven. We crowded around the little IKEA table with our heaping plates. For a long while, we couldn't even talk; the three of us just munched silently together, occasionally punctuated by a small moan of satisfaction.

"The Fey don't know what they're missing," I said at last, "not eating stuff like this."

Obadiah made a noise of agreement, his mouth full.

Eva beamed.

As we leaned back in our chairs at last in full-bellied contentment, I shared with Eva about the cure I had in my blood, how it could save countless fairies, and how the Queen had agreed to free her captives.

"Thank god." Eva breathed a long sigh. I knew she'd had nightmares of all those death-still little faces as well. "You did it; you really did it."

I smiled at her, a little weakly. I hadn't told her yet what the cost had been.

"There's one more thing, though," I said to her. "I think I may have also found the cure for girls like Quinn."

Eva's eyebrows raised.

"If I carry both the X-factor and the Y-factor, enough to synthesize Elixir, and anyone who receives from me can make their own, then it would be logical that someone like Quinn, who had their X-factor stolen from them, could get it replaced, if she got a donation from me."

Eva nodded, wide-eyed.

Obadiah steepled his fingers, thinking.

"They won't just be getting X-factor from you, though," he said.

"I know," I replied. "I thought of that."

"What do you mean?" Eva asked.

"I mean that if I donate to Quinn, I'll be giving her missing X-factor back, but I'll also be giving her my Y-factor. I'll be giving her the ability to do fairy magic."

The three of us looked at each other in silence for a while, processing the magnitude of what this could mean.

"It would be the first time in history that someone who was born fully mortal suddenly has innate magical powers, just like a fairy has," said Obadiah, "just like the immortal witches in the Vale have."

"Oh my god," Eva whispered.

"I know," I said. "It's world-changing."

"Even I couldn't give people that when I gave them my Elixir," Obadiah spoke up. "All I could give them was temporary, minor abilities. But this would be unlimited power, just grafted onto a mortal body."

"My mother will have kittens if she finds out I've done this," I said, laughing, but only on the outside.

"But by then it will be too late," Obadiah replied.

"Mab, are you sure this is a good idea?" Eva asked.

"No," I said. "But it's the only way I can possibly see to cure what's wrong with Quinn and those other girls. Korvus stole something from them, and we have the ability to give it back. Shouldn't we do it? I

mean, god forbid, if Quinn were to . . ." I didn't want
to say "kill herself," but I could tell Eva and Obadiah
knew what I was thinking. "It's worth taking the risk,
isn't it?"

Slowly, both of them nodded.

"We'd tell her, though. She should know exactly
what it is she'd be taking on, so she could make an
informed choice. If she doesn't want it, I won't push
it on her."

"But she will want it," Eva said quietly, and we all
looked at her.

"Quinn is a witch, like me. She's probably been
trying to do magic for years, buying crystals and
herbs at little new-agey bookstores, and staying up
late reading spell books under the covers with a flash-
light where her mom couldn't see. And now you're
about to come tell her that the power is absolutely
real, and she can have it?"

"She might say no," said Obadiah. "She might be
too scared to wield power like that. If she's scared, it
means she's wise. Any person with any sense would
be scared of that kind of power."

"Still, we have to give her a choice."

He was right, though. Suddenly having power,
especially without the immortality that usually ac-
companied it, could be dangerous. I didn't want to be
giving Quinn something that could get her killed.

"She needs a magic mentor," I mused. "Someone
who can help her learn to work with these new abilities. But I don't know if any of the fairies in the Vale

would sign up for something like that. They wouldn't trust her; they wouldn't know what to do with her as a mortal. I wish there was someone here."

"You can make someone," said Eva, and I looked up at her, the possibility of what she was suggesting dawning on me.

"I mean, you're making the donation of the X/Y-factors to Quinn because she's sick and she needs it. But you could give the same donation to someone who is well, and who is more experienced and could handle it better. And might really be able to mentor Quinn."

"Tiffany," we both said at once.

I thought of the vivacious, dark-haired leader of Eva's group. Tiffany might be human, but the magic I'd seen her tap into the night of the ritual was real. I'd never forget the way her eyes had glowed with otherworldly light, the way she'd spoken with another's voice. And instinctively I trusted her. She took her responsibilities seriously. She could mentor people like Quinn and anyone else from Korvus' list who'd been affected. Thinking of my conversation with her at their ritual, I knew in my bones I could trust Tiffany. She might be a little "out there," as Eva would say, but oddly enough, underneath all her Renaissance fair clothing and lopsided grins and cackling laughter, there was a maturity, a groundedness, a strength. I couldn't think of a better human candidate for handling power. Well, except maybe Reggie, but I couldn't go there with him. Magic definitely required someone humble, honest, strong. And then it hit me, and I was embarrassed I hadn't thought of it before.

"Eva," I said, and she looked up at me questioningly.

"It should be you."

"What?" She still didn't seem to understand, or maybe she did and her mind just couldn't accept it.

"I can't think of a better candidate for magic, a better mentor, than you."

When I looked up at Obadiah, he was nodding in agreement.

Eva blushed. "I can't," she said. "There are so many people in our group who would be better candidates than me. They've been involved longer, they're more experienced, they're better at it."

"The fact that you say that is all the more reason it should be you," Obadiah interjected. "I'd be terrified to give this level of power to someone arrogant."

Eva looked up at us. I could tell she was scared, but her eyes were shining.

"I can't believe you would trust me with that."

"I can't think of anyone I trust more," I said quietly, "than the people sitting at this table. Obadiah and I already got ours. You deserve it too."

Eva smiled sheepishly. "Oh god, how am I ever going to break this to my grandmother?" she said, and then laughed.

She turned back to us, a look of hesitant acceptance in her eyes.

"Okay, but if I say yes, you need to give it to Tiffany as well. I need a mentor too."

"Fair enough," I said. "Remember, you've got me also. We're in this together."

When I came in to work, Reggie was exactly the same. There was something deeply comforting about that, I realized. Everything else in life could be thrown upside down, but Reggie was always Reggie, despite how much the world changed around him.

He offered me his usual office breakfast, but today I declined. "I'll pop if I eat anything more—Eva already took care of that," I protested as he tried to thrust a bagel into my hand.

We sat down at his desk together.

"I don't know how to tell you this," I began, "but I think I may have some ideas for how to help Quinn."

Reggie's furry eyebrows rose. "Do tell," he said. "I'd pretty much given up on that case. What the kid has is a mental health issue. I was going to call her mother back and tell her there wasn't anything we could do for her, that she'd be better off trying elsewhere."

"I'm not sure if it'll work, but there's something I'd like to try. If you could call Mrs. Sheffield and ask for another meeting tomorrow, I'd appreciate that. I'd like to talk to Quinn one more time. It needs to be in person. There's something I want to try."

Reggie jotted something down on a legal pad.

"What did you have in mind?" he asked.

"I'm really sorry, but would it be alright if I don't talk about it yet? I just . . . I want to try something different. An experiment. See if it works . . ."

Reggie's brows rose up again, but he nodded.

"I trust you, kid," he said at last.

I smiled, touched by his faith in me.

I'd contacted Tiffany and made plans to meet her that night after work; Obadiah and Eva were going to come with me. At dusk, the air had turned deliciously cool as the three of us walked to the subway. We were going to meet her at their ritual space and lay out our plans for the transfer. I felt nervous as I walked along. I still wasn't totally sure about what we were doing, but Tiffany was the best access we had to the rest of the girls on Korvus' list. If I had something in my possession that could help them, it wouldn't be right of me to hold it back.

When we reached the loft, I saw Obadiah's eyebrows raise. It wasn't nearly as classy of an establishment as his store—then again, Tiffany hadn't had decades of semi-immortality to make it so. Obadiah opened the door for Eva and me and we stepped into the dim interior. We walked up the stairs. The loft space was eerily quiet without the crowd of ritual-goers. The paper moon hung silently over the sawdust sea. Tiffany was sitting on the ripped stuffed couch at the far corner of the room, wearing a black velvet dress, like something a Victorian lady would have worn in mourning. Her black hair was pulled back tight in a severe look, and she wore studious, cat-eye glasses.

Her chin was resting on her hands, and she jumped at our approach; I could tell she'd been deep in thought.

"Thank you so much for coming out," she said, rising, shaking Obadiah's hand and introducing herself, then giving all three of us walloping bear hugs.

"You got my message?" I asked. It had been the most awkward voicemail of my life. How do you tell someone that they could become part fairy?

She nodded, and I could see by the hope and fear mixed in her eyes that she believed every word I'd said. After all, after what she'd seen with Korvus, why wouldn't she believe in magic now?

"I'm honored that you'd consider me."

"I know that you'll take good care of Quinn and the rest of the people Korvus hurt. It may be rocky for a while; it's the first time humans have ever had this kind of power. But I'll never forget what I saw when I came to your ritual—you have magic of your own already, whether you know it or not. What you have, it's different than the fairy magic I know, but it's real and it's powerful. That's why I thought you'd be the perfect candidate. Plus, Eva has told me a lot about you, just how mature and honest and grounded you are. I know you'll watch out for everyone we give this transfer to, make sure they don't get hurt."

Tiffany looked in my eyes, her expression utterly serious.

"You have my word," she said.

I smiled. It was an expression Obadiah often used, quaintly old-fashioned, and yet deadly serious when he said it. And I got the sense that Tiffany was the same sort, even though she'd been born almost three centuries later.

I thought that Tiffany was going to want to do some kind of elaborate ritual around her magic transfer, but she didn't.

"Let's keep this simple," was all she said. I could get behind that.

Tiffany asked us to all close our eyes, and we did. Even Obadiah, though he gave me an amused eyebrow wiggle till I poked him in the ribs. We were just starting to act natural around each other as a couple again. It was going to take time, a lot of time, but I got these little glimmers that our normal life would come back. It would come back because we wouldn't settle for anything less.

Tiffany led us in a simple guided meditation, and when I opened my eyes again, I had to admit I did feel more grounded, relaxed.

"Okay." She smiled. "Let's do this."

She took a small black case out of her purse, and when she opened it I saw it contained a thin lancet that flashed silver when the light hit it. Something told me Tiffany had sterilized it. It would be a much safer tool than the pocket knife I'd used the first time, and just this one small, responsible and forward-thinking gesture made me feel even better about Tiffany being Quinn's mentor.

"I'll go first," I said. "Then when I ask, give me your arm."

Tiffany nodded, her eyes solemn.

I closed my eyes and whispered my intention. Then I pierced my hand with the blade.

I did the same to Tiffany, then clasped our hands together.

She closed her eyes, and I did too.

I opened them when I heard her let out a sharp gasp.

She looked up at me, and I could tell in her eyes that she felt the magic.

"Oh my god," she whispered. "I'd felt it before, but never like this."

Slowly, we released our hands from each other's.

"It will continue to get stronger over time as it infiltrates your system," I told her. "You have my cell number; call me if you have any questions. And call me before the first time you try to do a spell."

"Of course," she said, and I knew she would.

Obadiah was very quiet as he watched all this. I could tell he was deep in thought.

"What is it?" I asked him when Tiffany had walked out of earshot.

"It's funny," he said. "This is exactly what I tried to give to humans, the experience of magic. But I could only give it to them half-assed, by drinking Elixir. You gave it to them for real."

"I hope it's a good thing. I hope there aren't unintended consequences," I said, turning away, but he squeezed my hand.

"Everything in life has unintended consequences, but they aren't all bad."

"I just hope I can handle them when they happen."

"You don't have to handle them all alone. You've got me." He smiled.

Sheepishly, I smiled in return.

"And me," Eva called out. Clearly she'd heard our whole conversation from where she was seated on the couch.

I looked at all of their smiling faces under the paper moon. Tiffany had opened the window and the cool evening breeze drifted in, smelling of strange cooking and the crackle of a gathering storm. Traffic outside was a slow and rhythmic sound, like the tide. I'd always thought of myself as a loner, but I realized I wasn't, not if I didn't want to be. Whatever happened next, I had friends on my side. And we could handle it, together.

"Tiffany," I said as we were getting ready to leave. "Would you be willing to take a trip out to New Jersey with me to go visit Quinn Sheffield? I don't have the strength to do the transfer twice, but you could do it for her now that you have it."

"I'd be honored." Tiffany smiled, and I smiled back.

I was still nervous about what we were doing, but less so now that I had my friends.

CHAPTER 18

The next morning, I was back on New Jersey transit, taking the train out to West Tulip once more, but this time Tiffany was with me. I'd told Brenda over the phone that she was a friend of Quinn's and asked if she was okay with her coming along. Brenda had been happy enough to agree to the meeting. I think she would have agreed to anything at this point. Apparently Quinn was even worse, and her mother was desperate. It was hard to get exact information out of the woman, but something she'd said hinted that Quinn had tried to kill herself while I was in the Vale. Thankfully, she'd been unsuccessful. But I knew if there was any hope, we had to come soon.

"She's, um, still in her room," Brenda said, leading us up the stairs. She hadn't bothered this time with the formality of offering us a beverage.

I knocked on the door, then opened it. Tiffany followed me.

Quinn was still lying on the bed, looking as if she'd barely changed positions from the last time I saw her two weeks ago. In a way, she was. Her eyes shifted slightly in our direction. I wondered if she recognized Tiffany.

"Quinn, this is Tiffany. I think you've met before."

Quinn shivered almost imperceptibly. I think she associated Tiffany with her memories of Cory and for a moment I felt bad that I'd brought her here.

"Quinn, we know about Cory. We know who he really is, where he's really from," I said, and for the first time, I detected life in her eyes.

"I regret everything," she muttered, barely audible.

"Don't," I whispered. "It's not your fault. He's a powerful supernatural; he's seductive as hell." I paused, gulped and then decided this would go better if I was fully honest with Quinn. "He deceived me too."

Quinn looked at me, and for the first time, I saw a crack in her impenetrable gloom, an opening I could reach into.

"I know he took something from you, and I'm not speaking metaphorically here. He stole something real, and it's the reason you feel so bad right now. But it can be replaced. You can get your life, your joy, your *self*, back."

She nodded, but she didn't seem convinced.

So I started talking. I told her about X-factor, and Y-factor, and the cure I'd found for the fairies.

I wasn't sure if she believed me, but I kept talking for fear that if I stopped I'd lose the courage to do what I was about to do.

"I'd like to offer you some," I said at last.

"You would give that to me?" She sounded skeptical. "I don't deserve that."

"No one *deserves* magic. But if you have it, you can do good things with it or bad things with it. You won't be alone. I gave some to Tiffany too," I said. "And Eva Morales. And you'll also have me."

"I can't believe this," Quinn was muttering, but I could tell that finally she really did believe me.

"This is the first time in history that we've ever done this before, that mortals have been given magic. I don't know what the effects will be. It's a risk. There's an inherent danger in such an unknown. But it's the only thing I can think of that could help here."

"I'll take it," she whispered.

"You sure?" I asked.

She nodded.

I took Obadiah's pocket knife—now sterilized— from my jacket pocket, and Quinn stared at it, wide-eyed.

Now we had to make the actual switch, before her mother came in and found out in horror what we were doing.

Tiffany stepped forward, holding out her hand to me.

"I'm going to use the blade to make a small cut on your hand," I said to Quinn. "It creates an opening, for one thing to pass into another. It won't hurt much."

Quinn extended her hand at my words. I saw that it was shaking.

Closing my eyes and whispering a silent intention, I pressed the knife, first to Tiffany's hand and then to Quinn's. I waited silently as they clasped hands together, praying that it would work, praying that the mix of Feydust and X-factor would be able to transfer to the deeply depleted Quinn, to help her, to heal her.

I don't know how long we stayed like that, but when I opened my eyes, Quinn already looked like a different person. She was smiling, her eyes bright, a glow radiating from her face. I nodded, and she let go of Tiffany's hand.

"I feel . . . different," she whispered. Looking into her eyes was like seeing a rushing stream that had been locked up in ice. She was almost giddy. But then she took a deep breath, calming herself.

"I have magic in my blood now?" she said in a voice that sounded like she couldn't quite believe it.

I nodded. Tiffany did too.

"I don't want to try to . . . do anything without other people there to help, in case something goes wrong."

Wise girl, I thought.

"I'll be there for you," Tiffany said. "I'll give you my number. Seriously, call me whenever you need me."

"Me too," I offered.

"Quinn, everything alright?" I heard Brenda's voice calling from downstairs. We must have been in her room for quite a while.

"Ready to come down?" I asked.

Brenda's mouth fell open when she saw Quinn on the landing. Quinn walked over to her, smiled sheepishly and then threw her arms around her mother. Brenda started crying. They just stayed like that, locked in that hug. Truthfully, I don't think Quinn had ever hugged her mom like that ever, not even when she was well.

"We should go," I said, not wanting to interrupt their hug. "We can probably walk to the train station. It's not far. Um, Reggie will send you an invoice."

Over her mother's shoulder, Quinn smiled at me, mouthing the words "thank you" and "I'll call you."

With a grateful sigh, we slipped out of their house.

Tiffany and I walked in silence past trimly manicured lawns down the suburban street, until we reached the train station.

We rode back into the city together. When we got to Penn Station, I turned to Tiffany.

"Thank you," I said. "How are you holding up?"

"I feel a little tired, but I'll be okay."

"Good."

I reached into my purse, pulling out a sheet of

paper, which I'd copied off the bark parchment Korvus had given me.

I handed it to Tiffany.

"These are the names and as much personal information as I could get for all the young women who were affected," I said to her. "Are these people you know?"

Tiffany's eyes scanned the list. "I know most of them. And some of them that I don't know, their names sound familiar—they could be a friend of someone in the group; I'll ask around. We'll track them all down."

"If you can't find them, let me know. I am a P.I. after all." I smiled at her.

"I'll be in touch," she said as I hugged her goodbye.

When I got above ground, I saw I'd missed a call from Reggie.

Standing in the crisp, autumn sunshine outside Penn Station, I called him back.

"Mab, I don't know what you did to Quinn, but Brenda just called me. She was crying hysterically . . ."

"What?"

"No, no, with joy. She said she hadn't seen her daughter like that in eight months. She said it was like she was back to her old self. Quinn told her she wants to enroll back in college again, finish her last semester. She's going out to dinner with her parents tonight. A girl who didn't leave the house for six months. It's a miracle. And it was all you."

"Thanks." I beamed, smiling as I leaned up against the building, watching the crowds flow like tides in and out of Penn Station.

"I don't know what the heck you did or said in there," said Reggie, and I shifted uncomfortably at his words. Was he going to ask me how I'd done it? How could I tell him? How could I ever tell him?

Silence crackled through the line.

At last he spoke. "But all I can say is you did good."

I relaxed at his words.

"Thank you."

"Like I said, I'd written that case off as unsolvable," Reggie continued. "But you got through. You know, you've got a magic touch with people, Mab," he said, awe in his voice, "a real magic touch."

Yeah, magic, I thought. I couldn't help but smile at the unintentional perfection of his choice of words.

ACKNOWLEDGMENTS

This was the first sequel I'd ever written, and the first book I'd ever written under a deadline; it's been quite an adventure! And the outpouring of love and support I've received from friends, family, colleagues and readers for the Changeling P.I. series continues to touch my heart.

To my editor, Rebecca Lucash, a huge thank-you for everything you've done. I feel like I've grown so much as a writer under your guidance, and I will always be grateful to you for opening that first door. I wish you all the best as you begin the next chapter of your life!

To my new editor, Priyanka Krishnan, I know this is the beginning of a wonderful partnership!

To my awesome agent, Jennifer Udden, thank you for always being there for me, for your insightful feedback on the manuscript, your savvy advice on the business and your deep enthusiasm for my books! I look forward to working with you for many years to come!

To my critique partners, Amy Boyles and Michelle Dayton, thank you for all of your assistance in plotting out Book 2. This story would have never come together without your brainstorming!

To the members of LIRW, my Long Island RWA chapter, thank you for being such a warm and supportive community. Thank you to Kimberly Rocha of The Book Obsessed Chicks, for all you do for us authors, for your wonderful friendship and for always being the best part of our town!

To my fellow Harper Voyager Impulse authors in the Impulse Authors Unite forum, thank you for making me realize I'm not in this alone!

To my conference sisters Mia Hopkins, Sienna Snow, and Susan O'Connell—thank you for comforting me when I was freaking out and cheering me when I succeeded. As we pursue our different but shared paths, you continue to make it such a fun ride!

To Emma Carswell-Engle, Anna Michalczyk, Jeannine Pitas and Sarah Bitner—I am blessed with the best of friends! Thank you for sharing in my joy, for your unwavering support and for all your love!

Also to Sarah, an extra thank-you for beta reading Chapter Five!

To my friend Rebecca Himmelsbach—I think of you often, and wish you well. I miss you.

To everyone at Local One—I couldn't ask for a

better place to work. Thank you for all the camaraderie, your genuine enthusiasm for my author career and for making the office so entertaining!

Thank you to Mr. Bill Toole, my primary teacher from first through eighth grade—the love of storytelling you instilled in me as a child will be with me forever.

To my family—thank you for all the well-wishes I've received from relatives near and far!

But most of all, thank you to my parents, Jim and Rosie Vincent. You guys will always be my biggest fans, and I will always be grateful for the bedrock of your support. I love you!

And thank you to my husband, Matthew Schechtman. Thank you for everything you do that helps me live my dream. For your brilliant brainstorming input in plotting out this story, your excellent suggestions on the manuscript, your help with promo and events and, most of all, for always being so proud of me! In all our ups and downs, the one thing in life I never doubt is your love. Thank you for all the joy you bring. I adore you!